EDWARD EVERETT HALE

If, Yes, and Perhaps

The American Short Story Series

VOLUME 17

GARRETT PRESS

Library of Congress Catalog Card No. 68-55676

*This volume was reprinted from the 1868 edition
published by Ticknor & Fields*

First Garrett Press Edition published 1969

The American Short Story Series
Volume 17
© 1968

Manufactured in the United States of America

GARRETT PRESS, INC.
Publishers

250 West 54th Street, New York, N.Y. 10019

DEDICATION.

———◆———

I DEDICATE this book to the youngest of my friends, now two hours old. Fun, fact, and fancy,—may his fresh life mix the three in their just proportions.

MILTON, June 6, 1868.

CONTENTS.

———◆———

THE CHILDREN OF THE PUBLIC.

[THIS story originated in the advertisement of the humbug which it describes. Some fifteen or twenty years since, when gift enterprises rose to one of their climaxes, a gift of a large sum of money, I think $10,000, was offered in New York to the most successful ticket-holder in some scheme, and one of $5,000 to the second. It was arranged that one of these parties should be a man and the other a woman; and the amiable suggestion was added, on the part of the undertaker of the enterprise, that if the gentleman and lady who drew these prizes liked each other sufficiently well when the distribution was made, they might regard the decision as a match made for them in Heaven, and take the money as the dowry of the bride. This thoroughly practical, and, at the same time, thoroughly absurd suggestion, arrested the attention of a distinguished story-teller, a dear friend of mine, who proposed to me that we should each of us write the history of one of the two successful parties, to be woven together by their union at the end. The plan, however, lay latent for years, — the gift enterprise of course blew up, — and it was not until the summer of 1862 that I wrote my half of the proposed story, with the hope of eliciting the other half. My friend's more important engagements, however, have thus far kept Fausta's detailed biography from the light. I sent my half to Mr. Frank Leslie, in competition for a premium offered by him, as is stated in the second chapter of the story. And the story found such favor in the eyes of the judges, that it received one of his second premiums. The first was very properly awarded to Miss Louisa

Alcott, for a story of great spirit and power. " The Children of the Public" was printed in Frank Leslie's Illustrated Newspaper for January 24 and January 31, 1863. The moral which it tries to illustrate, which is, I believe, an important one, was thus commended to the attention of the very large circle of the readers of that journal, — a journal to which I am eager to say I think this nation has been very largely indebted for the loyalty, the good sense, and the high tone which seem always to characterize it. During the war, the pictorial journals had immense influence in the army, and they used this influence with an undeviating regard to the true honor of the country.]

CHAPTER I.

THE PORK-BARREL.

" FELIX," said my wife to me, as I came home to-night, " you will have to go to the pork-barrel."

" Are you quite sure," said I, — " quite sure ? ' Woe to him,' says the oracle, ' who goes to the pork-barrel before the moment of his need.' "

" And woe to him, say I," replied my brave wife, — " woe and disaster to him ; but the moment of our need has come. The figures are here, and you shall see. I have it all in black and in white."

And so it proved, indeed, that when Miss Sampson, the nurse, was paid for her month's service, and when the boys had their winter boots, and when my life-insurance assessment was provided for, and the new payment for the insurance on the house, — when the taxes were settled with the collector (and my wife had to lay aside double for the war), — when the pew-rent was paid for the year, and the water-rate, — we must have to start with, on the 1st of January, one hundred dollars. This, as we live, would pay, in cash, the butcher, and the grocer, and the baker, and all the dealers in things that perish, and would buy the omnibus tickets, and recompense Bridget till the 1st of April. And at my house, if we can see forward three months we are satisfied. But, at my house, we are never satisfied if there is a credit at any store for us. We are sworn to pay as we go. We owe no man anything.

So it was that my wife said : " Felix, you will have to go to the pork-barrel."

This is the story of the pork-barrel.

It happened once, in a little parish in the Green Mountains, that the deacon reported to Parson Plunkett, that, as he rode to meeting by Chung-a-baug Pond, he saw Michael Stowers fishing for pickerel through a hole in the ice on the Sabbath day. The parson made note of the complaint, and that after-noon drove over to the pond in his " one-horse shay." He made his visit, not unacceptable, on the poor Stowers household, and then crossed lots to the place where he saw poor Michael hoeing. He told Michael that he was charged with Sabbath breaking, and bade him plead to the charge. And poor Mike, like a man, plead guilty ; but, in extenuation, he said that there was nothing to eat in the house, and rather than see wife and children faint, he had cut a hole in the ice, had put in his hook again and again, and yet again, and coming home had delighted the waiting family with an unexpected breakfast. The good parson made no rebuke, nodded pensive, and drove straightway to the deacon's door.

"Deacon," said he, "what meat did you eat for breakfast yesterday?"

The deacon's family had eaten salt pork, fried.

"And where did you get the pork, Deacon?"

The Deacon stared, but said he had taken it from his pork-barrel.

"Yes, Deacon," said the old man; "I supposed so. I have been to see Brother Stowers, to talk to him about his Sabbath-breaking; and, Deacon, I find the pond is his pork-barrel."

The story is a favorite with me and with Fausta. But "woe," says the oracle, "to him who goes to the pork-barrel before the moment of his need." And to that "woe" both Fausta and I say "amen." For we know that there is no fish in our pond for spendthrifts or for lazy-bones; none for people who wear gold chains or Attleborough jewelry; none for people who are ashamed of cheap carpets or wooden mantelpieces. Not for those who run in debt will the fish bite; nor for those who pretend to be richer or better or wiser than they are. No! But we have found, in our lives, that in a great democracy there reigns a great and gracious sovereign. We have found that this sovereign, in a reckless and unconscious way, is, all the time, making the most profuse provision for all the citizens. We have found that those who are not too grand to trust him fare as well as they deserve. We have found, on the other hand, that those who lick his feet or flatter his follies fare worst of living men. We find that those who work honestly, and only seek a man's fair average of life, or a woman's, get that average, though sometimes by the most singular experiences in the long run. And thus we find that, when an extraordinary contingency arises in life, as just now in ours, we have only to go to our pork-barrel, and the fish rises to our hook or spear.

The sovereign brings this about in all sorts of ways, but he does not fail, if, without flattering him, you trust him. Of this sovereign the name is— "the Public." Fausta and I are apt to call ourselves his children, and so I name this story of our lives,

"THE CHILDREN OF THE PUBLIC."

CHAPTER II.

WHERE IS THE BARREL?

"WHERE is the barrel this time, Fausta?" said I, after I had added and subtracted her figures three times, to be sure she had carried her tens and hundreds rightly. For the units, in such accounts, in face of Dr. Franklin, I confess I do not care.

"The barrel," said she, "is in FRANK LESLIE'S OFFICE. Here is the mark!" and she handed me FRANK LESLIE'S NEWSPAPER, with a mark at this announcement: —

$100

for the best Short Tale of from one to two pages of FRANK LESLIE'S ILLUSTRATED NEWSPAPER, to be sent in on or before the 1st of November, 1862.

"There is another barrel," she said, "with $5,000 in it, and another with $1,000. But we do not want $5,000 or $1,000. There is a little barrel with $50 in it. But see here, with all this figuring, I cannot make it do. I have stopped the gas now, and I have turned the children's coats, — I wish you would see how well Robert's looks, — and I have had a new tile put in the cook-stove, instead of buying that lovely new 'Banner.' But all will not do. We must go to this barrel."

"And what is to be the hook, darling, this time?" said I.

"I have been thinking of it all day. I hope you will not hate it, — I know you will not like it exactly; but why not write down just the whole story of what it is to be 'Children of the Public.'; how we came to live here, you know; how we built the house, and — all about it?"

"How Felix knew Fausta," said I; "and how Fausta first met Felix, perhaps; and when they first kissed each other; and what she said to him when they did so."

"Tell that, if you dare," said Fausta; "but perhaps — the oracle says we must not be proud — perhaps you might tell just a little. You know — really almost everybody is named Carter now; and I do not believe the neighbors will notice, — perhaps they won't read the paper. And if they do notice it, I don't care! There!"

"It will not be so bad as —"

But I never finished the sentence. An imperative gesture closed my lips physically as well as metaphorically, and I was glad to turn the subject enough to sit down to tea with the children. After the bread and butter we agreed what we might and what we might not tell, and then I wrote what the reader is now to see.

CHAPTER III.

MY LIFE TO ITS CRISIS.

NEW-YORKERS of to-day see so many processions, and live through so many sensations, and hurrah for so many heroes in every year, that it is only the oldest of fogies who tells you of the triumphant procession of steamboats which, in the year 1824, welcomed General Lafayette on his arrival from his tour through the country he had so nobly served.

But, if the reader wishes to lengthen out this story, he may button the next silver-gray friend he meets, and ask him to tell of the broken English and broken French of the Marquis, of Levasseur, and the rest of them ; of the enthusiasm of the people and the readiness of the visitors, and he will please bear in mind that of all that am I.

For it so happened that on the morning when, for want of better lions to show, the mayor and governor and the rest of them took the Marquis and his secretary, and the rest of them, to see the orphan asylum in Deering Street, — as they passed into the first ward, after having had " a little refreshment " in the managers' room, Sally Eaton, the head nurse, dropped the first courtesy to them, and Sally Eaton, as it happened, held me screaming in her arms. I had been sent to the asylum that morning with a paper pinned to my bib, which said my name was Felix Carter.

" Eet ees verra fine," said the Marquis, smiling blandly.

" Ràvissant ! " said Levasseur, and he dropped a five-franc piece into Sally Eaton's hand. And so the procession of exhibiting managers talking bad French, and of exhibited Frenchmen talking bad English, passed on ; all but good old Elkanah Ogden — God bless him ! — who happened to have come there with the governor's party, and who loitered a minute to talk with Sally Eaton about me.

Years afterwards she told me how the old man

kissed me, how his eyes watered when he asked my
story, how she told again of the moment when I was
heard screaming on the doorstep, and how she offered
to go and bring the paper which had been pinned to
my bib. But the old man said it was no matter, —
"only we would have called him Marquis," said he,
"if his name was not provided for him. We must
not leave him here," he said; "he shall grow up a
farmer's lad, and not a little cockney." And so,
instead of going the grand round of infirmaries, kitch-
ens, bakeries, and dormitories with the rest, the good
old soul went back into the managers' room, and
wrote at the moment a letter to John Myers, who
took care of his wild land in St. Lawrence County for
him, to ask him if Mrs. Myers would not bring up
an orphan baby by hand for him; and if, both together, they would not train this baby till he said
"stop"; if, on the other hand, he allowed them, in
the yearly account, a hundred dollars each year for the
charge.

Anybody who knows how far a hundred dollars
goes in the backwoods, in St. Lawrence County, will
know that any settler would be glad to take a ward so
recommended. Anybody who knew Betsy Myers as
well as old Elkanah Ogden did, would know she
would have taken any orphan brought to her door,
even if he were not recommended at all.

So it happened, thanks to Lafayette and the ci+-
council! that I had not been a "Child of the Public"

1 *

a day, before, in its great, clumsy, liberal way, it had
provided for me. I owed my healthy, happy home
of the next fourteen years in the wilderness to those
marvellous habits, which I should else call absurd,
with which we lionize strangers. Because our hos-
pitals and poorhouses are the largest buildings we
have, we entertain the Prince of Wales and Jenny
Lind alike, by showing them crazy people and paupers.
Easy enough to laugh at is the display; but if, dear
Public, it happen, that by such a habit you ventilate
your Bridewell or your Bedlam, is not the ventilation,
perhaps, a compensation for the absurdity? I do not
know if Lafayette was any the better for his seeing
the Deering Street Asylum; but I do know I was.

This is no history of my life. It is only an illustration of one of its principles. I have no anecdotes
of wilderness life to tell, and no sketch of the lovely
rugged traits of John and Betsy Myers, — my real
father and mother. I have no quest for the pretended
parents, who threw me away in my babyhood, to record. They closed accounts with me when they left
me on the asylum steps, and I with them. I grew up
with such schooling as the public gave, — ten weeks
in winter always, and ten in summer, till I was big
enough to work on the farm, — better periods of schools,
I hold, than on the modern systems. Mr. Ogden I
never saw. Regularly he allowed for me the hundred
a year till I was nine years old, and then suddenly he
died, as the reader perhaps knows. But John Myers

kept me as his son, none the less. I knew no change until, when I was fourteen, he thought it time for me to see the world, and sent me to what, in those days, was called a " Manual-Labor School."

There was a theory coming up in those days, wholly unfounded in physiology, that if a man worked five hours with his hands, he could study better in the next five. It is all nonsense. Exhaustion is exhaustion ; and if you exhaust a vessel by one stopcock, nothing is gained or saved by closing that and opening another. The old up-country theory is the true one. Study ten weeks and chop wood fifteen ; study ten more and harvest fifteen. But the " Manual-Labor School" offered itself for really no pay, only John Myers and I carried over, I remember, a dozen barrels of potatoes when I went there with my books. The school was kept at Roscius, and if I would work in the carpenter's shop and on the school farm five hours, why they would feed me and teach me all they knew in what I had of the day beside.

" Felix," said John, as he left me, " I do not suppose this is the best school in the world, unless you make it so. But I do suppose you can make it so. If you and I went whining about, looking for the best school in the world, and for somebody to pay your way through it, I should die, and you would lose your voice with whining, and we should not find one after all. This is what the public happens to provide for you and me. We won't look a gift-horse in the mouth. Get on his back, Felix; groom him well as you can when you stop, feed him when you can, and at all events water him well and take care of him well. My last advice to you, Felix, is to take what is offered you, and never complain because nobody offers more."

Those words are to be cut on my seal-ring, if I ever have one, and if Dr. Anthon or Professor Webster will put them into short enough Latin for me. That is the motto of the "Children of the Public."

John Myers died before that term was out. And my more than mother, Betsy, went back to her friends in Maine. After the funeral I never saw them more. How I lived from that moment to what Fausta and I call the Crisis is nobody's concern. I worked in the shop at the school, or on the farm. Afterwards I taught school in neighboring districts. I never bought a ticket in a lottery or a raffle. But whenever there was a chance to do an honest stroke of work, I did it. I have walked fifteen miles at night to carry an election return to the *Tribune's* agent at Gouverneur. I have turned out in the snow to break open the road when the supervisor could not find another man in the township.

When Sartain started his magazine, I wrote an essay in competition for his premiums, and the essay earned its hundred dollars. When the managers of the "Orphan Home," in Baltimore, offered their prizes for papers on bad boys, I wrote for one of them, and that helped me on four hard months. There was no luck in those things. I needed the money, and I put my hook into the pork-barrel, — that is, I trusted the Public. I never had but one stroke of luck in my life. I wanted a new pair of boots badly. I was going to walk to Albany, to work in the State library on the history of the Six Nations, which had an interest for me. I did not have a dollar. Just then there passed Congress the bill dividing the surplus revenue. The State of New York received two or three millions, and divided it among the counties. The county of St. Lawrence divided it among the townships, and the township of Roscius divided it among the voters. Two dollars and sixty cents of Uncle Sam's money came to me, and with that money on my feet I walked to Albany. That I call luck! How many fools had to assent in an absurdity before I could study the history of the Six Nations!

But one instance told in detail is better than a thousand told in general, for the illustration of a principle. So I will detain you no longer from the history of what Fausta and I call

THE CRISIS.

CHAPTER IV.

THE CRISIS.

I WAS at work as a veneerer in a piano-forte factory at Attica, when some tariff or other was passed or repealed; there came a great financial explosion, and our boss, among the rest, failed. He owed us all six months' wages, and we were all very poor and very blue. Jonathan Whittemore — a real good fellow, who used to cover the hammers with leather — came to me the day the shop was closed, and told me he was going to take the chance to go to Europe. He was going to the Musical Conservatory at Leipsic, if he could. He would work his passage out as a stoker. He would wash himself for three or four days at Bremen, and then get work, if he could, with Voightlander or Von Hammer till he could enter the Conservatory. By way of preparation for this he wanted me to sell him my Adler's German Dictionary.

"I've nothing to give you for it, Felix, but this foolish thing, — it is one of Burrham's tickets, — which I bought in a frolic the night of our sleigh-ride. I'll transfer it to you."

I told Jonathan he might have the dictionary and welcome. He was doing a sensible thing, and he would use it twenty times as much as I should. As for the ticket, he had better keep it. I did not want it. But I saw he would feel better if I took it, — so he indorsed it to me.

Now the reader must know that this Burrham was a man who had got hold of one corner of the idea of what the Public could do for its children. He had found out that there were a thousand people who would be glad to make the tour of the mountains and the lakes every summer if they could do it for half-price. He found out that the railroad companies were glad enough to put the price down if they could be sure of the thousand people. He mediated between the two, and so "cheap excursions" came into being. They are one of the gifts the Public gives its children. Rising from step to step, Burrham had, just before the great financial crisis, conceived the idea of a great cheap combination, in which everybody was to receive a magazine for a year and a. cyclopædia, both at half-price; and not only so, but the money that was gained in the combination was to be given by lot to two ticket-holders, one a man and one a woman, for their dowry in marriage. I dare say the reader remembers the prospectus. It savors too much of the modern "Gift Enterprise" to be reprinted in full; but it had this honest element, that everybody got more than he could get for his money in retail. I have my magazine, the old *Boston Miscellany*, to this day, and I just now looked out Levasseur's name in my cyclopædia; and, as you will see, I have reason to know that all the other subscribers got theirs.

One of the tickets for these books, for which Whittemore had given five good dollars, was what he gave to me for my dictionary. And so we parted. I loitered at Attica, hoping for a place where I could put in my oar. But my hand was out at teaching, and in a time when all the world's veneers of different kinds were ripping off, nobody wanted me to put on more of my kind, — so that my cash ran low. I would not go in debt, — that is a thing I never did. More honest, I say, to go to the poorhouse, and make the Public care for its child there, than to borrow what you cannot pay. But I did not come quite to that, as you shall see.

I was counting up my money one night, — and it was easily done, — when I observed that the date on this Burrham order was the 15th of October, and it occurred to me that it was not quite a fortnight before those books were to be delivered. They were to be delivered at Castle Garden, at New York; and the thought struck me that I might go to New York, try my chance there for work, and at least see the city, which I had never seen, and get my cyclopædia and magazine. It was the least offer the Public ever made to me; but just then the Public was in a collapse, and the least was better than nothing. The plan of so long a journey was Quixotic enough, and I hesitated about it a good deal. Finally I came to this resolve: I would start in the morning to walk to the lock-station at Brockport on the canal. If a boat passed that night where they would give me my fare for any work I could do for them, I would go to Albany. If not, I would walk back to Lockport the next day, and try my fortune there. This gave me, for my first day's enterprise, a foot journey of about twenty-five miles. It was out of the question, with my finances, for me to think of compassing the train.

Every point of life is a pivot on which turns the whole action of our after-lives ; and so, indeed, of the after-lives of the whole world. But we are so pur-blind that we only see this of certain special enter-prises and endeavors, which we therefore call critical. I am sure I see it of that twenty-five miles of fresh autumnal walking. I was in tiptop spirits. I found the air all oxygen, and everything " all right." I did not loiter, and I did not hurry. I swung along with the feeling that every nerve and muscle drew, as in the trades a sailor feels of every rope and sail. And so I was not tired, not thirsty, till the brook appeared where I was to drink ; nor hungry till twelve o'clock came, when I was to dine. I called myself as I walked " The Child of Good Fortune," because the sun was on my right quarter, as the sun should be when you walk, because the rain of yesterday had laid the dust for me, and the frost of yesterday had painted the hills for me, and the northwest wind cooled the air for me. I came to Wilkie's Cross-Roads just in time to meet the Claremont baker and buy my dinner loaf of him. And when my walk was nearly

B

done, I came out on the low bridge at Sewell's, which
is a drawbridge, just before they raised it for a passing
boat, instead of the moment after. Because I was all
right I felt myself and called myself " The Child of Good
Fortune." Dear reader, in a world made by a loving
Father, we are all of us children of good fortune, if we
only have wit enough to find it out, as we stroll along.

The last stroke of good fortune which that day had
for me was the solution of my question whether or no
I would go to Babylon. I was to go if any good-natured boatman would take me. This is a question, Mr.
Millionnaire, more doubtful to those who have not
drawn their dividends than to those who have. As I
came down the village street at Brockport, I could see
the horses of a boat bound eastward, led along from
level to level at the last lock ; and, in spite of my de-
termination not to hurry, I put myself on the long,
loping trot which the St. Regis Indians taught me,
that I might overhaul this boat before she got under
way at her new speed. I came out on the upper gate
of the last lock just as she passed out from the lower
gate. The horses were just put on, and a reckless boy
gave them their first blow after two hours of rest and
corn. As the heavy boat started off under the new
motion, I saw, and her skipper saw at the same instant, that a long new tow-rope of his, which had lain
coiled on deck, was suddenly flying out to its full
length. The outer end of it had been carried upon
the lock-side by some chance or blunder, and there

some idle loafer had thrown the looped bight of it over a hawser-post. The loafers on the lock saw, as I did, that the rope was running out, and at the call of the skipper one of them condescended to throw the loop overboard, but he did it so carelessly that the lazy rope rolled over into the lock, and the loop caught on one of the valve-irons of the upper gate. The whole was the business of an instant, of course. But the poor skipper saw, what we did not, that the coil of the rope on deck was foul, and so entangled round his long tiller, that ten seconds would do one of three things, — they would snap his new rope in two, which was a trifle, or they would wrench his tiller-head off the rudder, which would cost him an hour to mend, or they would upset those two horses, at this instant on a trot, and put into the canal the rowdy youngster who had started them. It was this complex certainty which gave fire to the double cries which he addressed aft to us on the lock, and forward to the magnet boy, whose indifferent intelligence at that moment drew him along.

I was stepping upon the gate-head to walk across it. It took but an instant, not nearly all the ten seconds, to swing down by my arms into the lock, keeping myself hanging by my hands, to catch with my right foot the bight of the rope and lift it off the treacherous iron, to kick the whole into the water, and then to scramble up the wet lock-side again. I got a little wet, but that was nothing. I ran down the tow-path, beckoned to the skipper, who sheered his boat up to the shore, and I jumped on board.

At that moment, reader, Fausta was sitting in a
yellow chair on the deck of that musty old boat,
crocheting from a pattern in *Godey's Lady's Book.*
I remember it as I remember my breakfast of this
morning. Not that I fell in love with her, nor did I
fall in love with my breakfast; but I knew she was
there. And that was the first time I ever saw her.
It is many years since, and I have seen her every day
from that evening to this evening. But I had then no
business with her. My affair was with him whom I have
called the skipper, by way of adapting this fresh-water
narrative to ears accustomed to Marryat and Tom
Cringle. I told him that I had to go to New York;
that I had not time to walk, and had not money to
pay; that I should like to work my passage to Troy,
if there were any way in which I could; and to ask
him this I had come on board.

" Waal," said the skipper, " 'taint much that is to
be done, and Zekiel and I calc'late to do most of that;
and there's that blamed boy beside — "

This adjective " blamed " is the virtuous oath by
which simple people, who are improving their habits,
cure themselves of a stronger epithet, as men take to
flagroot who are abandoning tobacco.

" He ain't good for nothin', as you see," continued
the skipper meditatively, " and you air, anybody can
see that," he added. " Ef you've mind to come to
Albany, you can have your vittles, poor enough they
are too; and ef you are willing to ride sometimes, you

can ride. I guess where there's room for three in the
bunks there's room for four. 'Taint everybody would
have cast off that blamed hawser-rope as neat as you
did."

From which last remark I inferred, what I learned
as a certainty as we travelled farther, that but for the
timely assistance I had rendered him I should have
plead for my passage in vain.

This was my introduction to Fausta. That is to
say, she heard the whole of the conversation. The
formal introduction, which is omitted in no circle of
American life to which I have ever been admitted,
took place at tea half an hour after, when Mrs. Grills,
who always voyaged with her husband, brought in
the flapjacks from the kitchen. "Miss Jones," said
Grills, as I came into the meal, leaving Zekiel at the
tiller, — "Miss Jones, this is a young man who is going
to Albany. I don't rightly know how to call your
name, sir." I said my name was Carter. Then he
said, "Mr. Carter, this is Miss Jones. Mrs. Grills,
Mr. Carter. Mr. Carter, Mrs. Grills. She is my
wife." And so our *partie carrée* was established for
the voyage.

In these days there are few people who know that
a journey on a canal is the pleasantest journey in the
world. A canal has to go through fine scenery. It
cannot exist unless it follow through the valley of a
stream. The movement is so easy that, with your
eyes shut, you do not know you move. The route is

so direct, that when you are once shielded from the sun, you are safe for hours. You draw, you read, you write, or you sew, crochet, or knit. You play on your flute or your guitar, without one hint of inconvenience. At a "low bridge" you duck your head lest you lose your hat, — and that reminder teaches you that you are human. You are glad to know this, and you laugh at the memento. For the rest of the time you journey, if you are " all right " within, in elysium.

I rode one of those horses perhaps two or three hours a day. At locks I made myself generally useful. At night I walked the deck till one o'clock, with my pipe or without it, to keep guard against the lock-thieves. The skipper asked me sometimes, after he found I could " cipher," to disentangle some of the knots in his bills of lading for him. But all this made but a little inroad in those lovely autumn days, and for the eight days that we glided along, — there is one blessed level which is seventy miles long, — I spent most of my time with Fausta. We walked together on the tow-path to get our appetites for dinner and for supper. At sunrise I always made a cruise inland, and collected the gentians and black alder-berries and colored leaves, with which she dressed Mrs. Grill's table. She took an interest in my wretched sketch-book, and though she did not and does not draw well, she did show me how to spread an even tint, which I never knew before. I was working up my French.

She knew about as much and as little as I did, and we read Mad. Reybaud's Clementine together, guessing at the hard words, because we had no dictionary.

Dear old Grill offered to talk French at table, and we tried it for a few days. But it proved he picked up his pronunciation at St. Catherine's, among the boatmen there, and he would say *shwo* for "horses," where the book said *chevaux*. Our talk, on the other hand, was not Parisian, — but it was not Catherinian, — and we subsided into English again.

So sped along these blessed eight days. I told Fausta thus much of my story, that I was going to seek my fortune in New York. She, of course, knew nothing of me but what she saw, and she told me nothing of her story.

But I was very sorry when we came into the basin at Troy, for I knew then that in all reason I must take the steamboat down. And I was very glad, — I have seldom in my life been so glad, — when I found that she also was going to New York immediately. She accepted, very pleasantly, my offer to carry her trunk to the Isaac Newton for her, and to act as her escort to the city. For me, my trunk,

"in danger tried,"
Swung in my hand, — " nor left my side."

My earthly possessions were few anywhere. I had left at Attica most of what they were. Through the voyage I had been man enough to keep on a working-gear fit for a workman's duty. And old Grills had not

yet grace enough to keep his boat still on Sunday.
How one remembers little things! I can remember
each touch of the toilet, as, in that corner of a dark
cuddy where I had shared "Zekiel's" bunk with him,
I dressed myself with one of my two white shirts, and
with the change of raiment which had been tight
squeezed in my portmanteau. The old overcoat was
the best part of it, as in a finite world it often is. I
sold my felt hat to Zekiel, and appeared with a light
travelling-cap. I do not know how Fausta liked my
metamorphosis. I only know that, like butterflies,
for a day or two after they go through theirs, I felt
decidedly cold.

As Carter, the canal man, I had carried Fausta's
trunk on board. As Mr. Carter, I gave her my arm,
led her to the gangway of the Newton, took her passage and mine, and afterwards walked and sat through
the splendid moonlight of the first four hours down
the river.

Miss Jones determined that evening to breakfast on
the boat. Be it observed that I did not then know
her by any other name. She was to go to an aunt's
house, and she knew that if she left the boat on its
early arrival in New York, she would disturb that
lady by a premature ringing at her bell. I had no
reason for haste, as the reader knows. The distribution of the cyclopædias was not to take place till the
next day, and that absurd trifle was the only distinct
excuse I had to myself for being in New York at all.

I asked Miss Jones, therefore, if I might not be her escort still to her aunt's house. I had said it would be hard to break off our pleasant journey before I had seen where she lived, and I thought she seemed relieved to know that she should not be wholly a stranger on her arrival. It was clear enough that her aunt would send no one to meet her.

These preliminaries adjusted, we parted to our respective cabins. And when, the next morning, at that unearthly hour demanded by Philadelphia trains and other exigencies, the Newton made her dock, I rejoiced that breakfast was not till seven o'clock, that I had two hours more of the berth, which was luxury compared to Zekiel's bunk, — I turned upon my other side and slept on.

Sorry enough for that morning nap was I for the next thirty-six hours. For when I went on deck, and sent in the stewardess to tell Miss Jones that I was waiting for her, and then took from her the check for her trunk, I woke to the misery of finding that, in that treacherous two hours, some pirate from the pier had stepped on board, had seized the waiting trunk, left almost alone, while the baggage-master's back was turned, and that, to a certainty, it was lost. I did not return to Fausta with this story till the breakfast-bell had long passed and the breakfast was very cold. I did not then tell it to her till I had seen her eat her breakfast with an appetite much better than mine. I had already offered up stairs the largest reward to any-

body who would bring it back which my scanty purse
would pay. I had spoken to the clerk, who had sent
for a policeman. I could do nothing more, and I did
not choose to ruin her chop and coffee by ill-timed
news. The officer came before breakfast was over,
and called me from table.

On the whole, his business-like way encouraged
one. He had some clews which I had not thought
possible. It was not unlikely that they should pounce
on the trunk before it was broken open. I gave him
a written description of its marks ; and when he civilly
asked if "my lady" would give some description of
any books or other articles within, I readily promised
that I would call with such a description at the police
station. Somewhat encouraged, I returned to Miss
Jones, and, when I led her from the breakfast-table,
told her of her misfortune. I took all shame to myself for my own carelessness, to which I attributed the
loss. But I told her all that the officer had said to
me, and that I hoped to bring her the trunk at her
aunt's before the day was over.

Fausta took my news, however, with a start which
frightened me. All her money, but a shilling or two,
was in the trunk. To place money in trunks is a
weakness of the female mind which I have nowhere
seen accounted for. Worse than this, though, — as
appeared after a moment's examination of her travelling *sac*, — her portfolio in the trunk contained the
letter of the aunt whom she came to visit, giving her

her address in the city. To this address she had no
other clew but that her aunt was Mrs. Mary Mason,
had married a few years before a merchant named
Mason, whom Miss Jones had never seen, and of
whose name and business this was all she knew. They
lived in a numbered street, but whether it was Fourth
Street, or Fifty-fourth, or One Hundred and Twenty-
fourth, or whether it was something between, the
poor child had no idea. She had put up the letter
carefully, but had never thought of the importance of
the address. Besides this aunt, she knew no human
being in New York.

" Child of the Public," I said to myself, " what do
you do now ? " I had appealed to my great patron in
sending for the officer, and on the whole I felt that
my sovereign had been gracious to me, if not yet
hopeful. But now I must rub my lamp again, and
ask the genie where the unknown Mason lived. The
genie of course suggested the Directory, and I ran for
it to the clerk's office. But as we were toiling down
the pages of " Masons," and had written off thirteen
or fourteen who lived in numbered streets, Fausta
started, looked back at the preface and its date, flung
down her pencil in the only abandonment of dismay in
which I ever saw her, and cried, " First of May !
They were abroad until May. They have been
abroad since the day they were married ! " So that
genie had to put his glories into his pocket, and carry
his Directory back to the office again.

The natural thing to propose was, that I should find for Miss Jones a respectable boarding-house, and that she should remain there until her trunk was found, or till she could write to friends who had this fatal address, and receive an answer. But here she hesitated. She hardly liked to explain why, — did not explain wholly. But she did not say that she had no friends who knew this address. She had but few relations in the world, and her aunt had communicated with her alone since she came from Europe. As for the boarding-house, " I had rather look for work," she said bravely. " I have never promised to pay money when I did not know how to obtain it; and that " — and here she took out fifty or sixty cents from her purse — " and that is all now. In respectable boarding-houses, when people come without luggage, they are apt to ask for an advance. Or, at least," she added, with some pride, " I am apt to offer it."

I hastened to ask her to take all my little store ; but I had to own that I had not two dollars. I was sure, however, that my overcoat and the dress-suit I wore would avail me something, if I thrust them boldly up some spout. I was sure that I should be at work within a day or two. At all events, I was certain of the cyclopædia the next day. That should go to old Gowan's, — in Fulton Street it was then, — "the moral centre of the intellectual world," in the hour I got it. And at this moment, for the first time, the thought crossed me, " If mine could only be the name drawn, so that that foolish $5,000 should fall to me." In that case I felt that Fausta might live in "a respectable boarding-house" till she died. Of this, of course, I said nothing, only that she was welcome to my poor dollar and a half, and that I should receive the next day some more money that was due me.

"You forget, Mr. Carter," replied Fausta, as proudly as before, — "you forget that I cannot borrow of you any more than of a boarding-house-keeper. I never borrow. Please God, I never will. It must be," she added, "that in a Christian city like this there is some respectable and fit arrangement made for travellers who find themselves where I am. What that provision is I do not know; but I will find out what it is before this sun goes down."

I paused a moment before I replied. If I had been fascinated by this lovely girl before, I now bowed in respect before her dignity and resolution; and, with my sympathy, there was a delicious throb of self-respect united, when I heard her lay down so simply, as principles of her life, two principles on which I had always myself tried to live. The half-expressed habits of my boyhood and youth were now uttered for me as axioms by lips which I knew could speak nothing but right and truth.

I paused a moment. I stumbled a little as I expressed my regret that she would not let me help her, —joined with my certainty that she was in the right in refusing, — and then, in the only stiff speech I ever made to her, I said : —

"I am the 'Child of the Public.' If you ever hear my story, you will say so too. At the least, I can claim this, that I have a right to help you in your quest as to the way in which the public will help you. Thus far I am clearly the officer in his suite to whom he has intrusted you. Are you ready, then, to go on shore?"

Fausta looked around on that forlorn ladies' saloon, as if it were the last link holding her to her old safe world.

> "Looked upon skylight, lamp, and chain,
> As what she ne'er might see again."

Then she looked right through me; and if there had been one mean thought in me at that minute, she would have seen the viper. Then she said, sadly, —

"I have perfect confidence in you, though people would say we were strangers. Let us go."

And we left the boat together. We declined the invitations of the noisy hackmen, and walked slowly to Broadway.

We stopped at the station-house for that district, and to the attentive chief Fausta herself described those contents of her trunk which she thought would be most easily detected, if offered for sale. Her mother's Bible, at which the chief shook his head; Bibles, alas! brought nothing at the shops; a soldier's medal, such as were given as target prizes by the Montgomery regiment; and a little silver canteen, marked with the device of the same regiment, seemed to him better worthy of note. Her portfolio was wrought with a cipher, and she explained to him that she was most eager that this should be recovered. The pocket-book contained more than one hundred dollars, which she described, but he shook his head here, and gave her but little hope of that, if the trunk were once opened. His chief hope was for this morning.

" And where shall we send to you then, madam?" said he.

I had been proud, as if it were my merit, of the impression Fausta had made upon the officer, in her quiet, simple, ladylike dress and manner. For my-self, I thought that one slip of pretence in my dress or bearing, a scrap of gold or of pinchbeck, would have ruined both of us in our appeal. But, fortunately, I did not disgrace her, and the man looked at her as if he expected her to say " Fourteenth Street." What would she say ?

" That depends upon what the time will be. Mr. Carter will call at noon, and will let you know."

We bowed, and were gone. In an instant more she begged my pardon, almost with tears ; but I told her that if she also had been a " Child of the Public," she could not more fitly have spoken to one of her father's officers. I begged her to use me as her pro-tector, and not to apologize again. Then we laid out the plans which we followed out that day.

The officer's manner had reassured her, and I suc-ceeded in persuading her that it was certain we should have the trunk at noon. How much better to wait, at least so far, before she entered on any of the enterprises of which she talked so coolly, as of offering herself as a nursery-girl, or as a milliner, to whoever would employ her, if only she could thus secure an honest home till money or till aunt were found. Once persuaded that we were safe from this Quixotism, I told her that we must go on, as we did on the canal, and first we must take our constitutional walk for two hours.

"At least," she said, "our good papa, the Public, gives us wonderful sights to see, and good walking to our feet, as a better Father has given us this heavenly sky and this bracing air."

And with those words the last heaviness of despondency left her face for that day. And we plunged into the delicious adventure of exploring a new city, staring into windows as only strangers can, revelling in print-shops as only they do, really seeing the fine buildings as residents always forget to do, and laying up, in short, with those streets, nearly all the associations which to this day we have with them.

Two hours of this tired us with walking, of course. I do not know what she meant to do next; but at ten I said, "Time for French, Miss Jones." "*Ah oui*," said she, "*mais où?*" and I had calculated my distances, and led her at once into Lafayette Place ; and, in a moment, pushed open the door of the Astor Library, led her up the main stairway, and said,

"This is what the Public provides for his children when they have to study."

"This is the Astor," said she, delighted. "And we are all right, as you say, here?" Then she saw that our entrance excited no surprise among the few readers, men and women, who were beginning to assemble.

We took our seats at an unoccupied table, and began to revel in the luxuries for which we had only to ask that we might enjoy. I had a little memorandum of books which I had been waiting to see. She needed none; but looked for one and another, and yet another, and between us we kept the attendant well in motion. A pleasant thing to me to be finding out her thoroughbred tastes and lines of work, and I was happy enough to interest her in some of my pet readings; and, of course, for she was a woman, to get quick hints which had never dawned on me before. A very short hour and a half we spent there before I went to the station-house again. I went very quickly. I returned to her very slowly.

The trunk was not found. But they were now quite sure they were on its track. They felt certain it had been carried from pier to pier and taken back up the river. Nor was it hopeless to follow it. The particular rascal who was supposed to have it would certainly stop either at Piermont or at Newburg. They had telegraphed to both places, and were in time for both. "The day boat, sir, will bring your lady's trunk, and will bring me Rowdy Rob, too, I hope," said the officer. But at the same moment, as he rang his bell, he learned that no despatch had yet been received from either of the places named. I did not feel so certain as he did.

But Fausta showed no discomfort as I told my news. " Thus far," said she, " the Public serves me well. I will borrow no trouble by want of faith." And I — as Dante would say — and I, to her, " will you let me remind you, then, that at one we dine; that Mrs. Grills is now placing the salt-pork upon the cabin table, and Mr. Grills asking the blessing; and, as this is the only day when I can have the honor of your company, will you let me show you how a Child of the Public dines, when his finances are low ? "

Fausta laughed, and said again, less tragically than before, " I have perfect confidence in you," — little thinking how she started my blood with the words; but this time, as if in token, she let me take her hand upon my arm, as we walked down the street together.

If we had been snobs, or even if I had been one, I should have taken her to Taylor's, and have spent all the money I had on such a luncheon as neither of us had ever eaten before. Whatever else I am, I am not a snob of that sort. I show my colors. I led her into a little cross-street which I had noticed in our erratic morning pilgrimage. We stopped at a German baker's. I bade her sit down at the neat marble table, and I bought two rolls. She declined lager, which

I offered her in fun. We took water instead, and we had dined, and had paid two cents for our meal, and had had a very merry dinner, too, when the clock struck two.

"And now, Mr. Carter," said she, "I will steal no more of your day. You did not come to New York to escort lone damsels to the Astor Library or to dinner. Nor did I come only to see the lions or to read French. I insist on your going to your affairs, and leaving me to mine. If you will meet me at the Library half an hour before it closes, I will thank you ; till then," with a tragedy shake of the hand, and a merry laugh, "adieu!"

I knew very well that no harm could happen to her in two hours of an autumn afternoon. I was not sorry for her *congé*, for it gave me an opportunity to follow my own plans. I stopped at one or two cabinet-makers, and talked with the "jours" about work, that I might tell her with truth that I had been in search of it; — then I sedulously began on calling upon every man I could reach named Mason. O, how often I went through one phase or another of this colloquy : —

"Is Mr. Mason in ?"

"That's my name, sir."

"Can you give me the address of Mr. Mason who returned from Europe last May ?"

"Know no such person, sir."

The reader can imagine how many forms this dia-

logue could be repeated in, before, as I wrought my
way through a long line of dry-goods cases to a distant
counting-room, I heard some one in it say, "No,
madam, I know no such person as you describe"; and
from the recess Fausta emerged and met me. Her
plan for the afternoon had been the same with mine.
We laughed as we detected each other; then I told
her she had had quite enough of this, that it was time
she should rest, and took her, *nolens volens*, into the
ladies' parlor of the St. Nicholas, and bade her wait
there through the twilight, with my copy of Clementine, till I should return from the police-station. If
the reader has ever waited in such a place for some
one to come and attend to him, he will understand
that nobody will be apt to molest him when he has not
asked for attention.

Two hours I left Fausta in the rocking-chair, which
there the Public had provided for her. Then I returned, sadly enough. No tidings of Rowdy Rob,
none of trunk, Bible, money, letter, medal, or anything. Still was my district sergeant hopeful, and,
as always, respectful. But I was hopeless this time,
and I knew that the next day Fausta would be plung-
ing into the war with intelligence-houses and advertisements. For the night, I was determined that she
should spend it in my ideal "respectable boarding-
house." On my way down town, I stopped in at one
or two shops to make inquiries, and satisfied myself
where I would take her. Still I thought it wisest that

we should go after tea; and another cross-street baker, and another pair of rolls, and another tap at the Croton, provided that repast for us. Then I told Fausta of the respectable boarding-house, and that she must go there. She did not say no. But she did say she would rather not spend the evening there. "There must be some place open for us," said she. "There! there is a church-bell! The church is always home. Let us come there."

So to "evening meeting" we went, startling the sexton by arriving an hour early. If there were any who wondered what was the use of that Wednesday-evening service, we did not. In a dark gallery pew we sat, she at one end, I at the other; and, if the whole truth be told, each of us fell asleep at once, and slept till the heavy organ tones taught us that the service had begun. A hundred or more people had straggled in then, and the preacher, good soul, he took for his text, "Doth not God care for the ravens?" I cannot describe the ineffable feeling of home that came over me in that dark pew of that old church. I had never been in so large a church before. I had never heard so heavy an organ before. Perhaps I had heard better preaching, but never any that came to my occasions more. But it was none of these things which moved me. It was the fact that we were just where we had a right to be. No impudent waiter could ask us why we were sitting there, nor any petulant policeman propose that we should push on. It was God's house, and, because his, it was his children's.

All this feeling of repose grew upon me, and, as it proved, upon Fausta also. For when the service was ended, and I ventured to ask her whether she also had this sense of home and rest, she assented so eagerly, that I proposed, though with hesitation, a notion which had crossed me, that I should leave her there.

"I cannot think," I said, "of any possible harm that could come to you before morning."

"Do you know, I had thought of that very same thing, but I did not dare tell you," she said.

Was not I glad that she had considered me her keeper! But I only said, "At the 'respectable boarding-house' you might be annoyed by questions."

"And no one will speak to me here. I know that from Goody Two-Shoes."

"I will be here," said I, "at sunrise in the morning." And so I bade her good by, insisting on leaving in the pew my own great-coat. I knew she might need it before morning. I walked out as the sexton closed the door below on the last of the down-stairs worshippers. He passed along the aisles below, with his long poker which screwed down the gas. I saw at once that he had no intent of exploring the galleries. But I loitered outside till I saw him lock the doors and depart; and then, happy in the thought that Miss Jones was in the safest place in New York, — as comfortable as she was the night before, and much more comfortable than she had been any night upon the canal, I went in search of my own lodging.

" To the respectable boarding-house ? "

Not a bit, reader. I had no shillings for respectable or disrespectable boarding-houses. I asked the first policeman where his district station was. I went into its office, and told the captain that I was green in the city ; had got no work and no money. In truth, I had left my purse in Miss Jones's charge, and a five-cent piece, which I showed the chief, was all I had. He said no word but to bid me go up two flights and turn into the first bunk I found. I did so ; and in five minutes was asleep in a better bed than I had slept in for nine days.

That was what the Public did for me that night. I, too, was safe !

I am making this story too long. But with that night and its anxieties the end has come. At sunrise I rose and made my easy toilet. I bought and ate my roll, — varying the brand from yesterday's. I bought another, with a lump of butter, and an orange, for Fausta. I left my portmanteau at the station, while I rushed to the sexton's house, told his wife I had left my gloves in church the night before, — as was the truth, — and easily obtained from her the keys. In a moment I was in the vestibule — locked in — was in the gallery, and there found Fausta, just awake, as she declared, from a comfortable night, reading her morning lesson in the Bible, and sure, she said, that

I should soon appear. Nor ghost, nor wraith, had visited her. I spread for her a brown paper table-cloth on the table in the vestibule. I laid out her breakfast for her, called her, and wondered at her toilet. How is it that women always make themselves appear as neat and finished as if there were no conflict, dust, or wrinkle in the world.

[Here Fausta adds, in this manuscript, a parenthesis, to say that she folded her undersleeves neatly, and her collar, before she slept, and put them between the cushions, upon which she slept. In the morning they had been pressed — without a sad-iron.]

She finished her repast. I opened the church door for five minutes. She passed out when she had enough examined the monuments, and at a respect-able distance I followed her. We joined each other, and took our accustomed morning walk; but then she resolutely said, " Good by," for the day. She would find work before night, — work and a home. And I must do the same. Only when I pressed her to let me know of her success, she said she would meet me at the Astor Library just before it closed. No, she would not take my money. Enough, that for twenty-four hours she had been my guest. When she had found her aunt and told her the story, they should insist on repaying this hospitality. Hospitality, dear reader, which I had dispensed at the charge of six cents. Have you ever treated Miranda for a day and found the charge so low ? When I urged other assistance she said resolutely, " No." In fact, she had already made an appointment at two, she said, and she must not waste the day.

I also had an appointment at two ; for it was at that hour that Burrham was to distribute the cyclopædias at Castle Garden. The Emigrant Commission had not yet seized it for their own. I spent the morning in asking vainly for Masons fresh from Europe, and for work in cabinet-shops. I found neither, and so wrought my way to the appointed place, where, instead of such wretched birds in the bush, I was to get one so contemptible in my hand.

Those who remember Jenny Lind's first triumph night at Castle Garden have some idea of the crowd as it filled gallery and floor of that immense hall when I entered. I had given no thought to the machinery of this folly. I only know that my ticket bade me be there at two P. M. this day. But as I drew near, the throng, the bands of policemen, the long queues of persons entering, reminded me that here was an affair of ten thousand persons, and also that Mr. Burrham was not unwilling to make it as showy, perhaps as noisy, an affair as was respectable, by way of advertising future excursions and distributions. I was led to seat No. 3,671 with a good deal of parade, and when I came there I found I was very much of a prisoner. I was late, or rather on the stroke of two. Immediately, almost, Mr. Burrham arose in the front and made a long speech about his liberality, and the public's liberality, and everybody's liberality in general, and the method of the distribution in particular. The mayor and four or five other well-known and respectable gentlemen were kind enough to be present to guarantee the fairness of the arrangements. At the suggestion of the mayor and the police, the doors would now be closed, that no persons might interrupt the ceremony till it was ended. And the distribution of the cyclopædias would at once go forward, in the order in which the lots were drawn,— earliest numbers securing the earliest impressions; which, as Mr. Burrham almost regretted to say, were a little better than the latest. After these had been distributed two figures would be drawn, — one green and one red, to indicate the fortunate lady and gentleman who would receive respectively the profits which had arisen from this method of selling the cyclopædias, after the expenses of printing and distribution had been covered, and after the magazines had been ordered.

Great cheering followed this announcement from all but me. Here I had shut myself up in this humbug hall, for Heaven knew how long, on the most important day of my life. I would have given up willingly my cyclopædia and my chance at the "profits," for the certainty of seeing Fausta at five o'clock. If I did not see her then, what might befall her, and when might I see her again. An hour before this certainty was my own, now it was only mine by my liberating myself from this prison. Still I was encouraged by seeing that everything was conducted like clock-work. From literally a hundred stations they were distributing the books. We formed ourselves into queues as we pleased, drew our numbers, and then presented ourselves at the bureaux, ordered our magazines, and took our cyclopædias. It would be done, at that rate, by half past four. An omnibus might bring me to the Park, and a Bowery car do the rest in time. After a vain discussion for the right of exit with one or two of the attendants, I abandoned myself to this hope, and began studying my cyclopædia.

It was sufficiently amusing to see ten thousand people resign themselves to the same task, and affect to be unconcerned about the green and red figures which were to divide the "profits." I tried to make out who were as anxious to get out of that tawdry den as I was. Four o'clock struck, and the distribution was not done. I began to be very impatient. What if Fausta fell into trouble? I knew, or hoped I knew, that she would struggle to the Astor Library, as to her only place of rescue and refuge, — her asylum. What if I failed her there? I who had pretended to be her protector! "Protector, indeed!" she would say, if she knew I was at a theatre witnessing the greatest folly of the age. And if I did not meet her to-day, when should I meet her? If she found her aunt, how should I find her? If she did not find her, — good God? that was worse, — where might she not be before twelve hours were over? Then the fatal trunk! I had told the police agent he might send it to the St. Nicholas, because I had to give him some address. But Fausta did not know this, and the St. Nicholas people knew nothing of us. I grew more and more excited, and when at last my next neighbor told me that it was half past four, I rose and insisted on leaving my seat. Two ushers with blue sashes almost held me down; they showed me the whole assembly sinking into quiet. In fact, at that moment Mr. Burrham was begging every one to be seated. I would not be seated. I would go to the door. I would go out. " Go, if you please ! " said the usher next it, contemptuously. And I looked, and there was no handle! Yet this was not a dream. It is the way they arrange the doors in halls where they choose to keep people in their places. I could have collared that grinning blue sash. I did tell him I would wring his precious neck for him, if he did not let me out. I said I would sue him for false imprisonment; I would have a writ of *habeas corpus*.

" *Habeas corpus* be d—d ! " said the officer, with an irreverent disrespect to the palladium. " If you are not more civil, sir, I will call the police, of whom we have plenty. You say you want to go out; you are keeping everybody in."

And, in fact, at that moment the clear voice of the mayor was announcing that they would not go on until there was perfect quiet; and I felt that I was imprisoning all these people, not they me.

"Child of the Public," said my mourning genius; "are you better than other men?" So I sneaked back to seat No. 3,671, amid the contemptuous and reproachful looks and sneers of my more respectable neighbors, who had sat where they were told to do. We must be through in a moment, and perhaps Fausta would be late also. If only the Astor would keep open after sunset! How often have I wished that since, and for less reasons!

Silence thus restored, Mr. A——, the mayor, led forward his little daughter, blindfolded her, and bade her put her hand into a green box, from which she drew out a green ticket. He took it from her, and read, in his clear voice again, "No. 2,973!" By this time we all knew where the "two thousands" sat. Then "nine hundreds" were not far from the front, so that it was not far that that frightened girl, dressed all in black, and heavily veiled, had to walk, who answered to this call. Mr. A—— met her, helped her up the stair upon the stage, took from her her ticket, and read, "Jerusha Stillingfleet, of Yellow Springs, who, at her death, as it seems, transferred this right to the bearer."

The disappointed nine thousand nine hundred and ninety-nine joined in a rapturous cheer, each man and woman, to show that he or she was not disappointed. The bearer spoke with Mr. Burrham, in answer to his questions, and, with a good deal of ostentation, he opened a check-book, filled a check and passed it to

her, she signing a receipt as she took it, and transfer-
ring to him her ticket.   So far, in dumb show, all was
well.   What was more to my purpose, it was rapid, for
we should have been done in five minutes more, but
that some devil tempted some loafer in a gallery to
cry, "Face! face!"   Miss Stillingfleet's legatee was
still heavily veiled.

In one horrid minute that whole amphitheatre,
which seemed to me then more cruel than the Coliseum
ever was, rang out with a cry of "Face, face!" I tried
the counter-cry of "Shame! shame!" but I was in
disgrace among my neighbors, and a counter-cry
never takes as its prototype does, either.   At first, on
the stage, they affected not to hear or understand;
then there was a courtly whisper between Mr. Burrham and the lady; but Mr. A——, the mayor, and
the respectable gentlemen, instantly interfered.   It
was evident that she would not unveil, and that they
were prepared to indorse her refusal.   In a moment
more she courtesied to the assembly; the mayor gave
her his arm, and led her out through a side-door.

O, the yell that rose up then!   The whole assembly
stood up, and, as if they had lost some vested right,
hooted and shrieked, " Back! back!   Face! face!"
Mr. A—— returned, made as if he would speak,
came forward to the very front, and got a moment's
silence.

"It is not in the bond, gentlemen," said he.   "The
young lady is unwilling to unveil, and we must not
compel her."

" Face ! face ! " was the only answer, and oranges
from up stairs flew about his head and struck upon the
table, — an omen only fearful from what it prophesied.
Then there was such a row for five minutes as I hope
I may never see or hear again. People kept their
places fortunately, under a vague impression that they
should forfeit some magic rights if they left those numbered seats. But when, for a moment, a file of policemen appeared in the orchestra, a whole volley of
cyclopædias fell like rain upon their chief, with a re-
newed cry of " Face ! face ! "

At this juncture, with a good deal of knowledge of
popular feeling, Mr. A—— led forward his child again.
Frightened to death the poor thing was, and crying;
he tied his handkerchief round her eyes hastily, and
took her to the red box. For a minute the house was
hushed. A cry of " Down ! down ! " and every one
took his place as the child gave the red ticket to her
father. He read it as before, " No. 3,671 ! " I heard
the words as if he did not speak them. All excited
by the delay and the row, by the injustice to the
stranger and the personal injustice of everybody to me,
I did not know, for a dozen seconds, that every one
was looking towards our side of the house, nor was it
till my next neighbor with the watch said, " Go, you
fool," that I was aware that 3,671 was I ! Even then,
as I stepped down the passage and up the steps, my
only feeling was, that I should get out of this horrid
trap, and possibly find Miss Jones lingering near the

Astor, — not by any means that I was invited to take a check for $5,000.

There was not much cheering. Women never mean to cheer, of course. The men had cheered the green ticket, but they were mad with the red one. I gave up my ticket, signed my receipt, and took my check. shook hands with Mr. A—— and Mr. Burrham, and turned to bow to the mob, — for mob I must call it now. But the cheers died away. A few people tried to go out perhaps, but there was nothing now to retain any in their seats as before, and the generality rose, pressed down the passages, and howled, " Face ! face ! " I thought for a moment that I ought to say something, but they would not hear me, and, after a moment's pause, my passion to depart overwhelmed me. I muttered some apology to the gentlemen, and left the stage by the stage door.

I had forgotten that to Castle Garden there can be no back entrance. I came to door after door, which were all locked. It was growing dark. Evidently the sun was set, and I knew the library door would be shut at sunset. The passages were very obscure. All around me rang this horrid yell of the mob, in which all that I could discern was the cry, " Face, face ! " At last, as I groped round, I came to a practicable door. I entered a room where the western sunset glare dazzled me. I was not alone. The veiled lady in black was there. But the instant she saw me she sprang towards me, flung herself into my arms, and cried : —

"Felix, is it you? — you are indeed my protector!"

It was Miss Jones! It was Fausta! She was the legatee of Miss Stillingfleet. My first thought was, "O, if that beggarly usher had let me go! Will I ever, ever think I have better rights than the Public again?"

I took her in my arms. I carried her to the sofa. I could hardly speak for excitement. Then I did say that I had been wild with terror; that I had feared I had lost her, and lost her forever; that to have lost that interview would have been worse to me than death; for unless she knew that I loved her better than man ever loved woman, I could not face a lonely night, and another lonely day.

"My dear, dear child," I said, "you may think me wild; but I must say this, — it has been pent up too long."

"Say what you will," she said after a moment, in which still I held her in my arms; she was trembling so that she could not have sat upright alone, — " say what you will, if only you do not tell me to spend another day alone."

And I kissed her, and I kissed her, and I kissed her, and I said, "Never, darling, God helping me, till I die!"

How long we sat there I do not know. Neither of us spoke again. For one, I looked out on the sunset and the bay. We had but just time to rearrange our-

selves in positions more independent, when Mr. A——
came in, this time in alarm, to say : —

"Miss Jones, we must get you out of this place, or
we must hide you somewhere. I believe, before God,
they will storm this passage, and pull the house about
our ears."

He said this, not conscious as he began that I was
there. At that moment, however, I felt as if I could
have met a million men. I started forward and passed
him, saying, "Let me speak to them." I rushed upon
the stage, fairly pushing back two or three bullies who
were already upon it. I sprang upon the table, kick-
ing down the red box as I did so, so that the red
tickets fell on the floor and on the people below. One
stuck in an old man's spectacles in a way which made
the people in the galleries laugh. A laugh is a great
blessing at such a moment. Curiosity is another.
Three loud words spoken like thunder do a good deal
more. And after three words the house was hushed
to hear me. I said : —

"Be fair to the girl. She has no father nor mother.
She has no brother nor sister. She is alone in the
world, with nobody to help her but the Public — and
me ! "

The audacity of the speech brought out a cheer,
and we should have come off in triumph, when some
rowdy — the original "face" man, I suppose —
said, —

"And who are you ? "

If the laugh went against me now I was lost, of course. Fortunately I had no time to think. I said without thinking, —

"I am the Child of the Public, and her betrothed husband!"

O Heavens! what a yell of laughter, of hurrahings, of satisfaction with a *dénouement*, rang through the house, and showed that all was well. Burrham caught the moment, and started his band, this time successfully, — I believe with "See the Conquering Hero." The doors, of course, had been open long before. Well-disposed people saw they need stay no longer; ill-disposed people dared not stay; the blue-coated men with buttons sauntered on the stage in groups, and I suppose the worst rowdies disappeared as they saw them. I had made my single speech, and for the moment I was a hero.

I believe the mayor would have liked to kiss me. Burrham almost did. They overwhelmed me with thanks and congratulations. All these I received as well as I could, — somehow I did not feel at all sur-prised, — everything was as it should be. I scarcely thought of leaving the stage myself, till, to my surprise, the mayor asked me to go home with him to dinner.

Then I remembered that we were not to spend the rest of our lives in Castle Garden. I blundered out something about Miss Jones, that she had no escort except me, and pressed into her room to find her. A group of gentlemen was around her. Her veil was back now. She was very pale, but very lovely. Have I said that she was beautiful as heaven? She was the queen of the room, modestly and pleasantly receiving their felicitations that the danger was over, and owning that she had been very much frightened. "Until," she said, "my friend, Mr. Carter, was fortunate enough to guess that I was here. How he did it," she said, turning to me, "is yet an utter mystery to me."

She did not know till then that it was I who had shared with her the profits of the cyclopædias.

As soon as we could excuse ourselves, I asked some one to order a carriage. I sent to the ticket-office for my valise, and we rode to the St. Nicholas. I fairly laughed as I gave the hackman at the hotel door what would have been my last dollar and a half only two hours before. I entered Miss Jones's name and my own. The clerk looked, and said, inquiringly, —

"Is it Miss Jones's trunk which came this afternoon?"

I followed his finger to see the trunk on the marble floor. Rowdy Rob had deserted it, having seen, perhaps, a detective when he reached Piermont. The trunk had gone to Albany, had found no owner, and had returned by the day boat of that day.

Fausta went to her room, and I sent her supper after her. One kiss and "Good night" was all that I got from her then.

"In the morning," said she, "you shall explain."

It was not yet seven. I went to my own room and dressed, and tendered myself at the mayor's just before his gay party sat down to dine. I met, for the first time in my life, men whose books I had read, and whose speeches I had by heart, and women whom I have since known to honor ; and, in the midst of this brilliant group, so excited had Mr. A—— been in telling the strange story of the day, I was, for the hour, the lion.

I led Mrs. A—— to the table ; I made her laugh very heartily by telling her of the usher's threats to me, and mine to him, and of the disgrace into which I fell among the three thousand six hundreds. I had never been at any such party before. But I found it was only rather simpler and more quiet than most parties I had seen, that its good breeding was exactly that of dear Betsy Myers.

As the party broke up, Mrs. A—— said to me, —

"Mr. Carter, I am sure you are tired, with all this excitement. You say you are a stranger here. Let me send round for your trunk to the St. Nicholas, and you shall spend the night here. I know I can make you a better bed than they."

I thought as much myself, and assented. In half an hour more I was in bed in Mrs. A——'s " best room."

" I shall not sleep better," said I to myself, " than I did last night."

That was what the Public did for me that night. I was safe again !

CHAPTER LAST.

FAUSTA'S STORY.

FAUSTA slept late, poor child. I called for her before breakfast. I waited for her after. About ten she appeared, so radiant, so beautiful, and so kind! The trunk had revealed a dress I never saw before, and the sense of rest, and eternal security, and unbroken love had revealed a charm which was never there to see before. She was dressed for walking, and, as she met me, said, —

"Time for constitutional, Mr. Millionnaire."

So we walked again, quite up town, almost to the region of pig-pens and cabbage-gardens which is now the Central Park. And after just the first gush of my enthusiasm, Fausta said, very seriously: —

"I must teach you to be grave. You do not know whom you are asking to be your wife. Excepting Mrs. Mason, No. 27 Thirty-fourth Street, sir, there is no one in the world who is of kin to me, and she does not care for me one straw, Felix," she said, almost sadly now. "You call yourself 'Child of the Public.' I started when you first said so, for that is just what I am.

"I am twenty-two years old. My father died before I was born. My mother, a poor woman, disliked by his relatives and avoided by them, went to live in Hoboken

over there, with me.   How she lived, God knows!
but it happened that of a strange death she died, I in
her arms."

After a pause, the poor girl went on : —

"There was a great military review, an encampment.   She was tempted out to see it.   Of a sudden
by some mistake, a ramrod was fired from a careless
soldier's gun, and it pierced her through her heart.   I
tell you, Felix, it pinned my baby frock into the
wound, so that they could not part me from her till it
was cut away.

"Of course every one was filled with horror.   Nobody claimed poor me, the baby.   But the battalion,
the Montgomery Battalion, it was, which had, by mis-
chance, killed my mother, adopted me as their child.
I was voted 'Fille du Regiment.'   They paid an assessment annually, which the colonel expended for me.
A kind old woman nursed me."

"She was your Betsy Myers," interrupted I.

"And when I was old enough I was sent into Con-
necticut, to the best of schools.   This lasted till I was
sixteen.   Fortunately for me, perhaps, the Montgomery Battalion then dissolved.   I was finding it hard to
answer the colonel's annual letters.   I had my living
to earn, — it was best I should earn it.   I declined a
proposal to go out as a missionary.   I had no call.   I
answered one of Miss Beecher's appeals for Western
teachers.   Most of my life since has been a school-
ma'am's.   It has had ups and downs.   But I have al-

ways been proud that the Public was my godfather;
and, as you know," she said, "I have trusted the
Public well. I have never been lonely, wherever I
went. I tried to make myself of use. Where I was
of use I found society. The ministers have been kind
to me. I always offered my services in the Sunday
schools and sewing-rooms. The school committees
have been kind to me. They are the Public's high
chamberlains for poor girls. I have written for the
journals. I won one of Sartain's hundred-dollar
prizes —"

"And I another," interrupted I.

"When I was very poor, I won the first prize for
an essay on bad boys."

"And I the second," answered I.

"I think I know one bad boy better than he
knows himself," said she. But she went on. "I
watched with this poor Miss Stillingfleet the night she
died. This absurd 'distribution' had got hold of her,
and she would not be satisfied till she had transferred
that strange ticket, No. 2,973, to me, writing the in-
dorsement which you have heard. I had had a longing to visit New York and Hoboken again. This
ticket seemed to me to beckon me. I had money
enough to come, if I would come cheaply. I wrote
to my father's business partner, and enclosed a note to
his only sister. She is Mrs. Mason. She asked me,
coldly enough, to her house. Old Mr. Grills always
liked me, — he offered me escort and passage as far as

Troy or Albany. I accepted his proposal, and you know the rest."

When I told Fausta my story, she declared I made it up as I went along. When she believed it, — as she does believe it now, — she agreed with me in declaring that it was not fit that two people thus joined should ever be parted. Nor have we been, ever!

She made a hurried visit at Mrs. Mason's. She prepared there for her wedding. On the 1st of November we went into that same church which was our first home in New York; and that dear old raven-man made us

ONE!

A PIECE OF POSSIBLE HISTORY.

[THIS essay was first published in the Monthly Religious
Magazine, Boston, for October, 1851. One or another professor
of chronology has since taken pains to tell me that it is impossible. But until they satisfy themselves whether Homer ever
lived at all, I shall hold to the note which I wrote to Miss Dryasdust's cousin, which I printed originally at the end of the
article, and which will be found there in this collection. The
difficulties in the geography are perhaps worse than those of
chronology.]

A SUMMER bivouac had collected together a little
troop of soldiers from Joppa, under the shelter of
a grove, where they had spread their sheep-skins,
tethered their horses, and pitched a single tent. With
the carelessness of soldiers, they were chatting away
the time till sleep might come, and help them to to-
morrow with its chances; perhaps of fight, perhaps of
another day of this camp indolence. Below the garden
slope where they were lounging, the rapid torrent of
Kishon ran brawling along. A full moon was rising
above the rough edge of the Eastern hills, and the
whole scene was alive with the loveliness of an Eastern landscape.

As they talked together, the strains of a harp came borne down the stream by the wind, mingling with the rippling of the brook.

"The boys were right," said the captain of the little company. "They asked leave to go up the stream to spend their evening with the Carmel-men; and said that they had there a harper, who would sing and play for them."

"Singing at night, and fighting in the morning! It is the true soldier's life," said another.

"Who have they there?" asked a third.

"One of those Ziklag-men," replied the chief. "He came into camp a few days ago, seems to be an old favorite of the king's, and is posted with his men, by the old tomb on the edge of the hill. If you cross the brook, he is not far from the Carmel post; and some of his young men have made acquaintance there."

"One is not a soldier for nothing. If we make enemies at sight, we make friends at sight too."

"Echish here says that the harper is a Jew."

"What! — a deserter?"

"I do not know that; that is the king's lookout. Their company came up a week ago, were reviewed the day I was on guard at the outposts, and they had this post I tell you of assigned to them. So the king is satisfied; and, if he is, I am."

"Jew or Gentile, Jehovah's man or Dagon's man," said one of the younger soldiers, with a half-irreverent tone, "I wish we had him here to sing to us."

" And to keep us awake," yawned another.

" Or to keep us from thinking of to-morrow," said a third.

" Can nobody sing here, or play, or tell an old-time story ? "

There was nobody. The only two soldiers of the post, who affected musical skill, were the two who had gone up to the Carmelites' bivouac ; and the little company of Joppa — catching louder notes and louder, as the bard's inspiration carried him farther and farther away — crept as far up the stream as the limits of their station would permit ; and lay, without noise, to catch, as they best could, the rich tones of the music as it swept down the valley.

Soothed by the sound, and by the moonlight, and by the summer breeze, they were just in mood to welcome the first interruption which broke the quiet of the night. It was the approach of one of their company, who had been detached to Accho a day or two before ; and who came hurrying in to announce the speedy arrival of companions, for whom he bespoke a welcome. Just as they were to leave Accho, he said, that day, on their return to camp, an Ionian trading-vessel had entered port. He and his fellow-soldiers had waited to help her moor, and had been chatting with her seamen. They had told them of the chance of battle to which they were returning ; and two or three of the younger Ionians, enchanted at the relief from the sea's imprisonment, had begged

them to let them volunteer in company with them.
These men had come up into the country with the soldiers, therefore; and he who had broken the silence of
the listeners to the distant serenade had hurried on to
tell his comrades that such visitors were on their way.

They soon appeared on foot, but hardly burdened
by the light packs they bore.

A soldier's welcome soon made the Ionian sailors as
much at home with the men of the bivouac, as they
had been through the day with the detachment from
the sea-board. A few minutes were enough to draw
out sheep-skins for them to lie upon, a skin of wine for
their thirst, a bunch of raisins and some oat-cakes for
their hunger; a few minutes more had told the news
which each party asked from the other; and then
these sons of the sea and these war-bronzed Philistines
were as much at ease with each other as if they had
served under the same sky for years.

"We were listening to music," said the old chief,
"when you came up. Some of our young men have
gone up, indeed, to the picket yonder, to hear the
harper sing, whose voice you catch sometimes, when
we are not speaking."

"You find the Muses in the midst of arms, then,"
said one of the young Ionians.

"Muses?" said the old Philistine, laughing. "That
sounds like you Greeks. Ah! sir, in our rocks here
we have few enough Muses, but those who carry these
lances, or teach us how to trade with the islands for
tin."

"That's not quite fair," cried another. "The youngsters who are gone sing well; and one of them has a harp I should be glad you should see. He made it himself from a gnarled olive-root." And he turned to look for it.

"You'll not find it in the tent: the boy took it with him. They hoped the Ziklag minstrel might ask them to sing, I suppose."

"A harp of olive-wood," said the Ionian, "seems Muse-born and Pallas-blessed."

And, as he spoke, one of the new-comers of the Philistines leaned over, and whispered to the chief: "He is a bard himself, and we made him promise to sing to us. I brought his harp with me that he might cheer up our bivouac. Pray, do you ask him."

The old chief needed no persuasion; and the eyes of the whole force brightened as they found they had a minstrel "of their own" now, when the old man pressed the young Ionian courteously to let them hear him: "I told you, sir, that we had no Muses of our own; but we welcome all the more those who come to us from over seas."

Homer smiled; for it was Homer whom he spoke to, — Homer still in the freshness of his unblinded youth. He took the harp which the young Philistine handed to him, thrummed upon its chords, and as he tuned them said: "I have no harp of olive-wood; we cut this out, it was years ago, from an old oleander in the marshes behind Colophon. What will you hear, gentlemen?"

" The poet chooses for himself," said the courtly old captain.

" Let me sing you, then, of *the Olive Harp* " ; and he struck the chords in a gentle, quieting harmony, which attuned itself to his own spirit, pleased as he was to find music and harmony and the olive of peace in the midst of the rough bivouac, where he had come up to look for war. But he was destined to be disappointed. Just as his prelude closed, one of the young soldiers turned upon his elbow, and whispered contemptuously to his neighbor: " Always *olives*, always *peace :* that 's all your music 's good for ! ' "

The boy spoke too loud, and Homer caught the discontented tone and words with an ear quicker than the speaker had given him credit for. He ended the prelude with a sudden crash on the strings, and said shortly, " And what is better to sing of than the olive ? "

The more courteous Philistines looked sternly on the young soldier ; but he had gone too far to be frightened, and he flashed back : " War is better. My broadsword is better. If I could sing, I would sing to your Ares ; we call him Mars ! "

Homer smiled gravely. " Let it be so," said he ; and, in a lower tone, to the captain, who was troubled at the breach of courtesy, he added, " Let the boy see what war and Mars are for."

He struck another prelude and began. Then was it that Homer composed his " Hymn to Mars." In

wild measure, and impetuous, he swept along through
the list of Mars's titles and attributes; then his key
changed, and his hearers listened more intently, more
solemnly, as in a graver strain, with slower music, and
an almost awed dignity of voice, the bard went on: —

> "Helper of mortals, hear!
> As thy fires give
> The present boldnesses that strive
> In youth for honor;
> So would I likewise wish to have the power
> To keep off from my head thy bitter hour,
> And quench the false fire of my soul's low kind,
> By the fit ruling of my highest mind!
> Control that sting of wealth
> That stirs me on still to the horrid scath
> Of hideous battle!
>
> "Do thou, O ever blessed! give me still
> Presence of mind to put in act my will,
> Whate'er the occasion be;
> And so to live, unforced by any fear,
> Beneath those laws of peace, that never are
> Affected with pollutions popular
> Of unjust injury,
> As to bear safe the burden of hard fates,
> Of foes inflexive, and inhuman hates!"

The tones died away; the company was hushed for
a moment; and the old chief then said gravely to his
petulant follower, " That is what *men* fight for, boy."
But the boy did not need the counsel. Homer's manner, his voice, the music itself, the spirit of the song,
as much as the words, had overcome him; and the
boasting soldier was covering his tears with his hands.

Homer felt at once (the prince of gentlemen he) that the little outbreak, and the rebuke of it, had jarred the ease of their unexpected meeting. How blessed is the presence of mind with which the musician of real genius passes from song to song, "whate'er the occasion be!" With the ease of genius he changed the tone of his melody again, and sang his own hymn, "To Earth, the Mother of all."

The triumphant strain is one which harmonizes with every sentiment; and he commanded instantly the rapt attention of the circle. So engrossed was he, that he did not seem to observe, as he sang, an addition to their company of some soldiers from above in the valley, just as he entered on the passage : —

> "Happy, then, are they
> Whom thou, O great in reverence!
> Are bent to honor. They shall all things find
> In all abundance! All their pastures yield
> Herds in all plenty. All their roofs are filled
> With rich possessions.
> High happiness and wealth attend them,
> While, with laws well-ordered, they
> Cities of happy households sway;
> And their sons exult in the pleasure of youth,
> And their daughters dance with the flower-decked girls,
> Who play among the flowers of summer!
> Such are the honors thy full hands divide;
> Mother of Gods and starry Heaven's bride!" *

A buzz of pleasure and a smile ran round the circle, in which the new-comers joined. They were the

* After Chapman.

soldiers who had been to hear and join the music at
the Carmel-men's post.   The tones of Homer's harp
had tempted them to return; and they had brought
with them the Hebrew minstrel, to whom they had
been listening.   It was the outlaw David, of Bethlehem Ephrata.

David had listened to Homer more intently than
any one; and, as the pleased applause subsided, the
eyes of the circle gathered upon him, and the manner
of all showed that they expected him, in minstrel-
fashion, to take up the same strain.

He accepted the implied invitation, played a short
prelude, and taking Homer's suggestion of topic, sang
in parallel with it:—

"I will sing a new song unto thee, O God!
Upon psaltery and harp will I sing praise to thee.
Thou art He that giveth salvation to kings,
That delivereth David, thy servant, from the sword.
Rid me and save me from those who speak vanity,
Whose right hand is a right hand of falsehood, —
That our sons may be as plants in fresh youth ;
That our daughters may be as corner-stones, —
The polished stones of our palaces ;
That our garners may be full with all manner of store ;
That our sheep may bring forth thousands and ten thousands in the
    way ;
That there may be no cry nor complaint in our streets.
Happy is the people that is in such a case ;
Yea, happy is the people whose God is the Lord ! "

The melody was triumphant; and the enthusiastic
manner yet more so.   The Philistines listened delight-

ed,—too careless of religion, they, indeed not to be catholic in presence of religious enthusiasm; and Homer wore the exalted expression which his face seldom wore. For the first time since his childhood, Homer felt that he was not alone in the world!

Who shall venture to tell what passed between the two minstrels, when Homer, leaving his couch, crossed the circle at once, flung himself on the ground by David's side, gave him his hand; when they looked each other in the face, and sank down into the rapid murmuring of talk, which constant gesture illustrated, but did not fully explain to the rough men around them? They respected the poets' colloquy for a while; but then, eager again to hear one harp or the other, they persuaded one of the Ionian sailors to ask Homer again to sing to them.

It was hard to persuade Homer. He shook his head, and turned back to the soldier-poet.

"What should I sing?" he said.

They did not enter into his notion: hearers will not always. And so, taking his question literally, they replied, "Sing? Sing us of the snow-storm, the storm of stones, of which you sang at noon."

Poor Homer! It was easier to do it than to be pressed to do it; and he struck his harp again:—

> "It was as when, some wintry day, to men
>   Jove would, in might, his sharp artillery show;
> He wills his winds to sleep, and over plain
>   And mountains pours, in countless flakes, his snow.

> Deep it conceals the rocky cliffs and hills,
>> Then covers all the blooming meadows o'er,
> All the rich monuments of mortals' skill,
>> All ports and rocks that break the ocean-shore.
> Rock, haven, plain, are buried by its fall;
> But the near wave, unchanging, drinks it all.
> So while these stony tempests veil the skies,
> While this on Greeks, and that on Trojans flies,
> The walls unchanged above the clamor rise." *

The men looked round upon David, whose expression, as he returned the glance, showed that he had enjoyed the fragment as well as they. But when they still looked expectant, he did not decline the unspoken invitation; but, taking Homer's harp, sang, as if the words were familiar to him: —

> " He giveth snow like wool;
> He scattereth the hoar-frost like ashes;
> He casteth forth his ice like morsels;
> Who can stand before his cold?
> He sendeth forth his word, and melteth them;
> He causeth his wind to blow, and the waters flow."

" Always this ' *He*,' " said one of the young soldiers to another.

" Yes," he replied; " and it was so in the beginning of the evening, when we were above there."

" There is a strange difference between the two men, though the one plays as well as the other, and the Greek speaks with quite as little foreign accent as the Jew, and their subjects are the same."

" Yes," said the young Philistine harper; " if the

* After Cowper and Pope. Long after!

Greek should sing one of the Hebrew's songs, you would know he had borrowed it, in a moment."

"And so, if it were the other way."

"Of course," said their old captain, joining in this conversation. "Homer, if you call him so, sings the thing made: David sings the maker. Or, rather, Homer thinks of the thing made: David thinks of the maker, whatever they sing."

"I was going to say that Homer would sing of cities; and David, of the life in them."

"It is not what they say so much, as the way they look at it. The Greek sees the outside, — the beauty of the thing; the Hebrew —"

"Hush!"

For David and his new friend had been talking too. Homer had told him of the storm at sea they met a few days before; and David, I think, had spoken of a mountain-tornado, as he met it years before. In the excitement of his narrative he struck the harp, which was still in his hand, and sung: —

> " Then the earth shook and trembled,
>   The foundations of the hills moved and were shaken,
>   Because He was wroth ;
>   There went up a smoke out of his nostrils,
>   And fire out of his mouth devoured ;
>   It burned with living coal.
>   He bowed the heavens also, and came down,
>   And darkness was under his feet ;
>   He rode upon a cherub and did fly,
>   Yea, he did fly upon the wings of the wind.
>   He made darkness his resting-place,

His pavilion were dark waters and clouds of the skies;
At the brightness before him his clouds passed by,
 Hail-stones and coals of fire.
The Lord also thundered in the heavens,
 And the highest gave his voice;
  Hail-stones and coals of fire.
Yea, he sent out his arrows, and scattered them,
And he shot out his lightnings, and discomfited them.
 Then the channels of waters were seen,
 And the foundations of the world were made known,
  At thy rebuke, O Lord!
 At the blast of the breath of thy nostrils.
  He sent from above, he took me,
  He drew me out of many waters."

" Mine were but a few verses," said Homer. " I am more than repaid by yours. Imagine Neptune, our sea-god, looking on a battle : —

"There he sat high, retired from the seas;
 There looked with pity on his Grecians beaten;
 There burned with rage at the god-king who slew them.
 Then he rushed forward from the rugged mountains,
   Quickly descending;
 He bent the forests also as he came down,
 And the high cliffs shook under his feet.
   Three times he trod upon them,
 And with his fourth step reached the home he sought for.

"There was his palace, in the deep waters of the seas,
 Shining with gold, and builded forever.
 There he yoked him his swift-footed horses;
 Their hoofs are brazen, and their manes are golden.
  He binds them with golden thongs,
  He seizes his golden goad,
 He mounts upon his chariot, and doth fly:
 Yes! he drives them forth into the waves!

> And the whales rise under him from the depths,
>   For they know he is their king;
> And the glad sea is divided into parts,
> That his steeds may fly along quickly;
> And his brazen axle passes dry between the waves,
>   So, bounding fast, they bring him to his Grecians."*

And the poets sank again into talk.

"You see it," said the old Philistine. "He paints the picture. David sings the life of the picture."

"Yes: Homer sees what he sings; David feels his song."

"Homer's is perfect in its description."

"Yes; but for life, for the soul of the description, you need the Hebrew."

"Homer might be blind; and, with that fancy and word-painting power of his, and his study of everything new, he would paint pictures as he sang, though unseen."

"Yes," said another; "but David — " And he paused.

"But David?" asked the chief.

"I was going to say that he might be blind, deaf, imprisoned, exiled, sick, or all alone, and that yet he would never know he was alone; feeling as he does, as he must to sing so, of the presence of this Lord of his!"

"He does not think of a snow-flake, but as sent from him."

"While the snow-flake is reminding Homer of that

* Iliad, vi.

hard, worrying, slinging work of battle. He **must** have seen fight himself."

They were hushed again. For, though they no longer dared ask the poets to sing to them, — so engrossed were they in each other's society, - - the soldiers were hardly losers from this modest courtesy. For the poets were constantly arousing each other to strike a chord, or to sing some snatch of remembered song. And so it was that Homer, *àpropos* of I do not know what, sang in a sad tone : —

> " Like leaves on trees the race of man is found,
>   Now green in youth, now withering on the ground :
>   Another race the following spring supplies ;
>   They fall successive, and successive rise.
>   So generations in their course decay,
>   So flourish these, when those have passed away." *

David waited for a change in the strain ; but Homer stopped. The young Hebrew asked him to go on ; but Homer said that the passage which followed was mere narrative, from a long narrative poem. David looked surprised that his new friend had not pointed a moral as he sang ; and said simply, " We sing that thus : —

> " As for man, his days are as grass ;
>   As a flower of the field, so he flourisheth ;
>   For the wind passeth over it, and it is gone,
>   And the place thereof shall know it no more.
>   But the mercy of the Lord
>   Is from everlasting to everlasting
>   Of them that fear him ;

> * Iliad, vi. — POPE.

> And his righteousness
> Unto children's children,
>   To such as keep his covenant,
> As remember his commandments to do them!"

Homer's face flashed delighted. "I, like you, 'keep his covenant,'" he cried ; and then without a lyre, for his was still in David's hands, he sang, in clear tone : —

> "Thou bid'st me birds obey ; — I scorn their flight,
> If on the left they rise, or on the right !
> Heed them who may, the will of Jove I own,
> Who mortals and immortals rules alone !"*

"That is more in David's key," said the young Philistine harper, seeing that the poets had fallen to talk together again. "But how would it sound in one of the hymns on one of our feast-days ? "

> "Who mortals and immortals rules alone."

"How, indeed ? " cried one of his young companions. "There would be more sense in what the priests say and sing, if each were not quarrelling for his own, — Dagon against Astarte, and Astarte against Dagon.

The old captain bent over, that the poets might not hear him, and whispered : "There it is that the Hebrews have so much more heart than we in such things. Miserable fellows though they are, so many of them, yet, when I have gone through their whole land with the caravans, the chances have been that any serious-

---

* Iliad, xii., after Sotheby.

minded man spoke of no God but this '*He*' of David's."

"What is his name?"

"They do not know themselves, I believe."

"Well, as I said an hour ago, God's man or Dagon's man, — for those are good names enough for me, — I care little; but I should like to sing as that young fellow does."

"My boy," said the old man, "have not you heard him enough to see that it is not *he* that sings, near as much as this love of his for a Spirit he does not name? It is that spirited heart of his that sings."

"*You* sing like him? Find his life, boy; and perhaps it may sing for you."

"We should be more manly men, if he sang to us every night."

"Or if the other did," said an Ionian sailor.

"Yes," said the chief. "And yet, I think, if your countryman sang every night to me, he would make me want the other. Whether David's singing would send me to his, I do not feel sure. But how silly to compare them! As well compare the temple in Accho with the roar of a whirlwind — "

"Or the point of my lance with the flight of an eagle. The men are in two worlds."

"O, no! that is saying too much. You said that one could paint pictures — "

" — Into which the other puts life. Yes, I did say so. We are fortunate that we have them together."

"For this man sings of men quite as well as the other does; and to have the other sing of God —"

" — Why, it completes the song. Between them they bring the two worlds together."

" He bows the heavens, and comes down," said the boy of the olive-harp, trying to hum David's air.

" Let us ask them —"

And just then there rang along the valley the sound of a distant conch-shell. The soldiers groaned, roused up, and each looked for his own side-arms and his own skin.

But the poets talked on unheeding.

The old chief knocked down a stack of lances; but the crash did not rouse them. He was obliged himself to interrupt their eager converse.

" I am sorry to break in; but the night-horn has sounded to rest, and the guard will be round to inspect the posts. I am sorry to hurry you away, sir," he said to David.

David thanked him courteously.

" Welcome the coming, speed the parting guest," said Homer, with a smile.

" We will all meet to-morrow. And may to-night's dreams be good omens !"

" If we dream at all," said Homer again : —

> " Without a sign his sword the brave man draws,
> And asks no omen but his country's cause."

They were all standing together, as he made this careless reply to the captain; and one of the young

men drew him aside, and whispered that David was
in arms against his country.

Homer was troubled that he had spokén as he did.
But the young Jew looked little as if he needed
sympathy.   He saw the doubt and regret which hung
over their kindly faces ; told them not to fear for him ;
singing, as he bade them good night, and with one of
the Carmel-men walked home to his own outpost : —

> " The Lord who delivered me from the paw of the lion,
>   The Lord who delivered me from the paw of the bear,
>   He will deliver me."

And he smiled to think how his Carmelite companion would start, if he knew when first he used
those words.

So they parted, as men who should meet on the
morrow.

But God disposes.

David had left to-morrow's dangers for to-morrow
to care for.   It seemed to promise him that he must
be in arms against Saul.   But, unlike us in our eager-
ness to anticipate our conflicts of duty, David *waited.*

And the Lord delivered him.   While they were
singing by the brookside, the proud noblemen of the
Philistine army had forced an interview with their
king ; and, in true native Philistine arrogance, insisted that " this Hebrew " and his men should be sent
away.

With the light of morning the king sent for the
minstrel, and courteously dismissed him, because " the

princes of the Philistines have said, ' He shall not go up with us to the battle.' "

So David marched his men to Ziklag.

And David and Homer never met on earth again.

NOTE. — This will be a proper place to print the following note, which I was obliged to write to a second cousin of Miss Dryasdust after she had read the MS. of the article above : —

"DEAR MADAM : — I thank you for your kind suggestion, in returning my paper, that it involves a piece of impossible history. You inform me, that, ' according to the nomenclatured formulas and homophonic analogies of Professor Gouraud, of never-to-be-forgotten memory, " A NEEDLE is less useful for curing a DEAF HEAD, than for putting ear-rings into a *Miss's lily-ears* " ; and that this shows that the second king of Judah, named David (or Deaf-head) began to reign in 1055 B.C., and died 1040 B. C.' ; and further, that, according to the same authority, ' *Homer flourished* when the Greeks were fond of his POETRY ' ; which, being interpreted, signifies that he flourished in 914 B.C., and, consequently, could have had no more to do with David than to plant ivy over his grave, in some of his voyages to Phœnicia.

"I thank you for the suggestion. I knew the unforgetting professor ; and I do not doubt that he remembered David and Homer as his near friends. But, of course, to such a memory, a century or two might easily slip aside.

"Now, did you look up Clement ? And did you not forget the Arundelian Marbles ? For, if you will take the long estimates, you will find that some folks think Homer lived as long ago as the year 1150, and some that it was as ' short ago ' as 850. And some set David as long ago as 1170, and some bring him down to a hundred and fifty years later. These are the long measures and the short measures. So the long and short of it is, that you can keep the two poets 320 years apart, while I have rather more than a century which I can select any night of, for a bivouac scene, in which to bring them together. Believe me, my dear Miss D., always yours, &c.

" Confess that you forgot the Arundelian Marbles ! "

THE SOUTH AMERICAN EDITOR.

[I AM tempted to include this little burlesque in this collection simply in memory of the Boston Miscellany, the magazine in which it was published, which won for itself a brilliant reputation in its short career. There was not a large staff of writers for the Miscellany, but many of the names then unknown have since won distinction. To quote them in the accidental order in which I find them in the table of contents, where they are arranged by the alphabetical order of the several papers, the Miscellany contributors were Edward Everett, George Lunt, Nathan Hale, Jr., Nathaniel Hawthorne, N. P. Willis, W. W. Story, J. R. Lowell, C. N. Emerson, Alexander H. Everett, Sarah P. Hale, W. A. Jones, Cornelius Matthews, Mrs. Kirkland, J. W. Ingraham, H. T. Tuckerman, Evart A. Duyckinck, Francis A. Durivage, Mrs. J. Webb, Charles F. Powell, Charles W. Storey, Lucretia P. Hale, Charles F. Briggs, William E. Channing, Charles Lanman, G. H. Hastings, and Elizabeth B. Barrett, now Mrs. Browning, some of whose earliest poems were published in this magazine. These are all the contributors whose names appear, excepting the writers of a few verses. They furnished nine tenths of the contents of the magazine. The two Everetts, Lowell, William Story, and my brother, who was the editor, were the principal contributors. And I am tempted to say that I think they all put some of their best work upon this magazine.

The misfortune of the Miscellany, I suppose, was that its publishers had no capital. They had to resort to the claptraps of fashion-plates and other engravings, in the hope of forcing an immediate sale upon persons who, caring for fashion-plates, did not care for the literary character of the enterprise. It gave a very happy escape-pipe, however, for the high spirits of some of us who had just left college, and, through my brother's kindness, I was sometimes permitted to contribute to the journal. In memory of those early days of authorship, I select "The South American Editor" to publish here. For the benefit of the New York Observer, I will state that the story is not true. And lest any should complain that it advocates elopements, I beg to observe, in the seriousness of mature life, that the proposed elopement did not succeed, and that the parties who proposed it are represented as having no guardians or keepers but themselves. The article was first published in 1842.]

IT is now more than six years since I received the following letter from an old classmate of mine, Harry Barry, who had been studying divinity, and was then a settled minister. It was an answer to a communication I had sent him the week before.

"TOPSHAM, R. I., January 22, 1836.

"To say the truth, my dear George, your letter startled me a little. To think that I, scarcely six months settled in the profession, should be admitted so far into the romance of it as to unite forever two young runaways like yourself and Miss Julia What's-her-name is at least curious. But, to give you your due, you have made a strong case of it, and as Miss —— (what is her name, I have not yours at hand) is not under any real guardianship, I do not see but I am perfectly justified in complying with your rather odd request. You see I make a conscientious matter of it.

" Write me word when it shall be, and I will be sure to be ready. Jane is of course in my counsels, and she will make your little wife feel as much at home as in her father's parlor. Trust us for secrecy.

" I met her last week — "

But the rest of the letter has nothing to do with the story.

The elopement alluded to in it (if the little transaction deserves so high-sounding a name) was, in every sense of the words, strictly necessary. Julia Wentworth had resided for years with her grandfather, a pragmatic old gentleman, to whom from pure affection she had long yielded an obedience which he would have had no right to extort, and which he was sometimes disposed to abuse. He had declared in the most ingenuous manner that she should never marry with his consent any man of less fortune than her own would be ; and on his consent rested the prospect of her inheriting his property.

Julia and I, however, care little for money now, we cared still less then ; and her own little property and my own little salary made us esteem ourselves entirely independent of the old gentleman and his will.

His intention respecting the poor girl's marriage was thundered in her ears at least once a week, so that we both knew that I had no need to make court to him; indeed, I had never seen him, always having met her in walking, or in the evening at party, spectacle, concert, or lecture. He had lately been more domineering than usual, and I had but little difficulty in persuading the dear girl to let me write to Harry Barry, to make the arrangement to which he assented in the letter which I have copied above. The reasoning which I pressed upon her is obvious. We loved each other, —the old gentleman could not help that; and as he managed to make us very uncomfortable in Boston, in the existing state of affairs, we naturally came to the conclusion that the sooner we changed that state the better. Our excursion to Topsham would, we supposed, prove a very disagreeable business to him; but we knew it would result very agreeably for us, and so, though with a good deal of maidenly compunction and granddaughterly compassion on Julia's part, we outvoted him.

I have said that I had no fortune to enable me to come near the old gentleman's *beau ideal* of a grandson-in-law. I was then living on my salary as a South American editor. Does the reader know what that is? The South American editor of a newspaper has the uncontrolled charge of its South American news. Read any important commercial paper for a month, and at the end of it tell me if you have any clear conception of the condition of the various republics (!) of South America. If you have, it is because that journal employs an individual for the sole purpose of setting them in the clearest order before you, and that individual is its South American editor. The general-news editor of the paper will keep the run of all the details of all the histories of all the rest of the world, but he hardly attempts this in addition. If he does, he fails. It is therefore necessary, from the most cogent reasons, that any American news office which has a strong regard for the consistency or truth of its South American intelligence shall employ some person competent to take the charge which I held in the establishment of the Boston Daily Argus at the time of which I am speaking. Before that enterprising paper was sold, I was its "South American man"; this being my only employment, excepting that by a special agreement, in consideration of an addition to my salary, I was engaged to attend to the news from St. Domingo, Guatemala, and Mexico.*

---

* I do not know that this explanation is at all clear. Let me, as the mathematicians say, give an instance which will illustrate the importance of this profession. It is now a few months since I received the following note from a distinguished member of the Cabinet: —

"WASHINGTON, January —, 1842.

"DEAR SIR : — We are in a little trouble about a little thing. There are now in this city no less than three gentlemen bearing credentials to government as Chargés from the Republic of Oronoco. They are, of course, accredited from three several home governments. The President signified, when the first arrived, that he would receive the Chargé from that government, on the 2d proximo, but none of us know who the right Chargé is. The newspapers tell nothing satis-

Monday afternoon, just a fortnight after I received Harry Barry's letter, in taking my afternoon walk round the Common, I happened to meet Julia. I always walked in the same direction when I was alone. Julia always preferred to go the other way; it was the only thing in which we differed. When we were together I always went her way of course, and liked it best.

factory about it. I suppose you know: can you write me word before the 2d?

"The gentlemen are : Dr. Estremadura, accredited from the 'Constitutional Government,' — his credentials are dated the 2d of November; Don Paulo Vibeira, of the 'Friends of the People,' 5th of November; M. Antonio de Vesga, 'Constitution of 1823,' October 27th. They attach great importance to our decision, each having scrip to sell. In haste, truly yours."

To this letter I returned the following reply : —

"SIR : — Our latest dates from Oronoco are to the 13th ultimo. The 'Constitution of '23' was then in full power. If, however, the policy of our government be to recognize the gentlemen whose principals shall be in office on the 2d proximo, it is a very different affair.

"You may not be acquainted with the formulas for ascertaining the duration of any given modern revolution. I now use the following, which I find almost exactly correct.

"Multiply the age of the President by the number of statute miles from the equator, divide by the number of pages in the given Constitution; the result will be the length of the outbreak, in days. This formula includes, as you will see, an allowance for the heat of the climate, the zeal of the leader, and the verbosity of the theorists. The Constitution of 1823 was reproclaimed on the 25th of October last. If you will give the above formula into the hands of any of your clerks, the calculation from it will show that that government will **go**

I had told her, long before, all about Harry's letter,
and the dear girl in this walk, after a little blushing
and sighing, and half faltering and half hesitating and
feeling uncertain, yielded to my last and warmest
persuasions, and agreed to go to Mrs. Pollexfen's ball
that evening, ready to leave it with me in my
buggy sleigh, for a three hours' ride to Topsham,
where we both knew Harry would be waiting for
us. I do not know how she managed to get through
tea that evening with her lion of a grandfather, for
she could not then cover her tearful eyes with a veil
as she did through the last half of our walk together.

out of power on the 1st of February, at 25 minutes after 1, P. M. Your
choice, on the 2d, must be therefore between Vibeira and Estremadura; here you will have no difficulty. Bobádil (Vibeira's principal) was on the 13th ultimo confined under sentence of death, at such
a distance from the capital that he cannot possibly escape and get into
power before the 2d of February. The 'Friends of the People,' in
Oronoco, have always moved slowly; they never got up an insurrection
in less than nineteen days' canvassing; that was in 1839. Generally
they are even longer. Of course, Estremadura will be your man.

"Believe me, sir, very respectfully, your obedient servant,

"GEORGE HACKMATACK."

The Cabinet had the good sense to act on my advice. My information proved nearly correct, the only error being one of seven minutes
in the downfall of the 1823 Constitution. This arose from my making
no allowance for difference of longitude between Piaut, where their
government was established, and Opee, where it was crushed. The
difference of time between those places is six minutes and fifty-three
seconds, as the reader may see on a globe.

Estremadura was, of course, presented to the President, and sold
his scrip.

I know that I got through my tea and such like ordinary affairs by skipping them. I made all my arrangements, bade Gage and Streeter be ready with the sleigh at my lodgings (fortunately only two doors from Mrs. Pollexfen's) at half-past nine o'clock, and was the highest spirited of men when, on returning to those lodgings myself at eight o'clock, I found the following missives from the Argus office, which had been accumulating through the afternoon.

No. 1.

"4 o'clock, P. M.

"Dear Sir : — The southern mail, just in, brings Buenos Ayres papers six days later, by the Medora, at Baltimore.

"In haste,   J. C."

(Mr. C. was the gentleman who opened the newspapers, and arranged the deaths and marriages; he always kindly sent for me when I was out of the way.)

No. 2.

"5 o'clock, P. M.

"Dear Sir : — The U. S. ship Preble is in at Portsmouth; latest from Valparaiso. The mail is not sorted.

"Yours,   J. D."

(Mr. D. arranged the ship news for the Argus.)

No. 3.

" 6 o'clock, P. M.

"DEAR SIR: — I boarded, this morning, off Cape Cod, the Blunderhead, from Carthagena, and have a week's later papers.

"Truly yours,   J. E."

(Mr. E. was the enterprising commodore of our news-boats.)

No. 4.

" 6¼ o'clock, P. M.

"DEAR SIR: — I have just opened accidentally the enclosed letter, from our correspondent at Panama. You will see that it bears a New Orleans post-mark. I hope it may prove exclusive.

"Yours,   J. F."

(Mr. F. was general editor of the Argus.)

No. 5.

" 6½ o'clock, P. M.

"DEAR SIR: — A seaman, who appears to be an intelligent man, has arrived this morning at New Bedford, and says he has later news of the rebellion in Ecuador than any published. The Rosina (his vessel) brought no papers. I bade him call at your room at eight o'clock, which he promised to do.

"Truly yours,   J. G."

(Mr. G. was clerk in the Argus counting-room.)

No. 6.

"7½ o'clock, P. M.

"DEAR SIR:— The papers by the Ville de Lyon, from Havre, which I have just received, mention the reported escape of M. Bonpland from Paraguay, the presumed death of Dr. Francia, the probable overthrow of the government, the possible establishment of a republic, and a great deal more than I understand in the least.

"These papers had not come to hand when I wrote you this afternoon. I have left them on your desk at the office.

"In haste,   J. F."

I was taken all aback by this mass of odd-looking little notes. I had spent the afternoon in drilling Singelton, the kindest of friends, as to what he should do in any probable contingency of news of the next forty-eight hours, for I did not intend to be absent on a wedding tour even longer than that time; but I felt that Singleton was entirely unequal to such a storm of intelligence as this; and, as I hurried down to the office, my chief sensation was that of gratitude that the cloud had broken before I was out of the way; for I knew I could do a great deal in an hour, and I had faith that I might slur over my digest as quickly as possible, and be at Mrs. Pollexfen's within the time arranged.

I rushed into the office in that state of zeal in which a man may do anything in almost no time. But first,

I had to go into the conversation-room, and get the oral news from my sailor; then Mr. H., from one of the little news-boats, came to me in high glee, with some Venezuela Gazettes, which he had just extorted from a skipper, who, with great plausibility, told him that he knew his vessel had brought no news, for she never had before. (N. B. In this instance she was the only vessel to sail, after a three months' blockade.) And then I had handed to me by Mr. J., one of the commercial gentlemen, a private letter from Rio Janeiro, which had been lent him. After these delays, with full materials, I sprang to work — read, read, read; wonder, wonder, wonder; guess, guess, guess; scratch, scratch, scratch; and scribble, scribble, scribble, make the only transcript I can give of the operations which followed. At first, several of the other gentlemen in the room sat around me; but soon Mr. C., having settled the deaths and marriages, and the police and municipal reporters immediately after him, screwed out their lamps and went home; then the editor himself, then the legislative reporters, then the commercial editors, then the ship-news conductor, and left me alone.

I envied them that they got through so much earlier than usual, but scratched on, only interrupted by the compositors coming in for the pages of my copy as I finished them; and finally, having made my last translation from the last *Boletin Extraordinario*, sprang up, shouting, "Now for Mrs. P.'s," and looked at

my watch. It was half past one !* I thought of
course it had stopped, — no; and my last manuscript
page was numbered twenty-eight! Had I been writing there five hours? Yes!

Reader, when you are an editor, with a continent's
explosions to describe, you will understand how one
may be unconscious of the passage of time.

I walked home, sad at heart. There was no light in
all Mr. Wentworth's house; there was none in any
of Mrs. Pollexfen's windows; † and the last carriage of
her last relation had left her door. I stumbled up
stairs in the dark, and threw myself on my bed. What
should I say, what could I say, to Julia? Thus pon-
dering, I fell asleep.

If I were writing a novel, I should say that, at a late
hour the next day, I listlessly drew aside the azure
curtains of my couch, and languidly rang a silver bell
which stood on my dressing-table, and received from a
page dressed in an Oriental costume the notes and letters which had been left for me since morning, and the
newspapers of the day.

I am not writing a novel.

The next morning, about ten o'clock, I arose and

* Newspaper men of 1868 will be amused to think that half past
one was late in 1836. At that time the "Great Western Mail" was
due in Boston at 6 P. M., and there was no later news except "local,"
or an occasional horse express.

† The reader will observe the Arcadian habits of 1836, when the German was yet unknown.

went down to breakfast. As I sat at the littered table which every one else had left, dreading to attack my cold coffee and toast, I caught sight of the morning papers, and received some little consolation from them. There was the Argus with its three columns and a half of "Important from South America," while none of the other papers had a square of any intelligibility excepting what they had copied from the Argus the day before. I felt a grim smile creeping over my face as I observed this signal triumph of our paper, and ventured to take a sip of the black broth as I glanced down my own article to see if there were any glaring misprints in it. Before I took the second sip, however, a loud peal at the door-bell announced a stranger, and, immediately after, a note was brought in for me which I knew was in Julia's handwriting.

"DEAR GEORGE:— Don't be angry; it was not my fault, really it was not. Grandfather came home just as I was leaving last night, and was so angry, and said I should not go to the party, and I had to sit with him all the evening. Do write to me or let me see you; do something — "

What a load that note took off my mind! And yet, what must the poor girl have suffered! Could the old man suspect? Singleton was true to me as steel, I knew. He could not have whispered, — nor Barry;

but that Jane, Barry's wife. O woman! woman! what newsmongers they are! Here were Julia and I, made miserable for life, perhaps, merely that Jane Barry might have a good story to tell. What right had Barry to a wife? Not four years out of college, and hardly settled in his parish. To think that I had been fool enough to trust even him with the particulars of my all-important secret! But here I was again interrupted, coffee-cup still full, toast still untasted, by another missive.

" Tuesday morning.

" SIR: — I wish to see you this morning. Will you call upon me, or appoint a time and place where I may meet you?

"Yours, JEDEDIAH WENTWORTH."

" Send word by the bearer."

" Tell Mr. Wentworth I will call at his house at eleven o'clock."

The cat was certainly out; Mrs. Barry had told, or some one else had, who I did not know and hardly cared. The scene was to come now, and I was almost glad of it. Poor Julia! what a time she must have had with the old bear!

At eleven o'clock I was ushered into Mr. Wentworth's sitting-room. Julia was there, but before I had even spoken to her the old gentleman came bustling across

the room, with his "Mr. Hackmatack, I suppose"; and
then followed a formal introduction between me and
her, which both of us bore with the most praiseworthy
fortitude and composure, neither evincing, even by a
glance, that we had ever seen or heard of each other
before.   Here was another weight off my mind and
Julia's.   I had wronged poor Mrs. Barry.   The
secret was not out — what could he want?   It very
soon appeared.

After a minute's discussion of the weather, the
snow, and the thermometer, the old gentleman drew
up his chair to mine, with " I think, sir, you are con-
nected with the Argus office ? "

" Yes, sir ; I am its South American editor."

" Yes ! " roared the old man, in a sudden rage.
" Sir, I wish South America was sunk in the depths
of the sea ! "

" I am sure I do, sir," replied I, glancing at Julia,
who did not, however, understand me.   I had not
fully passed out of my last night's distress.

My sympathizing zeal soothed the old gentleman a
little, and he said more coolly, in an undertone: " Well,
sir, you are well informed, no doubt ; tell me, in strict
secrecy, sir, between you and me, do you — do you
place full credit — entire confidence in the intelligence
in this morning's paper ? "

" Excuse me, sir; what paper do you allude to ?
Ah ! the Argus, I see.   Certainly, sir ; I have not
the least doubt that it is perfectly correct."

"No doubt, sir! Do you mean to insult me? — Julia, I told you so; he says there is no doubt it is true. Tell me again there is some mistake, will you?" The poor girl had been trying to soothe him with the constant remark of uninformed people, that the newspapers are always in the wrong. He turned from her, and rose from his chair in a positive rage. She was half crying. I never saw her more distressed. What did all this mean? Were one, two, or all of us crazy?

It soon appeared. After pacing the length of the room once or twice, Wentworth came up to me again, and, attempting to appear cool, said between his closed lips: "Do you say you have no doubt that Rio Janeiro is strictly blockaded?"

"Not the slightest in the world," said I, trying to seem unconcerned.

"Not the slightest, sir? What are you so impudent and cool about it for? Do you think you are talking of the opening of a rose-bud or the death of a mosquito? Have you no sympathy with the sufferings of a fellow-creature? Why, sir!" and the old man's teeth chattered as he spoke, "I have five cargoes of flour on their way to Rio, and their captains will — Damn it, sir, I shall lose the whole venture."

The secret was out. The old fool had been sending flour to Rio, knowing as little of the state of affairs there as a child.

"And do you really mean, sir," continued the old

man, "that there is an embargo in force in Monte Video?"

"Certainly, sir; but I'm very sorry for it."

"Sorry for it! of course you are; — and that all foreigners are sent out of Buenos Ayres?"

"Undoubtedly, sir. I wish — "

"Who does not wish so? Why, sir, my corresponding friends there are half across the sea by this time. I wish Rosas was in —— and that the Indians have risen near Maranham?"

"Undoubtedly, sir."

"Undoubtedly! I tell you, sir, I have two vessels waiting for cargoes of India-rubbers there, under a blunder-headed captain, who will do nothing he has not been bidden to, — obey his orders if he breaks his owners. You smile, sir? Why, I should have made thirty thousand dollars this winter, sir, by my India-rubbers, if we had not had this devilish mild, open weather, you and Miss Julia there have been praising so. But next winter must be a severe one, and with those India-rubbers I should have made — But now those Indians, — pshaw! And a revolution in Chili?"

"Yes, sir."

"No trade there! And in Venezuela?"

"Yes, sir."

"Yes, sir; yes, sir; yes, sir; yes, sir! Sir, I am ruined. Say 'Yes, sir,' to that. I have thirteen vessels at this moment in the South American trade, sir; say 'Yes, sir,' to that.   Half of them will be taken by the piratical scoundrels; say 'Yes, sir,' to that.   Their insurance will not cover them ; say 'Yes, sir,' to that.   The other half will forfeit their cargoes, or sell them for next to nothing; say 'Yes, sir,' to that.   I tell you I am a ruined man, and I wish the South America, and your daily Argus, and you—"

Here the old gentleman's old-school breeding got the better of his rage, and he sank down in his arm-chair, and, bursting into tears, said : " Excuse me, sir, — excuse me, sir, — I am too warm."

We all sat for a few moments in silence, but then I took my share of the conversation.   I wish you could have seen the old man's face light up little by little, as I showed him that to a person who understood the politics and condition of the mercurial country with which he had ignorantly attempted to trade, his condition was not near so bad as he thought it; that though one port was blockaded, another was opened ; that though one revolution thwarted him, a few weeks would show another which would favor him ; that the goods which, as he saw, would be worthless at the port to which he had sent them, would be valuable elsewhere ; that the vessels which would fail in securing the cargoes he had ordered could secure others ; that the very revolutions and wars which troubled him would require in some instances large government purchases, perhaps large contracts for freight, possibly even for passage, — his vessels might be used for trans-

ports; that the very excitement of some districts
might be made to turn to our advantage; that, in
short, there were a thousand chances open to him
which skilful agents could readily improve. I reminded him that a quick run in a clipper schooner
could carry directions to half these skippers of his, to
whom, with an infatuation which I could not and
cannot conceive, he had left no discretion, and who
indeed were to be pardoned if they could use none,
seeing the tumult as they did with only half an eye.
I talked to him for half an hour, and went into details
to show that my plans were not impracticable. The old
gentleman grew brighter and brighter, and Julia, as I
saw, whenever I stole a glance across the room, felt
happier and happier. The poor girl had had a hard
time since he had first heard this news whispered the
evening before.

His difficulties were not over, however; for when I
talked to him of the necessity of sending out one or
two skilful agents immediately to take the personal
superintendence of his complicated affairs, the old man
sighed, and said he had no skilful agents to send.

With his customary suspicion, he had no partners,
and had never intrusted his clerks with any general
insight into his business. Besides, he considered them
all, like his captains, blunder-headed to the last degree.
I believe it was an idea of Julia's, communicated to
me in an eager, entreating glance, which induced me to
propose myself as one of these confidential agents,

and to be responsible for the other. I thought, as I spoke, of Singleton, to whom I knew I could explain my plans in full, and whose mercantile experience would make him a valuable coadjutor. The old gentleman accepted my offer eagerly. I told him that twenty-four hours were all I wanted to prepare myself. He immediately took measures for the charter of two little clipper schooners which lay in port then; and before two days were past, Singleton and I were on our voyage to South America. Imagine, if you can, how these two days were spent. Then, as now, I could prepare for any journey in twenty minutes, and of course I had no little time at my disposal for last words with Mr. and — Miss Wentworth. How I won on the old gentleman's heart in those two days! How he praised me to Julia, and then, in as natural affection, how he praised her to me! And how Julia and I smiled through our tears, when, in the last good-bys, he said he was too old to write or read any but business letters, and charged me and her to keep up a close correspondence, which on one side should tell all that I saw and did, and on the other hand remind me of all at home.

I have neither time nor room to give the details of that South American expedition. I have no right to. There were revolutions accomplished in those days without any object in the world's eyes; and, even in mine, only serving to sell certain cargoes of long cloths and flour. The details of those outbreaks now told would make some patriotic presidents tremble in their seats; and I have no right to betray confidence at whatever rate I purchased it. Usually, indeed, my feats and Singleton's were only obtaining the best information and communicating the most speedy instructions to Mr. Wentworth's vessels, which were made to move from port to port with a rapidity and intricacy of movement which none besides us two understood in the least. It was in that expedition that I travelled almost alone across the continent. I was, I think, the first white man who ever passed through the mountain path of Xamaulipas, now so famous in all the Chilian picturesque annuals. I was carrying directions for some vessels which had gone round the Cape; and what a time Burrows and Wheatland and I had a week after, when we rode into the public square of Valparaiso shouting, "Muera la Constitucion, — Viva Libertad!" by our own unassisted lungs actually raising a rebellion, and, which was of more importance, a prohibition on foreign flour, while Bahamarra and his army were within a hundred miles of us. How those vessels came up the harbor, and how we unloaded them, knowing that at best our revolution could only last five days! But as I said, I must be careful, or I shall be telling other people's secrets.

The result of that expedition was that those thirteen vessels all made good outward voyages, and all but one or two eventually made profitable home voyages.

When I returned home, the old gentleman received me with open arms. I had rescued, as he said, a large share of that fortune which he valued so highly. To say the truth, I felt and feel that he had planned his voyages so blindly, that, without some wiser head than his, they would never have resulted in anything. They were his last, as they were almost his first, South American ventures. He returned to his old course of more methodical trading for the few remaining years of his life. They were, thank Heaven, the only taste of mercantile business which I ever had. Living as I did, in the very sunshine of Mr. Wentworth's favor, I went through the amusing farce of paying my addresses to Julia in approved form, and in due time received the old gentleman's cordial assent to our union, and his blessing upon it. In six months after my return, we were married; the old man as happy as a king. He would have preferred a little that the ceremony should have been performed by Mr. B——, his friend and pastor, but readily assented to my wishes to call upon a dear and early friend of my own.

Harry Barry came from Topsham and performed the ceremony, "assisted by Rev. Mr. B."

G. H.

Argus Cottage, April 1, 1842.

THE OLD AND THE NEW, FACE TO FACE.

A THUMB-NAIL SKETCH.

[THIS essay was published in Sartain's Magazine, in 1852, as "A Thumb-nail Sketch," having received one of ten premiums which Mr. Sartain offered to encourage young writers. It had been written a few years earlier, some time before the studies of St. Paul's life by Conybeare and Howson, now so well known, were made public. The chronology of my essay does not precisely agree with that of these distinguished scholars. But I make no attempt now either to recast the essay or to discuss the delicate and complicated questions which belong to the chronology of Paul's life or to that of Nero; for there is no question with regard to the leading facts. At the end of twenty years I may again express the wish that some master competent to the greatest themes might take the trial of Paul as the subject of a picture.]

IN a Roman audience-chamber, the old civilization and the new civilization brought out, at the very birth of the new, their chosen champions.

In that little scene, as in one of Rembrandt's thumbnail studies for a great picture, the lights and shades are as distinct as they will ever be in the largest scene of history. The champions were perfect representatives of the parties. And any man, with the soul of a man, looking on, could have prophesied the issue of the great battle from the issue of that contest.

The old civilization of the Roman Empire, just at that time, had reached a point which, in all those outward forms which strike the eye, would regard our times as mean indeed. It had palaces of marble, where even modern kings would build of brick with a marble front to catch the eye ; it counted its armies by thousands, where we count ours by hundreds ; it surmounted long colonnades with its exquisite statues, for which modern labor digs deep in ruined cities, because it cannot equal them from its own genius ; it had roads, which are almost eternal, and which, for their purposes, show a luxury of wealth and labor that our boasted locomotion cannot rival. These are its works of a larger scale. And if you enter the palaces, you find pictures of matchless worth, rich dresses which modern looms cannot rival, and sumptuous furniture at which modern times can only wonder. The outside of the ancient civilization is unequalled by the outside of ours, and for centuries will be unequalled by it. We have not surpassed it there. And we see how it attained this distinction, such as it was. It came by the constant concentration of power. Power in few hands is the secret of its display and glory. And thus that form of civilization attained its very climax in the moment of the greatest unity of the Roman Empire. When the Empire nestled into rest, after the convulsions in which it was born; when a generation had passed away of those who had been Roman citizens; when a generation arose, which, excepting one man, the emperor, was a nation of Roman subjects, — then the Empire was at its height of power, its centralization was complete, the system of its civilization was at the zenith of its success.

At that moment it was that there dawned at Rome the first gray morning-light of the new civilization.

At that moment it was that that short scene, in that one chamber, contrasted the two as clearly as they can be contrasted even in long centuries.

There is one man, the emperor, who is a precise type, an exact representative, of the old. That man is brought face to face with another who is a precise type, an exact representative, of the new.

Only look at them as they stand there! The man who best illustrates the old civilization owes to it the most careful nurture. From his childhood he has been its petted darling. Its principal is concentration under one head. He is that head. When he is a child, men know he will be emperor of the world. The wise men of the world teach him; the poets of the world flatter him; the princes of the world bow to him. He is trained in all elegant accomplishments; he is led forward through a graceful, luxurious society. His bearing is that of an emperor; his face is the face of fine physical beauty. Imagine for yourself the

sensual countenance of a young Bacchus, beautiful as
Milton's devils; imagine him clad in splendor before
which even English luxury is mean; arrayed in
jewels, to which even Eastern pomp is tinsel; imagine an expression of tired hate, of low, brutal lust,
hanging on those exquisite licentious features, and you
have before you the type of Roman civilization. It is
the boy just budding into manhood, whom later times
will name as the lowest embodiment of meanness and
cruelty! You are looking upon Nero!

Not only is this man an exact type of the ancient civilization, its central power, its outside beauty, but the
precise time of this sketch of ours is the exact climax
of the *moral* results of the ancient civilization. We
are to look at Nero just when he has returned to
Rome from a Southern journey.* That journey had
one object, which succeeded. To his after-life it gives
one memory, which never dies. He has travelled to
his beautiful country palace, that he might kill his
mother!

We can picture to ourselves Agrippina, by knowing
that she was Nero's mother, and our picture will not
fail in one feature. She has all the beauty of sense,
all the attraction of passion. Indeed, she is the Empress of Rome, because she is queen of beauty —
and of lust. She is most beautiful among the beautiful of Rome; but what is that beauty of feature in a
state of whose matrons not one is virtuous, of whose

* Anno Christi, 60.

daughters not one is chaste? It is the beauty of sense alone, fit adornment of that external grandeur, of that old society.

In the infancy of her son, this beautiful Agrippina consulted a troop of fortune-tellers as to his fate; and they told her that he would live to be Emperor of Rome, and to kill his mother. With all the ecstasy of a mother's pride fused so strangely with all the excess of an ambitious woman's love of power, she cried in answer, "He may kill me, if only he rules Rome!" *

She spoke her own fate in these words.

Here is the account of it by Tacitus. Nero had made all the preparations; had arranged a barge, that of a sudden its deck might fall heavily upon those in the cabin, and crush them in an instant. He meant thus to give to the murder which he planned the aspect of an accident. To this fatal vessel he led Agrippina. He talked with her affectionately and gravely on the way; "and when they parted at the lakeside, with his old boyish familiarity he pressed her closely to his heart, either to conceal his purpose, or because the last sight of a mother, on the eve of death, touched even his cruel nature, and then bade her farewell."

Just at the point upon the lake where he had directed, as the Empress sat in her cabin talking with her attendants, the treacherous deck was let fall upon them all. But the plot failed. She saw dead at her

* Tacit. Annal., xiv. 9.

feet one of her favorites, crushed by the sudden blow. But she had escaped it. She saw that death awaited them all upon the vessel. The men around sprang forward, ready to do their master's bidding in a less clumsy and more certain way. But the Empress, with one of her attendants, sprang from the treacherous vessel into the less treacherous waves. And there, this faithful friend of hers, with a woman's wit and a woman's devotion, drew on her own head the blows and stabs of the murderers above, by crying, as if in drowning, " Save me, I am Nero's mother ! " Uttering those words of self-devotion, she was killed by the murderers above, while the Empress, in safer silence, buoyed up by fragments of the wreck, floated to the shore.

Nero had failed thus in secret crime, and yet he knew that he could not stop here. And the next day after his mother's deliverance, he sent a soldier to her palace, with a guard ; and there, where she was deserted even by her last attendant, without pretence of secrecy, they put to death the daughter and the mother of a Cæsar. And Nero only waits to look with a laugh upon the beauty of the corpse, before he returns to resume his government at Rome.

That moment was the culminating moment of the ancient civilization. It is complete in its centralizing power ; it is complete in its external beauty ; it is complete in its crime. Beautiful as Eden to the eye, with luxury, with comfort, with easy indolence to all ; but dust and ashes beneath the surface ! It is corrupted at the head! It is corrupted at the heart! There is nothing firm!

This is the moment which I take for our little picture. At this very moment there is announced the first germ of the new civilization. In the very midst of this falsehood, there sounds one voice of truth; in the very arms of this giant, there plays the baby boy who is to cleave him to the ground. This Nero slowly returns to the city. He meets the congratulations of a senate, which thank him and the gods that he has murdered his own mother. With the agony of an undying conscience torturing him, he strives to avert care by amusement. He hopes to turn the mob from despising him by the grandeur of their public entertainments. He enlarges for them the circus. He calls unheard-of beasts to be baited and killed for their enjoyment. The finest actors rant, the sweetest musicians sing, that Nero may forget his mother, and that his people may forget him.

At that period, the statesmen who direct the machinery of affairs inform him that his personal attention is required one morning for a state trial, to be argued before the Emperor in person. Must the Emperor be there? May he not waste the hours in the blandishments of lying courtiers, or the honeyed falsehoods of a mistress? If he chooses thus to postpone the audience, be it so; Seneca, Burrhus, and his other counsellors will obey. But the time will come when the worn-out boy will be pleased some morning with

5 *

the almost forgotten majesty of state.   The time comes one day.   Worn out by the dissipation of the week, fretted by some blunder of his flatterers, he sends for his wiser counsellers, and bids them lead him to the audience-chamber, where he will attend to these cases which need an Emperor's decision.   It is at that moment that we are to look upon him.

He sits there, upon that unequalled throne, his face sickly pale with boyish debauchery; his young forehead worn with the premature sensual wrinkles of lust; and his eyes bloodshot with last night's intemperance.   He sits there, the Emperor-boy, vainly trying to excite himself, and forget her, in the blazonry of that pomp, and bids them call in the prisoner.

A soldier enters, at whose side the prisoner has been chained for years.   This soldier is a tried veteran of the Prætorian cohorts.   He was selected, that from him this criminal could not escape; and for that purpose they have been inseparably bound.   But, as he leads that other through the hall, he looks at him with a regard and earnestness which say he is no criminal to him.   Long since, the criminal has been the guardian of his keeper.   Long since, the keeper has cared for the prisoner with all the ardor of a new-found son's affection.

They lead that gray-haired captive forward, and with his eagle eye he glances keenly round the hall. That flashing eye has ere now bade monarchs quail; and those thin lips have uttered words which shall make the world ring till the last moment of the world shall come. The stately Eastern captive moves un- awed through the assembly, till he makes a subject's salutation to the Emperor-judge who is to hear him. And when, then, the gray-haired sage kneels before the sensual boy, you see the prophet of the new civilization kneel before the monarch of the old! You see Paul make a subject's formal reverence to Nero! *

Let me do justice to the court which is to try him. In that judgment-hall there are not only the pomp of Rome, and its crime; we have also the best of its wisdom. By the dissolute boy, Nero, there stands the prime minister Seneca, the chief of the philosophers of his time; "Seneca the saint," cry the Christians of the next century. We will own him to be Seneca the wise, Seneca almost the good. To this sage had been given the education of the monster who was to rule the world. This sage had introduced him into power, had restrained his madness when he could, and with his colleague had conducted the general administration of the Empire with the greatest honor, while the boy was wearing out his life in debauchery in the palace. Seneca dared say more to Nero, to venture more with him, than did any other man. For the young tiger was afraid of his old master long after he had tasted blood. Yet Seneca's system was a cowardly system. It was the best of Roman morality and Greek philoso- phy, and still it was mean. His daring was the brav-

---

* Anno Christi, 60.   See Neander, P. & T., B. iii. ch. x

est of the men of the old civilization.   He is the type
of their excellences, as is Nero the model of their
power and their adornments.   And yet all that Seneca's
daring could venture was to seduce the baby-tyrant
into the least injurious of tyrannies.   From the plunder of a province he would divert him by the carnage
of the circus.   From the murder of a senator he could
lure him by some new lust at home.   From the ruin
of the Empire, he could seduce him by diverting him
with the ruin of a noble family.   And Seneca did
this with the best of motives.   He said he used all
the power in his hands, and he thought he did.   He
was one of those men of whom all times have their
share.   The bravest of his time, he satisfied himself
with alluring the beardless Emperor by petty crime
from public wrong; he could flatter him to the expedient.   He dared not order him to the right.

But Seneca knew what was right.   Seneca also had
a well-trained conscience, which told him of right and
of wrong.   Seneca's brother, Gallio, had saved Paul's
life when a Jewish mob would have dragged him to
pieces in Corinth; and the legend is that Seneca and
Paul had corresponded with each other before they
stood together in Nero's presence, the one as counsel-
lor, the other as the criminal.*   When Paul arose

* This correspondence, as preserved in the collections of fragments,
has too much the aspect of a school-boy exercise to claim much credit,
though high authorities support it as genuine.   But the probability
that there was such a correspondence, though now lost, is very strong.

from that formal salutation, when the apostle of the new civilization spoke to the tottering monarch of the old, if there had been one man in that assemblage, could he have failed to see that that was a turning-point in the world's history? Before him in that little hall, in that little hour, was passing the scene which for centuries would be acted out upon the larger stage.

Faith on the one side, before expediency and cruelty on the other! Paul before Seneca and Nero! He was ready to address Nero, with the eloquence and vehemence which for years had been demanding utterance.

He stood at length before the baby Cæsar, to whose tribunal he had appealed from the provincial court of a doubting Festus and a trembling Agrippa.

And who shall ask what words the vigorous Christian spoke to the dastard boy! Who that knows the eloquence which rung out on the ears of astonished Stoics at Athens, which commanded the incense and the hecatombs of wandering peasants in Asia, which stilled the gabbling clamor of a wild mob at Jerusalem, — who will doubt the tone in which Paul spoke to Nero! The boy quailed for the moment before the man! The gilded dotard shrunk back from the home truths of the new, young, vigorous faith: the ruler of a hundred legions was nothing before the God-commissioned prisoner.

No; though at this audience all men forsook Paul, as he tells us; though not one of the timid converts were there, but the soldier chained at his side, — still he triumphed over Nero and Nero's minister.

From that audience-hall those three men retire. The boy, grown old in lust, goes thence to be an hour alone, to ponder for an hour on this God, this resurrection, and this truth, of which the Jew, in such uncourtly phrase, has harangued him. To be alone, until the spectre of a dying mother rises again to haunt him, to persecute him and drive him forth to his followers and feasters, where he will try to forget Paul and the Saviour and God, where he would be glad to banish them forever. He does not banish them forever! Henceforward, whenever that spectre of a mother comes before him, it must re-echo the words of God and eternity which Paul has spoken. Whenever the chained and bleeding captive of the arena bends suppliant before him, there must return the memory of the only captive who was never suppliant before him, and his words of sturdy power!

And Seneca? Seneca goes home with the mortified feelings of a great man who has detected his own meanness.

We all know the feeling; for all God's children might be great, and it is with miserable mortification that we detect ourselves in one or another pettiness. Seneca goes home to say: " This wild *Easterner* has rebuked the Emperor as I have so often wanted to rebuke him. He stood there, as I have wanted to stand, a man before a brute.

" He said what I have thought, and have been afraid
to say. Downright, straightforward, he told the Emperor truths as to Rome, as to man, and as to his vices,
which I have longed to tell him. He has done what I
am afraid to do. He has dared this, which I have
dallied with, and left undone. *What is the mystery of
his power?*"

Seneca did not know. Nero did not know. The
" Eastern mystery " was in presence before them, and
they knew it not!

What was the mystery of Paul's power?

Paul leaves them with the triumph of a man who
has accomplished the hope of long years. Those
solemn words of his, " After that, I *must* also see
Rome," expressed the longing of years, whose object
now, in part, at least, is gratified. He must see
Rome!

It is God's mission to him that he see Rome and its
Emperor. Paul has seen with the spirit's eye what
we have seen since in history, — that he is to be the
living link by which the electric fire of life should
pass first from religious Asia to quicken this dead,
brutish Europe. He knows that he is God's messenger to bear this mystery of life eternal from the one
land to the other, and to unfold it there. And to-day
has made real, in fact, this his inward confidence.
To-day has put the seal of fact on that vision of his,
years since, when he first left his Asiatic home. A
prisoner in chains, still he has to-day seen the accom-

plishment of the vows, hopes, and resolutions of that field of Troy, most truly famous from the night he spent there.   There was another of these hours when God brings into one spot the acts which shall be the *argument* of centuries of history.   Paul had come down there in his long Asiatic journeys, — Eastern in his lineage, Eastern in his temperament, Eastern in his outward life, and Eastern in his faith, — to that narrow Hellespont, which for long ages has separated East from West, tore madly up the chains which would unite them, overwhelmed even love when it sought to intermarry them, and left their cliffs frowning eternal hate from shore to shore.   Paul stood upon the Asian shore and looked across upon the Western.   There were Macedonia and the hills of Greece, here Troas and the ruins of Ilium.   The names speak war.   The blue Hellespont has no voice but separation, except to Paul.   But to Paul, sleeping, it might be, on the tomb of Achilles, that night the "man of Macedonia" appears, and bids him come over to avenge Asia, to pay back the debt of Troy.

"Come over *and help us.*"   Give us life, for we gave you death.   Give us help for we gave you ruin. Paul was not disobedient to the heavenly vision.   The Christian Alexander, he crosses to Macedon with the words of peace instead of war, — the Christian shepherd of the people, he carries to Greece, from Troy, the tidings of salvation instead of carnage, of charity instead of license.   And he knows that to

Europe it is the beginning of her new civilization, it is the dawn of her new warfare, of her new poetry, of her reign of heroes who are immortal.

That *faith* of his, now years old, has this day received its crowning victory. This day, when he has faced Nero and Seneca together, may well stand in his mind as undoing centuries of bloodshed and of license.

And in this effort, and in that spiritual strength which had nerved him in planning it and carrying it through, was the " Asian mystery." Ask what was the secret of Paul's power as he bearded the baby Emperor, and abashed the baby Philosopher? What did he give the praise to, as he left that scene? What was the principle in action there, but faith in the new life, faith in the God who gave it!

We do not wonder, as Seneca wondered, that such a man as Paul dared say anything to such a boy as Nero! The absolute courage of the new faith was the motive-power which forced it upon the world. Here were the sternest of morals driven forward with the most ultra bravery.

Perfect faith gave perfect courage to the first witnesses. And there was the " mystery " of their victories.

And so, in this case, when after a while Seneca again reminded Nero of his captive, poor Nero did not dare but meet him again. Yet, when he met him again in that same judgment-hall, he did not dare hear him long; and we may be sure that there were but few words before, with such affectation of dignity as he could summon, he bade them set the prisoner free.

Paul free!   The old had faced the new.   Each had named its champion.   And the new conquers!

THE DOT AND LINE ALPHABET.

[THIS sketch was originally published in the Atlantic Monthly for October, 1858, just at the time that the first Atlantic Cable, whose first prattle had been welcomed by the acclamations of a continent, gasped its last under the manipulations of De Sauty. It has since been copied by Mr. Prescott in his valuable hand-book of the electric telegraph.

The war, which has taught us all so much, has given a brilliant illustration of the dot and line alphabet, wholly apart from the electric use of it, which will undoubtedly be often repeated. In the movements of our troops under General Foster in North Carolina, Dr. J. B. Upham of Boston, the distinguished medical director in that department, equally distinguished for the success with which he has led forward the musical education of New England, trained a corps of buglers to converse with each other by long and short bugle-notes, and thus to carry information with literal accuracy from point to point at any distance within which the tones of a bugle could be heard. It will readily be seen that there are many occasions in military affairs when such means of conversation might prove of inestimable value. Mr. Tuttle, the astronomer, on duty in the same campaign, made a similar arrangement with long and short flashes of light.]

JUST in the triumph week of that Great Telegraph which takes its name from the Atlantic Monthly, I read in the September number of that journal the revelations of an observer who was surprised to find that he had the power of reading, as they run, the revelations of the wire. I had the hope that he was about to explain to the public the more general use of this instrument, — which, with a stupid fatuity, the public has as yet failed to grasp. Because its signals have been first applied by means of electro-magnetism, and afterwards by means of the chemical power of electricity, the many-headed people refuses to avail itself, as it might do very easily, of the same signals for the simpler transmission of intelligence, whatever the power employed.

The great invention of Mr. Morse is his register and alphabet. He himself eagerly disclaims any pretension to the original conception of the use of electricity as an errand-boy. Hundreds of people had thought of that and suggested it; but Morse was the first to give the errand-boy such a written message, that he could not lose it on the way, nor mistake it when he arrived. The public, eager to thank Morse, as he deserves, thanks him for something he did not invent. For this he probably cares very little; nor do I care more. But the public does not thank him for what he did originate, — this invaluable and simple alphabet. Now, as I use it myself in every detail of life, and see every hour how the public might use it, if it chose, I am really sorry for this negligence, — both on the score of his fame, and of general convenience.

Please to understand, then, ignorant Reader, that this curious alphabet reduces all the complex machinery of Cadmus and the rest of the writing-masters to characters as simple as can be made by a dot, a space, and a line, variously combined. Thus, the marks . ___ designate the letter A. The marks ___ . . . designate the letter B. All the other letters are designated in as simple a manner.

Now I am stripping myself of one of the private comforts of my life, (but what will one not do for mankind?) when I explain that this simple alphabet need not be confined to electrical signals. *Long* and *short* make it all, — and wherever long and short can be combined, be it in marks, sounds, sneezes, fainting-fits, canes, or children, ideas can be conveyed by this arrangement of the long and short together. Only last night I was talking scandal with Mrs. Wilberforce at a summer party at the Hammersmiths. To my amazement, my wife, who scarcely can play "The Fisher's Hornpipe," interrupted us by asking Mrs. Wilberforce if she could give her the idea of an air in "The Butcher of Turin." Mrs. Wilberforce had never heard that opera, — indeed, had never heard of it. My angel-wife was surprised, — stood thrumming at the piano, — wondered she could not catch this very odd bit of discordant accord at all, — but checked herself in her effort, as soon as I observed that her long notes and short notes, in their tum-tee, tee, — tee-tee, tee-tum tum, meant, "He's her brother."

The conversation on her side turned from " The Butcher of Turin," and I had just time on the hint thus given me by Mrs. I. to pass a grateful eulogium on the distinguished statesman whom Mrs. Wilberforce, with all a sister's care, had rocked in his baby-cradle, — whom, but for my wife's long and short notes, I should have clumsily abused among the other statesmen of the day.

You will see, in an instant, awakening Reader, that it is not the business simply of " operators " in telegraphic dens to know this Morse alphabet, but your business, and that of every man and woman. If our school committees understood the times, it would be taught, even before phonography or physiology, at school. I believe both these sciences now precede the old English alphabet.

As I write these words, the bell of the South Congregational strikes dong, dong, dong, — dong, dong, dong, dong, — dong, — dong. Nobody has unlocked the church-door. I know that, for I am locked up in the vestry. The old tin sign, " In case of fire, the key will be found at the opposite house," has long since been taken down, and made into the nose of a water-pot. Yet there is no Goody Two-Shoes locked in. No one except me, and certainly I am not ringing the bell. No! But, thanks to Dr. Channing's Fire Alarm,* the bell is informing the South End that

---

* The Fire Alarm is the invention of Dr. William F. Channing:

> " A wizard of such dreaded fame,
>   That when in Salamanca's cave,
>   Him listed his magic wand to wave,
> The bells would ring in Notre Dame."

there is a fire in District Dong-dong-dong,—that is to say, District No. 3. Before I have explained to you so far, the " Eagle " engine, with a good deal of noise, has passed the house on its way to that fated district. An immense improvement this on the old system, when the engines radiated from their houses in every possible direction, and the fire was extinguished by the few machines whose lines of quest happened to cross each other at the particular place where the child had been building cob-houses out of lucifer-matches in a paper warehouse. Yes, it is a very great improvement. All those persons, like you and me, who have no property in District Dong-dong-dong, can now sit at home at ease;—and little need we think upon the mud above the knees of those who have property in that district and are running to look after it. But for them the improvement only brings misery. You arrive wet, hot or cold, or both, at the large District No. 3, to find that the lucifer-matches were half a mile away from your store,—and that your own private watchman, even, had not been waked by the working of the distant engines. Wet property holder, as you walk home, consider this. When you are next in the Common Council, vote an appropriation for applying Morse's alphabet of long and short to the bells. Then they can be made to sound intelligibly. Daūng dĭng dĭng,—dĭng,—dĭng daūng,—daūng daūng daūng, and so on, will tell you as you wake in the night that it is Mr. B.'s store which is on fire, and not yours, or that

it is yours and not his. This is not only a convenience to you and a relief to your wife and family, who
will thus be spared your excursions to unavailable and
unsatisfactory fires, and your somewhat irritated return,
— it will be a great relief to the Fire Department.
How placid the operations of a fire where none attend
except on business! The various engines arrive, but
no throng of distant citizens, men and boys, fearful of
the destruction of their all. They have all roused on
their pillows to learn that it is No. 530 Pearl Street
which is in flames. All but the owner of No. 530
Pearl Street have dropped back to sleep. He alone
has rapidly repaired to the scene. That is he, who
stands in the uncrowded street with the Chief Engineer,
on the deck of No. 18, as she plays away. His property destroyed, the engines retire, — he mentions the
amount of his insurance to those persons who repre-
sent the daily press, they all retire to their homes, —
and the whole is finished as simply, almost, as was his
private entry in his day-book the afternoon before.*

This is what might be, if the magnetic alarm only
struck *long* and *short*, and we had all learned Morse's
alphabet. Indeed, there is nothing the bells could not
tell, if you would only give them time enough. We
have only one chime, for musical purposes, in the

* I am proud to say that such suggestions have had so much weight,
that in 1868 the alarm strikes the number of the box which first telegraphs danger, six-four, six-four, &c., six being the district number,
and four the box number in that district.

town. But, without attempting tunes, only give the bells the Morse alphabet, and every bell in Boston might chant in monotone the words of " Hail Columbia " at length, every Fourth of July. Indeed, if Mr. Barnard should report any day that a discouraged 'prentice-boy had left town for his country home, all the bells could instantly be set to work to speak articulately, in language regarding which the dullest imagination need not be at loss,

> " Turn again, Higginbottom,
> Lord Mayor of Boston ! "

I have suggested the propriety of introducing this alphabet into the primary schools. I need not say I have taught it to my own children, — and I have been gratified to see how rapidly it made head, against the more complex alphabet, in the grammar schools. Of course it does ; — an alphabet of two characters matched against one of twenty-six, — or of forty-odd, as the very odd one of the phonotypists employ ! On the Franklin-medal day I went to the Johnson-School examination. One of the committee asked a nice girl what was the capital of Brazil. The child looked tired and pale, and, for an instant, hesitated. But, before she had time to commit herself, all answering was rendered impossible by an awful turn of whooping-cough which one of my own sons was seized with, — who had gone to the examination with me. Hawm, hem hem ; — hem hem hem ; — hem, hem ; — hawm, hem hem ; — hem hem hem ; — hem, hem, — barked the poor child, who was at the opposite extreme of the school-room. The spectators and the committee looked to see him fall dead with a broken blood-vessel. I confess that I felt no alarm, after I observed that some of his gasps were long and some very *staccato ;* — nor did pretty little Mabel Warren. She recovered her color,— and, as soon as silence was in the least restored, answered, "*Rio* is the capital of Brazil," — as modestly and properly as if she had been taught it in her cradle. They are nothing but children, any of them, — but that afternoon, after they had done all the singing the city needed for its annual entertainment of the singers, I saw Bob and Mabel start for a long expedition into West Roxbury, — and when he came back, I know it was a long featherfew, from her prize school-bouquet, that he pressed in his Greene's " Analysis," with a short frond of maiden's hair.

I hope nobody will write a letter to " The Atlantic," to say that these are very trifling uses. The communication of useful information is never trifling. It is as important to save a nice child from mortification on examination-day, as it is to tell Mr. Fremont that he is not elected President. If, however, the reader is distressed, because these illustrations do not seem to his more benighted observation to belong to the big bow-wow strain of human life, let him consider the arrangement which ought to have been made years since, for lee shores, railroad collisions, and that curious class of maritime accidents where one steamer runs into another under the impression that she is a light-house. Imagine the Morse alphabet applied to a steam-whistle, which is often heard five miles. It needs only *long* and *short* again. "*Stop Comet*," for instance, when you send it down the railroad line, by the wire, is expressed thus: ... — . . ..

.. .. .. — — . —

Very good message, if Comet happens to be at the telegraph station when it comes! But what if Comet has gone by? Much good will your trumpery message do then! If, however, you have the wit to sound your long and short on an engine-whistle, thus; — Scre scre, scre ; screeee; scre scre ; scre scre scre scre scre ; scre scre scre, — scre scre ; screeeee screeeee ; scre ; screeeee ; — why, then the whole neighborhood, for five miles around, will know that Comet must stop, if only they understand spoken language, — and among others, the engineman of Comet will understand it; and Comet will not run into that wreck of worlds which gives the order, — with the nucleus of hot iron and his tail of five hundred tons of coal. — So, of the signals which fog-bells can give, attached to light-houses. How excellent to have them proclaim through the darkness, "I am Wall"! Or of signals for steamship-engineers. When our friends were on board the "Arabia" the other day, and she and the "Europa" pitched into each other, — as if, on that happy week, all the continents were to kiss and join hands all round, — how great the relief to the passengers on each, if, through every night of their passage, collision had been prevented by this simple expedient! One boat would have screamed, " Europa, Europa, Europa," from night to morning, — and the other, " Arabia, Arabia, Arabia," — and neither would have been mistaken, as one unfortunately was, for a light-house.

The long and short of it is, that whoever can mark distinctions of time can use this alphabet of long-and-short, however he may mark them. It is therefore within the compass of all intelligent beings, except those who are no longer conscious of the passage of time, having exchanged its limitations for the wider sweep of eternity. The illimitable range of this alphabet, however, is not half disclosed when this has been said. Most articulate language addresses itself to one sense, or at most to two, sight and sound. I see, as I write, that the particular illustrations I have given are all of them confined to signals seen or signals heard. But the dot-and-line alphabet, in the few years of its history, has already shown that it is not restricted to these two senses, but makes itself intelligible to all. Its message, of course, is heard as well as read. Any good operator understands the sounds of its ticks upon the flowing strip of paper, as well as when he sees it. As he lies in his cot at midnight, he will expound the passing message without striking a light to see it. But this is only what may be said of any written language. You can read this article to your wife, or she can read it, as she prefers ; that is, she chooses whether it shall address her eye or her ear. But the long-and-short alphabet of Morse and his imitators despises such narrow range. It addresses whichever of the five senses the listener chooses. This fact is illustrated by a curious set of anecdotes, — never yet put in print, I think, — of that critical despatch which in one night announced General Taylor's death to this whole land. Most of the readers of these lines probably read that despatch in the morning's paper. The compositors and editors had read it. To them it was a despatch to the eye. But half the operators at the stations *heard* it ticked out, by the register stroke, and knew it before they wrote it down for the press. To them it was a despatch to the ear. My good friend Langenzunge had not that resource. He had just been promised, by the General himself (under whom he served at Palo Alto), the office of Superintendent of the Rocky Mountain Lines. He was returning from Washington over the Baltimore and Ohio Railroad, on a freight-train, when he heard of the President's danger. Langenzunge loved Old Rough and Ready, — and he felt badly about his own office, too. But his extempore train chose to stop at a forsaken shanty-village on the Potomac, for four mortal hours, at midnight. What does he do, but walk down the line into the darkness, climb a telegraph-post, cut a wire, and applied the two ends to his tongue, to *taste*, at the fatal moment, the words, " Died at half past ten." Poor

Langenzunge! he hardly had nerve to solder the wire again. Cogs told me that they had just fitted up the Naguadavick stations with Bain's chemical revolving disk. This disk is charged with a salt of potash, which, when the electric spark passes through it, is changed to Prussian blue. Your despatch is noise-lessly written in dark blue dots and lines. Just as the disk started on that fatal despatch, and Cogs bent over it to read, his spirit-lamp blew up, — as the dear things will. They were beside themselves in the lonely, dark office; but, while the men were fumbling for matches, which would not go, Cogs's sister, Nydia, a sweet blind girl, who had learned Bain's alphabet from Dr. Howe at South Boston, bent over the chemical paper, and *smelt* out the prussiate of potash, as it formed itself in lines and dots to tell the sad story. Almost anybody used to reading the blind books can read the embossed Morse messages with the finger, — and so this message was read at all the midnight way-stations where no night-work is expected, and where the com-panies do not supply fluid or oil. Within my narrow circle of acquaintance, therefore, there were these simultaneous instances, where the same message was seen, heard, smelled, tasted, and felt. So universal is the dot-and-line alphabet, — for Bain's is on the same principle as Morse's.

The reader sees, therefore, first, that the dot-and-line alphabet can be employed by any being who has command of any long and short symbols, — be they

long and short notches, such as Robinson Crusoe kept
his accounts with, or long and short waves of electricity, such as these which Valentia is sending across to
the Newfoundland bay, so prophetically and appropri-
ately named "The Bay of Bulls." Also, I hope the
reader sees that the alphabet can be understood by any
intelligent being who has any one of the five senses
left him, — by all rational men, that is, excepting the
few eyeless deaf persons who have lost both taste and
smell in some complete paralysis. The use of Morse's
telegraph is by no means confined to the small clique
who possess or who understand electrical batteries. It
is not only the torpedo or the *Gymnotus electricus* that
can send us messages from the ocean. Whales in the
sea can telegraph as well as senators on land, if they
will only note the difference between long spoutings
and short ones. And they can listen, too. If they
will only note the difference between long and short,
the eel of Ocean's bottom may feel on his slippery skin
the smooth messages of our Presidents, and the catfish,
in his darkness, look fearless on the secrets of a Queen.
Any beast, bird, fish, or insect, which can discriminate
between long and short, may use the telegraph alphabet, if he have sense enough. Any creature, which
can hear, smell, taste, feel, or see, may take note of its
signals, if he can understand them. A tired listener
at church, by properly varying his long yawns and his
short ones, may express his opinion of the sermon to
the opposite gallery before the sermon is done. A

dumb tobacconist may trade with his customers in an alphabet of short-sixes and long-nines. A beleaguered Sebastopol may explain its wants to the relieving army beyond the line of the Chernaya, by the lispings of its short Paixhans and its long twenty-fours.

THE LAST VOYAGE OF THE RESOLUTE.

[I HAD some opportunities, which no other writer for the press had, I believe, of examining the Resolute on her return from that weird voyage which is the most remarkable in the history of the navies of the world. And, as I know of no other printed record of the whole of that voyage than this, which was published in the Boston Daily Advertiser of June 11, 1856, I reprint it here. Readers should remember that the English government abandoned all claim on the vessel; that the American government then bought her of the salvors, refitted her completely, and sent her to England as a present to the Queen. The Queen visited the ship, and accepted the present in person. The Resolute has never since been to sea. I do not load the page with authorities; but I studied the original reports of the Arctic expeditions carefully in preparing the paper, and I believe it to be accurate throughout.

The voyage from New London to England, when she was thus returned, is strictly her last voyage. But when this article was printed its name was correct.]

IT was in early spring in 1852, early on the morning of the 21st of April, that the stout English discovery ship Resolute, manned by a large crew, commanded by a most manly man, Henry Kellett, left her moorings in the great river Thames, a little below the old town of London, was taken in tow by a fussy steam-tug, and proudly started as one of a fine English squadron in the great search of the nations for the lost Sir John Franklin. It was late in the year 1855, on the 24th of December, that the same ship, weather-worn, scantily rigged, without her lighter masts, all in the trim of a vessel which has had a hard fight with wind, water, ice, and time, made the light-house of *New* London, — waited for day and came round to anchor in the other river Thames, of *New* England. Not one man of the English crew was on board. The gallant Captain Kellett was not there; but in his place an American master, who had shown, in his way, equal gallantry. The sixty or seventy men with whom she sailed were all in their homes more than a year ago. The eleven men with whom she returned had had to double parts, and to work hard to make good the places of the sixty. And between the day when the Englishmen left her, and the day the Americans found her, she had spent fifteen months and more alone. She was girt in by the ice of the Arctic seas. No man knows where she went, what narrow scapes she passed through, how low her thermometers marked cold; — it is a bit of her history which was never written. Nor what befell her little tender, the "Intrepid," which was left in her neighborhood, "ready for occupation," just as she was left. No man will ever tell of the nip that proved too much for her, —

of the opening of her seams, and her disappearance beneath the ice. But here is the hardy Resolute, which, on the 15th of May, 1854, her brave commander left, as he was ordered, " ready for occupation," — which the brave Captain Buddington found September 10, 1855, more than a thousand miles from there, and pronounced still " ready for occupation " ; — and of what can be known of her history from Old London to New London, from Old England's Thames to New England's Thames, we will try to tell the story ; as it is written in the letters of her old officers and told by the lips of her new rescuers.

For Arctic work, if ships are to go into every nook and lane of ice that will yield at all to wind and steam, they must be as nearly indestructible as man can make them. For Arctic work, therefore, and for discovery work, ships built of the *teak* wood of Malabar and Java are considered most precisely fitted. Ships built of teak are said to be wholly indestructible by time. To this we owe the fact, which now becomes part of a strange coincidence, that one of the old Captain Cook's ships which went round the world with him has been, till within a few years, a whaling among the American whalers, revisiting, as a familiar thing, the shores which she was first to discover. The English admiralty, eager to fit out for Arctic service a ship of the best build they could find, bought the two teak-built ships Baboo and Ptarmigan in 1850, — sent them to their own dock-yards to be refitted, and the Baboo became the

Assistance, — the Ptarmigan became the Resolute, of their squadrons of Arctic discovery.

Does the reader know that in the desolation of the Arctic shores the Ptarmigan is the bird most often found? It is the Arctic grouse or partridge,* and often have the ptarmigans of Melville Island furnished sport and even dinners to the hungry officers of the " Resolute," wholly unconscious that she had ever been their god-child, and had thrown off their name only to take that which she now wears.

Early in May, 1850, just at the time we now know that brave Sir John Franklin and the remnant of his crew were dying of starvation at the mouth of Back's River, the " Resolute " sailed first for the Arctic seas, the flag-ship of Commodore Austin, with whose little squadron our own De Haven and his men had such pleasant intercourse near Beechey Island. In the course of that expedition she wintered off Cornwallis Island, — and in autumn of the next year returned to England.

Whenever a squadron or a man or an army returns to England, unless in the extreme and exceptional case of complete victory over obstacle invincible, there is always dissatisfaction. This is the English way. And so there was dissatisfaction when Captain Austin returned with his ships and men. There was also still a lingering hope that some trace of Franklin might yet be found, perhaps some of his party. Yet more, there

* Tetrao lagopus.

were two of the searching ships which had entered the Polar seas from Behring's Straits on the west, the " Enterprise " and " Investigator," which might need relief before they came through or returned. Arctic search became a passion by this time, and at once a new squadron was fitted out to take the seas in the spring of 1852. This squadron consisted of the " Assistance " and " Resolute " again, which had been refitted since their return, of the " Intrepid " and " Pioneer," two steamships used as tenders to the " Assistance " and " Resolute " respectively, and of the " North Star," which had also been in those regions, and now went as a storeship to the rest of the squadron. To the command of the whole Sir Edward Belcher was appointed, an officer who had served in some of the earlier Arctic expeditions. Officers and men volunteered in full numbers for the service, and these five vessels therefore carried out a body of men who brought more experience of the Northern seas together than any expedition which had ever visited them.

Of these, Captain Henry Kellett had command of the " Resolute," and was second in seniority to Sir Edward Belcher, who made the "Assistance" the flagship. It shows what sort of man he was, to say that for more than ten years he spent only part of one in England, and was the rest of the time in an antipodean hemisphere or a hyperborean zone. Before brave Sir John Franklin sailed, Captain Kellett was in the Pacific. Just as he was to return home, he was ordered

into the Arctic seas to search for Sir John.   Three
years successively, in his ship the "Herald," he passed
inside Behring's Straits, and far into the Arctic Ocean.
He discovered "Herald Island," the farthest land
known there.   He was one of the last men to see Mc-
Clure in the "Investigator" before she entered the
Polar seas from the northwest.   He sent three of his
men on board that ship to meet them all again, as will
be seen, in strange surroundings.   After more than
seven years of this Pacific and Arctic life, he returned
to England, in May or June, 1851, and in the next
winter volunteered to try the eastern approach to the
same Arctic seas in our ship, the "Resolute."   Some
of his old officers sailed with him.

We know nothing of Captain Kellett but what his
own letters, despatches, and instructions show, as they
are now printed in enormous parliamentary blue-books,
and what the despatches and letters of his officers and
of his commander show.   But these papers present the
picture of a vigorous, hearty man, kind to his crew
and a great favorite with them, brave in whatever trial,
always considerate, generous to his officers, reposing
confidence in their integrity ; a man, in short, of whom
the world will be apt to hear more.   His commander,
Sir Edward Belcher, tried by the same standard, appears a brave and ready man, apt to talk of himself,
not very considerate of his inferiors, confident in his
own opinion ; in short, a man with whom one would
not care to spend three Arctic winters.   With him, as

we trace the "Resolute's" fortunes, we shall have much to do. Of Captain Kellett we shall see something all along till the day when he sadly left her, as bidden by Sir Edward Belcher, "ready for occupation."

With such a captain, and with sixty-odd men, the "Resolute" cast off her moorings in the gray of the morning on the 21st of April, 1852, to go in search of Sir John Franklin. The brave Sir John had died two years before, but no one knew that, nor whispered it. The river steam-tug "Monkey" took her in tow, other steamers took the "Assistance" and the "North Star"; the "Intrepid" and "Pioneer" got up their own steam, and to the cheers of the little company gathered at Greenhithe to see them off, they went down the Thames. At the Nore, the steamship "Desperate" took the "Resolute" in charge, Sir Edward Belcher made the signal "Orkneys" as the place of rendezvous, and in four days she was there, in Stromness outer harbor. Here there was a little shifting of provisions and coal-bags, those of the men who could get on shore squandered their spending-money, and then, on the 28th of April, she and hers bade good by to British soil. And, though they have welcomed it again long since, she has not seen it from then till now.

The "Desperate" steamer took her in tow, she sent her own tow-lines to the "North Star," and for three days in this procession of so wild and weird a name,

they three forged on westward toward Greenland, —
a train which would have startled any old Viking had
he fallen in with it, with a fresh gale blowing all the
time and "a nasty sea." On the fourth day all the
tow-lines broke or were cast off however, Neptune and
the winds claimed their own, and the "Resolute"
tried her own resources. The towing steamers were
sent home in a few days more, and the squadron left
to itself.

We have too much to tell in this short article to be
able to dwell on the details of her visits to the hospi-
table Danes of Greenland, or of her passage through
the ice of Baffin's Bay. But here is one incident,
which, as the event has proved, is part of a singular
coincidence. On the 6th of July all the squadron,
tangled in the ice, joined a fleet of whalers beset in it,
by a temporary opening between the gigantic masses.
Caught at the head of a bight in the ice, with the "Assistance" and the "Pioneer," the "Resolute" was,
for the emergency, docked there, and, by the ice closing behind her, was, for a while, detained. Meanwhile
the rest of the fleet, whalers and discovery ships, passed
on by a little lane of water, the American whaler "Mc-
Lellan" leading. This "McLellan" was one of the
ships of the spirited New London merchants, Messrs.
Perkins & Smith, another of whose vessels has now
found the "Resolute" and befriended her in her need
in those seas. The "McLellan" was their pioneer
vessel there.

The " North Star " of the English squadron followed
the " McLellan." A long train stretched out behind.
Whalers and government ships, as they happened to
fall into line, — a long three quarters of a mile. It
was lovely weather, and, though the long lane closed
up so that they could neither go back nor forward, —
nobody apprehended injury till it was announced on
the morning of the 7th that the poor " McLellan " was
nipped in the ice and her crew were deserting her.
Sir Edward Belcher was then in condition to befriend
her, sent his carpenters to examine her, — put a few
charges of powder into the ice to relieve the pressure
upon her, — and by the end of the day it was agreed
that her injuries could be repaired, and her crew went
on board again. But there is no saying what ice will
do next. The next morning there was a fresh wind,
the " McLellan " was caught again, and the water
poured into her, a steady stream. She drifted about
unmanageable, now into one ship, now into another,
and the English whalemen began to pour on board, to
help themselves to such plunder as they chose. At
the Captain's request, Sir Edward Belcher put an end
to this, sent sentries on board, and working parties, to
clear her as far as might be, and keep account of what
her stores were and where they went to. In a day or
two more she sank to the water's edge and a friendly
charge or two of powder put her out of the way of harm
to the rest of the fleet. After such a week spent together it will easily be understood that the New London

whalemen did not feel strangers on board one of Sir Edward's vessels when they found her " ready for occupation " three years and more afterwards.

In this tussle with the ice, the " Resolute " was nipped once or twice, but she has known harder nips than that since. As July wore away, she made her way across Baffin's Bay, and on the 10th of August made Beechey Island, — known now as the head-quarters for years of the searching squadrons, because, as it happened, the place where the last traces of Franklin's ships were found, — the wintering place of his first winter. But Captain Kellett was on what is called the " western search," and he only stayed at Beechey Island to complete his provisions from the storeships, and in the few days which this took, to see for himself the sad memorials of Franklin's party, — and then the " Resolute " and " Intrepid " were away, through Barrow's Straits, — on the track which Parry ran along with such success thirty-three years before, — and which no one had followed with as good fortune as he, until now.

On the 15th of August Captain Kellett was off; bade good by to the party at Beechey Island, and was to try his fortune in independent command. He had not the best of luck at starting. The reader must remember that one great object of these Arctic expeditions was to leave provisions for starving men. For such a purpose, and for travelling parties of his own over the ice, Captain Kellett was to leave a depot at

Assistance Bay, some thirty miles only from Beechey Island. In nearing for that purpose the "Resolute" grounded, was left with but seven feet of water, the ice threw her over on her starboard bilge, and she was almost lost. Not quite lost, however, or we should not be telling her story. At midnight she was got off, leaving sixty feet of her false keel behind. Captain Kellett forged on in her, — left a depot here and another there, — and at the end of the short Arctic summer had come as far westward as Sir Edward Parry came. Here is the most westerly point the reader will find on most maps far north in America, — the Melville Island of Captain Parry. Captain Kellett's associate, Captain McClintock of the "Intrepid," had commanded the only party which had been here since Parry. In 1851 he came over from Austin's squadron with a sledge party. So confident is every one there that nobody has visited those parts unless he was sent, that McClintock encouraged his men one day by telling them that if they got on well, they should have an old cart Parry had left thirty-odd years before, to make a fire of. Sure enough; they came to the place, and there was the wreck of the cart just as Parry left it. They even found the ruts the old cart left in the ground as if they had not been left a week.

Captain Kellett came into harbor, and with great spirit he and his officers began to prepare for the extended searching parties of the next spring. The "Resolute" and her tender came to anchor off Dealy

Island, and there she spent the next eleven months of her life, with great news around her in that time.

There is not much time for travelling in autumn. The days grow very short and very cold. But what days there were were spent in sending out carts and sledges with depots of provisions, which the parties of the next spring could use. Different officers were already assigned to different lines of search in spring. On their journeys they would be gone three months and more, with a party of some eight men, — dragging a sled very like a Yankee wood-sled with their instruments and provisions, over ice and snow. To extend those searches as much as possible, and to prepare the men for that work when it should come, advanced depots were now sent forward in the autumn, under the charge of the gentlemen who would have to use them in the spring.

One of these parties, the "South line of Melville Island" party, was under a spirited young officer Mr. Mecham, who had tried such service in the last expedition. He had two of "her Majesty's sledges," "The Discovery" and "The Fearless," a depot of twenty days' provision to be used in the spring, and enough for twenty-five days' present use. All the sledges had little flags, made by some young lady friends of Sir Edward Belcher's. Mr. Mecham's bore an armed hand and sword on a white ground, with the motto, "*Per mare, per terram, per glaciem.*" Over mud, land, snow, and ice they carried their dépôt, and were nearly back, when, on the 12th of October, 1852, Mr. Mecham made the great discovery of the expedition.

On the shore of Melville Island, above Winter Harbor, is a great sandstone boulder, ten feet high, seven or eight broad, and twenty and more long, which is known to all those who have anything to do with those regions as " Parry's sandstone," for it stood near Parry's observatory the winter he spent here, and Mr. Fisher, his surgeon, cut on a flat face of it this inscription : —

HIS BRITANNIC MAJESTY'S
SHIPS HECLA AND GRIPER,
COMMANDED BY
W. E. PARRY AND MR. LIDDON,
WINTERED IN THE ADJACENT
HARBOR 1819 – 20.

A. FISHER, SCULPT.

It was a sort of God Terminus put up to mark the end of that expedition, as the Danish gentlemen tell us our Dighton rock is the last point of Thorfinn's expedition to these parts. Nobody came to read Mr. Fisher's inscription for thirty years and more, — a little Arctic hare took up her home under the great rock, and saw the face of man for the first time when, on the 5th of June, 1851, Mr. McClintock, on his first expedition this way, had stopped to see whether possibly any of Franklin's men had ever visited it. He found no signs of them, had not so much time as Mr. Fisher for stone-cutting, but carved the figures 1851 on the stone, and left it and the hare. To this stone, on his way back to the " Resolute," Mr. Mecham came again (as we said) on the 12th of October, one memorable Tuesday morning, having been bidden to leave a record there. He went on in advance of his party, meaning to cut 1852 on the stone. On top of it was a small cairn of stones built by Mr. McClintock the year before. Mecham examined this, and to his surprise a copper cylinder rolled out from under a spirit tin. " On opening it, I drew out a roll folded in a bladder, which, being frozen, broke and crumbled. From its dilapidated appearance, I thought at the moment it must be some record of Sir Edward Parry, and, fearing I might damage it, laid it down with the intention of lighting the fire to thaw it. My curiosity, however, overcame my prudence, and on opening it carefully with my knife, I came to a roll of cartridge paper with the impression fresh upon the seals. My astonishment may be conceived on finding it contained an account of the proceedings of H. M. ship ' Investigator ' since parting company with the ' Herald ' [Captain Kellett's old ship] in August, 1850, in Behring's Straits. Also a chart which disclosed to view not only the long-sought Northwest Passage, but the completion of the survey of Banks and Wollaston lands. Opened and indorsed Commander McClintock's despatch ; found it contained the following additions : —

" ' Opened and copied by his old friend and messmate upon this date, April 28, 1852.   ROBERT McCLURE
" ' Party all well and return to Investigator to-day.' "

A great discovery indeed to flash across one in a minute. The "Investigator" had not been heard from for more than two years. Here was news of her not yet six months old. The Northwest Passage had been dreamed of for three centuries and more. Here was news of its discovery, — news that had been known to Captain McClure for two years. McClure and McClintock were lieutenants together in the "Enterprise" when she was sent after Sir John Franklin in 1848, and wintered together at Port Leopold the next winter. Now, from different hemispheres, they had come so near meeting at this old block of sandstone. Mr. Mecham bade his mate build a new cairn, to put the record of the story in, and hurried on to the "Resolute" with his great news, — news of almost everybody but Sir John Franklin. Strangely enough, the other expedition, Captain Collinson's, had had a party in that neighborhood, between the other two, under Mr. Parks; but it was his extreme point possible, and he could not reach the Sandstone, though he saw the ruts of McClure's sleigh. This was not known till long afterwards.

The "Investigator," as it appeared from this despatch of Captain McClure's, had been frozen up in the Bay of Mercy of Banks Land: Banks Land having been for thirty years at once an Ultima Thule and Terra Incognita, put down on the maps where Captain Parry saw it across thirty miles of ice and water in 1819. Perhaps she was still in that same bay: these old

friends wintering there, while the "Resolute" and
"Intrepid" were lying under Dealy Island, and only
one hundred and seventy miles between.   It must have
been tantalizing to all parties to wait the winter through,
and not even get a message across.   But until winter
made it too cold and dark to travel, the ice in the strait
was so broken up that it was impossible to attempt to
traverse it, even with a light boat, for the lanes of water.
So the different autumn parties came in, the last on the
last of October, and the officers and men entered on
their winter's work and play, to push off the winter
days as quickly as they could.

The winter was very severe ; and it proved that,
as the "Resolute" lay, they were a good deal exposed
to the wind.   But they kept themselves busy, — ex-
ercised freely, — found game quite abundant within
reasonable distances on shore, whenever the light
served, — kept schools for the men, — delivered scientific lectures to whoever would listen, — established
the theatre for which the ship had been provided at
home, — and gave juggler's exhibitions by way of va-
riety.   The recent system of travelling in the fall and
spring cuts in materially to the length of the Arctic
winters as Ross, Parry, and Back used to experience
it, and it was only from the 1st of November to the
10th of March that they were left to their own resources.   Late in October one of the "Resolute's" men
died, and in December one of the "Intrepid's," but,
excepting these cases, they had little sickness, for

weeks no one on the sick-list; indeed, Captain Kellett says cheerfully that a sufficiency of good provisions, with plenty of work in the open air, will insure good health in that climate.

As early in the spring as he dared risk a travelling party, namely, on the 10th of March, 1853, he sent what they all called a forlorn hope across to the Bay of Mercy, to find any traces of the "Investigator"; for they scarcely ventured to hope that she was still there. This start was earlier by thirty-five days than the early parties had started on the preceding expedition. But it was every way essential that, if Captain McClure had wintered in the Bay of Mercy, the messenger should reach him before he sent off any or all his men, in travelling parties, in the spring. The little forlorn hope consisted of ten men under the command of Lieutenant Pim, an officer who had been with Captain Kellett in the "Herald" on the Pacific side, had spent a winter in the "Plover" up Behring's Straits, and had been one of the last men whom the "Investigator" had seen before they put into the Arctic Ocean, to discover, as it proved, the Northwest Passage.

Here we must stop a moment, to tell what one of these sledge parties is by whose efforts so much has been added to our knowledge of Arctic geography, in journeys which could never have been achieved in ships or boats. In the work of the "Resolute's" parties, in this spring of 1852, Commander McClintock travelled 1,325 miles with his sledge, and Lieutenant

Mecham 1,163 miles with his, through regions before wholly unexplored. The sledge, as we have said, is in general contour not unlike a Yankee wood-sled, about eleven feet long. The runners are curved at each end. The sled is fitted with a light canvas trough, so adjusted that, in case of necessity, all the stores, &c., can be ferried over any narrow lane of water in the ice. There are packed on this sled a tent for eight or ten men ; five or six pikes, one or more of which is fitted as an ice-chisel ; two large buffalo-skins, a water-tight floor-cloth, which contrives

> " a double debt to pay,
> A floor by night, the sledge's sail by day "

(and it must be remembered that " day " and " night " in those regions are very equivocal terms). There are, besides, a cooking-apparatus, of which the fire is made in spirit or tallow lamps, one or two guns, a pick and shovel, instruments for observation, panni-kins, spoons, and a little magazine of such necessaries, with the extra clothing of the party. Then the pro-vision, the supply of which measures the length of the expedition, consists of about a pound of bread and a pound of pemmican per man per day, six ounces of pork, and a little preserved potato, rum, lime-juice, tea, chocolate, sugar, tobacco, or other such creature comforts. The sled is fitted with two drag-ropes, at which the men haul. The officer goes ahead to find the best way among hummocks of ice or masses of snow. Sometimes on a smooth floe, before the wind, the floor-cloth is set for a sail, and she runs off merrily, perhaps with several of the crew on board, and the rest running to keep up. But sometimes over broken ice it is a constant task to get her on at all. You hear, " One, two, three, *haul*," all day long, as she is worked out of one ice " cradle-hole" over a hummock into another. Different parties select different hours for travelling. Captain Kellett finally considered that the best division of time, when, as usual, they had constant daylight, was to start at four in the afternoon, travel till ten P. M., *breakfast* then, tent and rest four hours; travel four more, tent, dine, and sleep nine hours. This secured sleep, when the sun was the highest and most trying to the eyes. The distances accomplished with this equipment are truly surprising.

Each man, of course, is dressed as warmly as flannel, woollen cloth, leather, and seal-skin will dress him. For such long journeying, the study of boots becomes a science, and our authorities are full of discussions as to canvas or woollen, or carpet or leather boots, of strings and of buckles. When the time " to tent " comes, the pikes are fitted for tent-poles, and the tent set up, its door to leeward, on the ice or snow. The floor-cloth is laid for the carpet. At an hour fixed, all talking must stop. There is just room enough for the party to lie side by side on the floor-cloth. Each man gets into a long felt bag, made of heavy felting literally nearly half an inch thick. He brings this up wholly over his head, and buttons himself in. He has a little hole in it to breathe through.   Over the felt is sometimes a brown holland bag, meant to keep out moisture.   The officer lies farthest in the tent, — as being next the wind, the point of hardship and so of honor. The cook for the day lies next the doorway, as being first to be called.   Side by side the others lie between. Over them all Mackintosh blankets with the buffalo-robes are drawn, by what power this deponent sayeth not, not knowing.   No watch is kept, for there is little danger of intrusion.   Once a whole party was startled by a white bear smelling at them, who waked one of their dogs, and a droll time they had of it, springing to their arms while enveloped in their sacks.   But we remember no other instance where a sentinel was needed.   And occasionally in the journals the officer notes that he overslept in the morning, and did not " call the cook" early enough.   What a passion is sleep, to be sure, that one should oversleep with such comforts round him!

Some thirty or forty parties, thus equipped, set out from the "Resolute" while she was under Captain Kellett's charge, on various expeditions.   As the journey of Lieutenant Pim to the "Investigator" at Banks Land was that on which turned the great victory of her voyage, we will let that stand as a specimen of all. None of the others, however, were undertaken at so early a period of the year, and, on the other hand, several others were much longer, — some of them, as has been said, occupying three months and more.

Lieutenant Pim had been appointed in the autumn to the "Banks Land search," and had carried out his depots of provisions when the other officers took theirs. Captain McClure's chart and despatch made it no longer necessary to have that coast surveyed, but made it all the more necessary to have some one go and see if he was still there. The chances were against this, as a whole summer had intervened since he was heard from. Lieutenant Pim proposed, however, to travel all round Banks Land, which is an island about the size and shape of Ireland, in search of him, Collinson, Franklin, or anybody. Captain Kellett, however, told him not to attempt this with his force, but to return to the ship by the route he went. First he was to go to the Bay of Mercy; if the "Investigator" was gone, he was to follow any traces of her, and, if possible, communicate with her or her consort, the "Enterprise."

Lieutenant Pim started with a sledge and seven men, and a dog-sledge with two under Dr. Domville, the surgeon, who was to bring back the earliest news from the Bay of Mercy to the captain. There was a relief sledge to go part way and return. For the intense cold of this early season they had even more careful arrangements than those we have described. Their tent was doubled. They had extra Mackintoshes, and whatever else could be devised. They had bad luck at starting, — broke down one sledge and had to send back for another; had bad weather, and must encamp, once for three days. "Fortunately," says the lieutenant of this encampment, "the temperature arose from fifty-one below zero to thirty-six below, and there remained," while the drift accumulated to such a degree around the tents, that within them the thermometer was only twenty below, and, when they cooked, rose to zero. A pleasant time of it they must have had there on the ice, for those three days, in their bags smoking and sleeping! No wonder that on the fourth day they found they moved slowly, so cramped and benumbed were they. This morning a new sledge came to them from the ship; they got out of their bags, packed, and got under way again. They were still running along shore, but soon sent back the relief party which had brought the new sled, and in a few days more set out to cross the strait, some twenty-five to thirty miles wide, which, when it is open, as no man has ever seen it, is one of the Northwest Passages discovered by these expeditions.

Horrible work it was! Foggy and dark, so they could not choose the road, and, as it happened, lit on the very worst mass of broken ice in the channel. Just as they entered on it, one black raven must needs appear. "Bad luck," said the men. And when Mr. Pim shot a musk-ox, their first, and the wounded creature got away, "So much for the raven," they croaked again. Only three miles the first day, four miles the second day, two and a half the third, and half a mile the fourth; this was all they gained by most laborious hauling over the broken ice, dragging one sledge at a time, and sometimes carrying forward the stores separately and going back for the sledges. Two days more gave them eight miles more, but on the seventh day on this narrow strait, the dragging being a little better, the great sledge slipped off a smooth hummock, broke one runner to smash, and " there they were."

If the two officers had a little bit of a "tiff" out there on the ice, with the thermometer at eighteen below, only a little dog-sledge to get them anywhere, their ship a hundred miles off, fourteen days' travel as they had come, nobody ever knew it ; they kept their secret from us, it is nobody's business, and it is not to be wondered at. Certainly they did not agree. The Doctor, whose sled, the " James Fitzjames," was still sound, thought they had best leave the stores and all go back ; but the Lieutenant, who had the command, did not like to give it up, so he took the dogs and the " James Fitzjames " and its two men and went on, leaving the Doctor on the floe, but giving him directions to go back to land with the wounded sledge and wait for him to return. And the Doctor did it, like a spirited fellow, travelling back and forth for what he could not take in one journey, as the man did in the story who had a peck of corn, a goose, and a wolf to get across the river. Over ice, over hummock, the Lieutenant went on his way with his dogs, not a bear nor a seal nor a hare nor a wolf to feed them with ;

preserved meats, which had been put up with dainty
care for men and women, all he had for the ravenous,
tasteless creatures, who would have been more pleased
with blubber, came to Banks Land at last, but no game
there; awful drifts; shut up in the tent for a whole
day, and he himself so sick he could scarcely stand!
There were but three of them in all; and the captain
of the sledge not unnaturally asked poor Pim, when he
was at the worst, "What shall I do, sir, if you die?"
Not a very comforting question!

He did not die. He got a few hours' sleep, felt
better and started again, but had the discourage-
ment of finding such tokens of an open strait the last
year that he felt sure that the ship he was going to
look for would be gone. One morning, he had been
off for game for the dogs unsuccessfully, and, when he
came back to his men, learned that they had seen seventeen deer. After them goes Pim; finds them to
be *three hares*, magnified by fog and mirage, and their
long ears answering for horns. This same day they
got upon the Bay of Mercy. No ship in sight!
Right across it goes the Lieutenant to look for records;
when, at two in the afternoon, Robert Hoile sees
something black up the bay. Through the glass the
Lieutenant makes it out to be a ship. They change
their direction at once. Over the ice towards her!
He leaves the sledge at three and goes on. How far it
seems! At four he can see people walking about, and a
pile of stones and flag-staff on the beach. Keep on,

Pim; shall one never get there ?   At five he is within a
hundred yards of her, and no one has seen him.   But
just then the very persons see him who ought to!
Pim beckons, waves his arms as the Esquimaux do in
sign of friendship.   Captain McClure and his lieutenant Haswell are "taking their exercise," the chief
business of those winters, and at last see him!   Pim is
black as Erebus from the smoke of cooking in the
little tent.   McClure owns, not to surprise only, but
to a twinge of dismay.   " I paused in my advance,"
says he, " doubting who or what it could be, a denizen
of this or the other world."   But this only lasts a
moment.   Pim speaks.   Brave man that he can.
How his voice must have choked, as if he were in
a dream.   "I am Lieutenant Pim, late of ' Herald.'
Captain Kellett is at Melville Island."   Well-chosen
words, Pim, to be sent in advance over the hundred
yards of floe !   Nothing about the " Resolute," —
that would have confused them.   But " Pim," " Herald," and " Kellett " were among the last signs of England they had seen, — all this was intelligible.   An excellent little speech, which the brave man had been
getting ready, perhaps, as one does a telegraphic despatch, for the hours that he had been walking over
the floe to her.   Then such shaking hands, such a
greeting.   Poor McClure could not speak at first.
One of the men at work got the news on board;
and up through the hatches poured everybody, sick
and well, to see the black stranger, and to hear his

news from England. It was nearly three years since they had seen any civilized man but themselves.

The 28th of July, three years before, Commander McClure had sent his last despatch to the Admiralty. He had then prophesied just what in three years he had almost accomplished. In the winter of 1850 he had discovered the Northwest Passage. He had come round into one branch of it, Banks Straits, in the next summer ; had gladly taken refuge on the Bay of Mercy in a gale ; and his ship had never left it since. Let it be said, in passing, that most likely she is there now. In his last despatches he had told the Admiralty not to be anxious about him if he did not arrive home before the autumn of 1854. As it proved, that autumn he did come with all his men, except those whom he had sent home before, and those who had died. When Pim found them, all the crew but thirty were under orders for marching, some to Baffin's Bay, some to the Mackenzie River, on their return to England. McClure was going to stay with the rest, and come home with the ship, if they could ; if not, by sledges to Port Leopold, and so by a steam-launch which he had seen left there for Franklin in 1849. But the arrival of Mr. Pim put an end to all these plans. We have his long despatch to the Admiralty explaining them, finished only the day before Pim arrived. It gives the history of his three years' exile from the world, — an exile crowded full of effective work, — in a record which gives a noble picture of the

man. The Queen has made him Sir Robert Le Mesu-
rier McClure since, in honor of his great discovery.

Banks Land, or Baring Island, the two names belong to the same island, on the shores of which Mc-
Clure and his men had spent most of these two years
or more, is an island on which they were first of civilized men to land. For people who are not very particular, the measurement of it which we gave before,
namely, that it is about the size and shape of Ireland,
is precise enough. There is high land in the interior
probably, as the winds from in shore are cold. The
crew found coal and dwarf willow which they could
burn ; lemmings, ptarmigan, hares, reindeer, and
musk-oxen, which they could eat.

> " Farewell to the land where I often have wended
> My way o'er its mountains and valleys of snow ;
>   Farewell to the rocks and the hills I 've ascended,
> The bleak arctic homes of the buck and the doe ;
>   Farewell to the deep glens where oft has resounded
> The snow-bunting's song, as she carolled her lay
>   To hillside and plain, by the green sorrel bounded,
> Till struck by the blast of a cold winter's day."

There is a bit of description of Banks Land, from
the anthology of that country, which, so far as we
know, consists of two poems by a seaman named Nel-
son, one of Captain McClure's crew. The highest
temperature ever observed on this " gem of the sea "
was 53° in midsummer. The lowest was 65° below
zero in January, 1853 ; that day the thermometer did
not rise to 60° below, that month was never warmer

than 16° below, and the average of the month was
43° below. A pleasant climate to spend three years
in !

One day for talk was all that could be allowed, after
Mr. Pim's amazing appearance. On the 8th of
April, he and his dogs, and Captain McClure and a
party, were ready to return to our friend the "Resolute." They picked up Dr. Domville on the way; he
had got the broken sledge mended, and killed five
musk-oxen, against they came along. He went on in
the dog-sledge to tell the news, but McClure and his
men kept pace with them; and he and Dr. Domville
had the telling of the news together.

It was decided that the "Investigator" should be
abandoned, and the "Intrepid" and "Resolute" made
room for her men. Glad greeting they gave them
too, as British seamen can give. More than half the
crews were away when the "Investigator's" parties
came in, but by July everybody had returned. They
had found islands where the charts had guessed there
was sea, and sea where they had guessed there was
land; had changed peninsulas into islands and islands into peninsulas. Away off beyond the seventy-
eighth parallel, Mr. McClintock had christened the farthest dot of land "Ireland's Eye," as if his native island
were peering off into the unknown there;—a great
island, which will be our farthest now, for years to
come, had been named "Prince Patrick's Land," in
honor of the baby prince who was the youngest when

7 *

they left home.   Will he not be tempted, when he is
a man, to take a crew, like another Madoc, and, as
younger sons of queens should, go and settle upon this
tempting god-child?   They had heard from Sir Edward Belcher's part of the squadron; they had heard
from England; had heard of everything but Sir
John Franklin.   They had even found an ale-bottle
of Captain Collinson's expedition, — but not a stick
nor straw to show where Franklin or his men had
lived or died.   Two officers of the "Investigator"
were sent home to England this summer by a ship
from Beechey Island, the head-quarters; and thus
we heard, in October, 1853, of the discovery of the
Northwest Passage.

After their crews were on board again, and the
" Investigator's " sixty stowed away also, the " Resolute " and " Intrepid " had a dreary summer of it.
The ice would not break up.   They had hunting-par-
ties on shore and races on the floe; but the captain
could not send the " Investigators " home as he wanted to, in his steam tender.   All his plans were made,
and made on a manly scale, — if only the ice would
open.   He built a storehouse on the island for Collinson's people, or for you, reader, and us, if we
should happen there, and stored it well, and left this
record: —

" This is a house which I have named the ' Sailor's
Home,' under the especial patronage of my Lords
Commissioners of the Admiralty.

" *Here* royal sailors and marines are fed, clothed, and receive double pay for inhabiting it."

In that house is a little of everything, and a good deal of victuals and drink; but nobody has been there since the last of the " Resolute's" men came away.

At last, the 17th of August, a day of foot-racing and jumping in bags and wrestling, all hands present, as at a sort of " Isthmian games," ended with a gale, a cracking up of ice, and the " Investigators" thought they were on their way home, and Kellett thought he was to have a month of summer yet.   But no; "there is nothing certain in this navigation from one hour to the next."   The " Resolute " and " Intrepid " were never really free of ice all that autumn; drove and drifted to and fro in Barrow's Straits till the 12th of November; and then froze up, without anchoring, off Cape Cockburn, perhaps one hundred and forty miles from their harbor of the last winter. The log-book of that winter is a curious record ; the ingenuity of the officer in charge was well tasked to make one day differ from another.   Each day has the first entry for " ship's position " thus: " In the floe off Cape Cockburn."   And the blank for the second entry, thus: " In the same position."   Lectures, theatricals, schools, &c., whiled away the time; but there could be no autumn travelling parties, and not much hope for discovery in the summer.

Spring came.   The captain went over ice in his

little dog-sled to Beechey Island, and received his directions to abandon his ships. It appears that he
would rather have sent most of his men forward, and
with a small crew brought the " Resolute " home
that autumn or the next. But Sir Edward Belcher
considered his orders peremptory " that the safety of
the crews must preclude any idea of extricating the
ships." Both ships were to be abandoned. Two
distant travelling parties were away, one at the " Investigator," one looking for traces of Collinson, which
they found. Word was left for them, at a proper
point, not to seek the ship again, but to come on to
Beechey Island. And at last, having fitted the
" Intrepid's " engines so that she could be under
steam in two hours, having stored both ships with
equal proportions of provisions, and made both vessels
" ready for occupation," the captain calked down the
hatches, and with all the crew he had not sent on
before, — forty-two persons in all, — left her Monday,
the 15th of May, 1854, and started with the sledges
for Beechey Island.

Poor old " Resolute "! All this gay company is gone
who have made her sides split with their laughter.
Here is Harlequin's dress, lying in one of the ward-
rooms, but there is nobody to dance Harlequin's
dances. " Here is a lovely clear day, — surely to-day
they will come on deck and take a meridian ! " No,
nobody comes. The sun grows hot on the decks ;
but it is all one, nobody looks at the thermome-

ter ! " And so the poor ship was left all alone." Such
gay times she has had with all these brave young men
on board! Such merry winters, such a lightsome
summer! So much fun, so much nonsense! So
much science and wisdom, and now it is all so still!
Is the poor " Resolute" conscious of the change? Does
she miss the races on the ice, the scientific lecture
every Tuesday, the occasional racket and bustle of
the theatre, and the worship of every Sunday? Has
not she shared the hope of Captain Kellett, of Mc-
Clure, and of the crew, that she may *break out well !*
She sees the last sledge leave her. The captain drives
off his six dogs, — vanishes over the ice, and they are
all gone. " Will they not come back again ? " says
the poor ship. And she looks wistfully across the ice
to her little friend the steam tender " Intrepid," and she
sees there is no one there. " Intrepid ! Intrepid !
have they really deserted us ? We have served them so
well, and have they really left us alone ? A great
many were away travelling last year, but they came
home. Will not any of these come home now ? "
No, poor " Resolute "! Not one of them ever came back
again ! Not one of them meant to. Summer came.
August came. No one can tell how soon, but some
day or other this her icy prison broke up, and the
good ship found herself on her own element again;
shook herself proudly, we cannot doubt, nodded joy-
fully across to the " Intrepid," and was free. But
alas ! there was no master to take latitude and longi-

K

tude, no helmsman at the wheel. In clear letters cast in brass over her helm there are these words, "England expects each man to do his duty." But here is no man to heed the warning, and the rudder flaps this way and that way, no longer directing her course, but stupidly swinging to and fro. And she drifts here and there, — drifts out of sight of her little consort, — strands on a bit of ice floe now, and then is swept off from it, — and finds herself, without even the "Intrepid's" company, alone on these blue seas with those white shores. But what utter loneliness! Poor "Resolute"! She longed for freedom, — but what is freedom where there is no law? What is freedom without a helmsman! And the "Resolute" looks back so sadly to the old days when she had a master. And the short bright summer passes. And again she sees the sun set from her decks. And now even her topmasts see it set. And now it does not rise to her deck. And the next day it does not rise to her topmast. Winter and night together! She has known them before! But now it is winter and night and loneliness all together. This horrid ice closes up round her again. And there is no one to bring her into harbor, — she is out in the open sound. If the ice drifts west, she must go west. If it goes east, she must go east. Her seeming freedom is over, and for that long winter she is chained again. But her heart is true to old England. And when she can go east, she is so happy! and when she must go west, she is so sad!

Eastward she does go! Southward she does go! True to the instinct which sends us all home, she tracks undirected and without a sail fifteen hundred miles of that sea, without a beacon, which separates her from her own. And so goes a dismal year. " Perhaps another spring they will come and find me out, and fix things below. It is getting dreadfully damp down there ; and I cannot keep the guns bright and the floors dry." No, good old " Resolute." May and June pass off the next year, and nobody comes ; and here you are all alone out in the bay, drifting in this dismal pack. July and August, — the days are growing shorter again. " Will nobody come and take care of me, and cut off these horrid blocks of ice, and see to these sides of bacon in the hold, and all these mouldy sails, and this powder, and the bread and the spirit that I have kept for them so well? It is September, and the sun begins to set again. And here is another of those awful gales. Will it be my very last? I all alone here, — who have done so much, — and if they would only take care of me I can do so much more. Will nobody come ? Nobody ? . . . . What! Is it ice blink, — are my poor old lookouts blind ? Is not there the ' Intrepid ' ? Dear ' Intrepid,' I will never look down on you again ! No ! there is no smoke-stack, it is not the ' Intrepid.' But it is somebody. Pray see me, good somebody. Are you a Yankee whaler ? I am glad to see the Yankee whalers. I remember the Yankee whalers very pleasantly.

We had a happy summer together once. . . . . It will
be dreadful if they do not see me! But this ice, this
wretched ice! They do see me, — I know they see
me, but they cannot get at me. Do not go away, good
Yankees; pray come and help me. I know I can get
out, if you will help a little. . . . . But now it is a
whole week and they do not come! Are there any
Yankees, or am I getting crazy? I have heard them
talk of crazy old ships, in my young days. . . . . No!
I am not crazy. They are coming! they are coming.
Brave Yankees! over the hummocks, down into the
sludge. Do not give it up for the cold. There is
coal below, and we will have a fire in the Sylvester,
and in the captain's cabin. . . . . There is a horrid lane
of water. They have not got a Halkett. O, if one
of these boats of mine would only start for them, instead of lying so stupidly on my deck here! But the
men are not afraid of water! See them ferry over on
that ice block! Come on, good friends! Welcome,
whoever you be, — Dane, Dutch, French, or Yankee,
come on! come on! It is coming up a gale, but I
can bear a gale. Up the side, men. I wish I could
let down the gangway alone. But here are all these
blocks of ice piled up, — you can scramble over them!
Why do you stop? Do not be afraid. I will make
you very comfortable and jolly. Do not stay talking
there. Pray come in. There is port in the captain's
cabin, and a little preserved meat in the pantry.
You must be hungry; pray come in! O, he is com-

ing, and now all four are coming. It would be dreadful if they had gone back! They are on deck. Now I shall go home! How lonely it has been!"

It was true enough that when Mr. Quail, the brother of the captain of the "McLellan," whom the "Resolute" had befriended, the mate of the George Henry, whaler, whose master, Captain Buddington, had discovered the "Resolute" in the ice, came to her after a hard day's journey with his men, the men faltered with a little superstitious feeling, and hesitated for a minute about going on board. But the poor lonely ship wooed them too lovingly, and they climbed over the broken ice and came on deck. She was lying over on her larboard side, with a heavy weight of ice holding her down. Hatches and companion were made fast, as Captain Kellett had left them. But, knocking open the companion, groping down stairs to the after cabin they found their way to the captain's table; somebody put his hand on a box of lucifers, struck a light, and revealed — books scattered in confusion, a candle standing, which he lighted at once, the glasses and the decanters from which Kellett and his officers had drunk good by to the vessel. The whalemen filled them again, and undoubtedly felt less discouraged. Meanwhile night came on, and a gale arose. So hard did it blow, that for two days these four were the whole crew of the "Resolute," and it was not till the 19th of September that they returned to their own ship, and reported what their prize was.

All these ten days, since Captain Buddington had
first seen her, the vessels had been nearing each other.
On the 19th he boarded her himself; found that in
her hold, on the larboard side, was a good deal of ice;
on the starboard side there seemed to be water. In
fact, her tanks had burst from the extreme cold; and
she was full of water, nearly to her lower deck.
Everything that could move from its place had moved;
everything was wet; everything that would mould
was mouldy. "A sort of perspiration" settled on the
beams above. Clothes were wringing wet. The captain's party made a fire in Captain Kellett's stove, and
soon started a sort of shower from the vapor with
which it filled the air. The "Resolute" has, however, four fine force-pumps. For three days the captain and six men worked fourteen hours a day on one
of these, and had the pleasure of finding that they
freed her of water, — that she was tight still. They
cut away upon the masses of ice; and on the 23d of
September, in the evening, she freed herself from her
encumbrances, and took an even keel. This was off
the west shore of Baffin's Bay, in latitude 67°. On
the shortest tack she was twelve hundred miles from
where Captain Kellett left her.

There was work enough still to be done. The rudder was to be shipped, the rigging to be made taut,
sail to be set; and it proved, by the way, that the sail
on the yards was much of it still serviceable, while
a suit of new linen sails below were greatly injured by

moisture. In a week more they had her ready to make sail. The pack of ice still drifted with both ships; but on the 21st of October, after a long northwest gale, the " Resolute " was free, — more free than she had been for more than two years.

Her " last voyage " is almost told. Captain Buddington had resolved to bring her home. He had picked ten men from the " George Henry," leaving her fifteen, and with a rough tracing of the American coast drawn on a sheet of foolscap, with his lever watch and a quadrant for his instruments, he squared off for New London. A rough, hard passage they had of it. The ship's ballast was gone, by the bursting of the tanks; she was top-heavy and under manned. He spoke a British whaling bark, and by her sent to Captain Kellett his epaulettes, and to his own owners news that he was coming. They had heavy gales and head winds, were driven as far down as the Bermudas; the water left in the ship's tanks was brackish, and it needed all the seasoning which the ship's chocolate would give to make it drinkable. " For sixty hours at a time," says the spirited captain, " I frequently had no sleep "; but his perseverance was crowned with success at last, and on the night of the 23d – 24th of December he made the light off the magnificent harbor from which he sailed; and on Sunday morning, the 24th, dropped anchor in the Thames, opposite *New* London, ran up the royal ensign on the shorn masts of the " Resolute," and the good people of the town knew that he and his were safe, and that one of the victories of peace was won.

As the fine ship lies opposite the piers of that beautiful town, she attracts visitors from everywhere, and is, indeed, a very remarkable curiosity. Seals were at once placed, and very properly, on the captain's book-cases, lockers, and drawers, and wherever private property might be injured by wanton curiosity, and two keepers are on duty on the vessel, till her destination is decided. But nothing is changed from what she was when she came into harbor. And, from stem to stern, every detail of her equipment is a curiosity, to the sailor or to the landsman. The candlestick in the cabin is not like a Yankee candlestick. The hawse hole for the chain cable is fitted as has not been seen before. And so of everything between. There is the aspect of wet over everything now, after months of ventilation; — the rifles, which were last fired at musk-oxen in Melville Island, are red with rust, as if they had lain in the bottom of the sea; the volume of Shakespeare, which you find in an officer's berth, has a damp feel, as if you had been reading it in the open air in a March northeaster. The old seamen look with most amazement, perhaps, on the preparations for amusement, — the juggler's cups and balls, or Harlequin's spangled dress; the quiet landsman wonders at the gigantic ice-saws, at the cast-off canvas boots, the long thick Arctic stockings. It seems almost wrong to go into

Mr. Hamilton's wardroom, and see how he arranged his soap-cup and his tooth-brush; and one does not tell of it, if he finds on a blank leaf the secret prayer a sister wrote down for the brother to whom she gave a prayer-book.   There is a good deal of disorder now, — thanks to her sudden abandonment, and perhaps to her three months' voyage home.   A little union-jack lies over a heap of unmended and unwashed underclothes; when Kellett left the ship, he left his country's flag over his arm-chair as if to keep possession. Two officers' swords and a pair of epaulettes were on the cabin table.   Indeed, what is there not there, — which should make an Arctic winter endurable, — make a long night into day, — or while long days away?

The ship is stanch and sound.   The "last voyage" which we have described will not, let us hope, be the last voyage of her career.   But wherever she goes, under the English flag or under our own, she will scarcely ever crowd more adventure into one cruise than into that which sealed the discovery of the Northwest Passage; which gave new lands to England, nearest to the pole of all she has; which spent more than a year, no man knows where, self-governed and unguided; and which, having begun under the strict *régime* of the English navy, ended under the remarkable mutual rules, adopted by common consent, in the business of American whalemen.

Is it not worth noting that in this chivalry of Arctic adventure, the ships which have been wrecked have been those of the fight or horror? They are the "Fury," the "Victory," the "Erebus," the "Terror." But the ships which never failed their crews, — which, for all that man knows, are as sound now as ever, — bear the names of peaceful adventure ; the "Hecla," the "Enterprise," and "Investigator," the "Assistance" and "Resolute," the "Pioneer" and "Intrepid," and our "Advance" and "Rescue" and "Arctic," never threatened any one, even in their names. And they never failed the men who commanded them or who sailed in them.

MY DOUBLE, AND HOW HE UNDID ME.

ONE OF THE INGHAM PAPERS.

[A Boston journal, in noticing this story, called it improbable. I think it is. But I think the moral important. It was first published in the Atlantic Monthly for September, 1859.]

It is not often that I trouble the readers of the Atlantic Monthly. I should not trouble them now, but for the importunities of my wife, who "feels to insist" that a duty to society is unfulfilled, till I have told why I had to have a double, and how he undid me. She is sure, she says, that intelligent persons cannot understand that pressure upon public servants which alone drives any man into the employment of a double. And while I fear she thinks, at the bottom of her heart, that my fortunes will never be remade, she has a faint hope that, as another Rasselas, I may teach a lesson to future publics, from which they may profit, though we die. Owing to the behavior of my double, or, if you please, to that public pressure which compelled me to employ him, I have plenty of leisure to write this communication.

I am, or rather was, a minister, of the Sandemanian

connection. I was settled in the active, wide-awake
town of Naguadavick, on one of the finest water-powers
in Maine. We used to call it a Western town in the
heart of the civilization of New England. A charming place it was and is. A spirited, brave young parish had I; and it seemed as if we might have all "the
joy of eventful living" to our heart's content.

Alas! how little we knew on the day of my ordina-
tion, and in those halcyon moments of our first house-
keeping! To be the confidential friend in a hundred
families in the town, — cutting the social trifle, as my
friend Haliburton says, "from the top of the whipped
syllabub to the bottom of the sponge-cake, which is
the foundation," — to keep abreast of the thought of
the age in one's study, and to do one's best on Sunday to
interweave that thought with the active life of an active town, and to inspirit both and make both infinite
by glimpses of the Eternal Glory, seemed such an exquisite forelook into one's life! Enough to do, and all
so real and so grand! If this vision could only have
lasted!

The truth is, that this vision was not in itself a de-
lusion, nor, indeed, half bright enough. If one could
only have been left to do his own business, the vision
would have accomplished itself and brought out new
paraheliacal visions, each as bright as the original.
The misery was and is, as we found out, I and Polly,
before long, that besides the vision, and besides the
usual human and finite failures in life (such as break-

ing the old pitcher that came over in the "Mayflower," and putting into the fire the Alpenstock with which her father climbed Mont Blanc), — besides these, I say (imitating the style of Robinson Crusoe), there were pitchforked in on us a great rowen-heap of humbugs, handed down from some unknown seed-time, in which we were expected, and I chiefly, to fulfil certain public functions before the community, of the character of those fulfilled by the third row of supernumeraries who stand behind the Sepoys in the spectacle of the "Cataract of the Ganges." They were the duties, in a word, which one performs as member of one or another social class or subdivision, wholly distinct from what one does as A. by himself A. What invisible power put these functions on me, it would be very hard to tell. But such power there was and is. And I had not been at work a year before I found I was living two lives, one real and one merely functional, — for two sets of people, one my parish, whom I loved, and the other a vague public, for whom I did not care two straws. All this was in a vague notion, which everybody had and has, that this second life would eventually bring out some great results, unknown at present, to somebody somewhere.

Crazed by this duality of life, I first read Dr. Wigan on the "Duality of the Brain," hoping that I could train one side of my head to do these outside jobs, and the other to do my intimate and real duties. For Richard Greenough once told me, that, in studying

for the statue of Franklin, he found that the left side
of the great man's face was philosophic and reflective,
and the right side funny and smiling. If you will go
and look at the bronze statue, you will find he has repeated this observation there for posterity. The eastern profile is the portrait of the statesman Franklin, the
western of poor Richard. But Dr. Wigan does not go
into these niceties of this subject, and I failed. It was
then that, on my wife's suggestion, I resolved to look
out for a Double.

I was, at first, singularly successful. We happened
to be recreating at Stafford Springs that summer.
We rode out one day, for one of the relaxations of
that watering-place, to the great Monson Poorhouse.
We were passing through one of the large halls, when
my destiny was fulfilled!

He was not shaven. He had on no spectacles.
He was dressed in a green baize roundabout and faded
blue overalls, worn sadly at the knee. But I saw at
once that he was of my height, five feet four and a half.
He had black hair, worn off by his hat. So have and
have not I. He stooped in walking. So do I. His
hands were large, and mine. And — choicest gift of
Fate in all — he had, not "a strawberry-mark on his
left arm," but a cut from a juvenile brickbat over his
right eye, slightly affecting the play of that eyebrow.
Reader, so have I! My fate was sealed!

A word with Mr. Holley, one of the inspectors, settled the whole thing. It proved that this Dennis

Shea was a harmless, amiable fellow, of the class known as shiftless, who had sealed his fate by marrying a dumb wife, who was at that moment ironing in the laundry. Before I left Stafford, I had hired both for five years. We had applied to Judge Pynchon, then the probate judge at Springfield, to change the name of Dennis Shea to Frederic Ingham. We had explained to the Judge, what was the precise truth, that an eccentric gentleman wished to adopt Dennis, under this new name, into his family. It never occurred to him that Dennis might be more than fourteen years old. And thus, to shorten this preface, when we returned at night to my parsonage at Naguadavick, there entered Mrs. Ingham, her new dumb laundress, myself, who am Mr. Frederic Ingham, and my double, who was Mr. Frederic Ingham by as good right as I.

O the fun we had the next morning in shaving his beard to my pattern, cutting his hair to match mine, and teaching him how to wear and how to take off gold-bowed spectacles ! Really, they were electro-plate, and the glass was plain (for the poor fellow's eyes were excellent). Then in four successive afternoons I taught him four speeches. I had found these would be quite enough for the supernumerary-Sepoy line of life, and it was well for me they were ; for though he was good-natured, he was very shiftless, and it was, as our national proverb says, " like pulling teeth " to teach him. But at the end of the next week he could say, with quite my easy and frisky air, —

1. " Very well, thank you.   And you? "   This for
an answer to casual salutations.

2. " I am very glad you liked it."

3. " There has been so much said, and, on the whole,
so well said, that I will not occupy the time."

4. " I agree, in general, with my friend the other
side of the room."

At first I had a feeling that I was going to be at
great cost for clothing him.   But it proved, of course,
at once, that, whenever he was out, I should be at
home.   And I went, during the bright period of his
success, to so few of those awful pageants which require a black dress-coat and what the ungodly call,
after Mr. Dickens, a white choker, that in the happy
retreat of my own dressing-gowns and jackets my days
went by as happily and cheaply as those of another
Thalaba.   And Polly declares there was never a year
when the tailoring cost so little.   He lived (Dennis,
not Thalaba) in his wife's room over the kitchen.   He
had orders never to show himself at that window.
When he appeared in the front of the house, I retired
to my sanctissimum and my dressing-gown.   In short,
the Dutchman and his wife, in the old weather-box,
had not less to do with each other than he and I.   He
made the furnace-fire and split the wood before daylight; then he went to sleep again, and slept late ;
then came for orders, with a red silk bandanna tied
round his head, with his overalls on, and his dress-
coat and spectacles off.   If we happened to be inter-

rupted, no one guessed that he was Frederic Ingham as well as I; and, in the neighborhood, there grew up an impression that the minister's Irishman worked day-times in the factory-village at New Coventry. After I had given him his orders, I never saw him till the next day.

I launched him by sending him to a meeting of the Enlightenment Board. The Enlightenment Board consists of seventy-four members, of whom sixty-seven are necessary to form a quorum. One becomes a member under the regulations laid down in old Judge Dudley's will. I became one by being ordained pastor of a church in Naguadavick. You see you cannot help yourself, if you would. At this particular time we had had four successive meetings, averaging four hours each, — wholly occupied in whipping in a quorum. At the first only eleven men were present; at the next, by force of three circulars, twenty-seven; at the third, thanks to two days' canvassing by Auchmuty and myself, begging men to come, we had sixty. Half the others were in Europe. But without a quorum we could do nothing. All the rest of us waited grimly for our four hours, and adjourned without any action. At the fourth meeting we had flagged, and only got fifty-nine together. But on the first appear-ance of my double, — whom I sent on this fatal Mon-day to the fifth meeting, — he was the *sixty-seventh* man who entered the room. He was greeted with a storm of applause! The poor fellow had missed his

way, — read the street signs ill through his spectacles
(very ill, in fact, without them), — and had not dared
to inquire.   He entered the room, — finding the president and secretary holding to their chairs two judges
of the Supreme Court, who were also members *ex
officio*, and were begging leave to go away.   On his
entrance all was changed.   *Presto*, the by-laws were
suspended, and the Western property was given away.
Nobody stopped to converse with him.   He voted, as
I had charged him to do, in every instance, with the
minority.   I won new laurels as a man of sense, though
a little unpunctual, — and Dennis, *alias* Ingham, returned to the parsonage, astonished to see with how
little wisdom the world is governed.   He cut a few of
my parishioners in the street ; but he had his glasses
off, and I am known to be near-sighted.   Eventually
he recognized them more readily than I.

I "set him again" at the exhibition of the New
Coventry Academy ; and here he undertook a "speaking part," — as, in my boyish, worldly days, I remember the bills used to say of Mlle. Celeste.   We are all
trustees of the New Coventry Academy ; and there
has lately been "a good deal of feeling" because the
Sandemanian trustees did not regularly attend the exhibitions.   It has been intimated, indeed, that the Sandemanians are leaning towards Free-Will, and that we
have, therefore, neglected these semiannual exhibitions, while there is no doubt that Auchmuty last year
went to Commencement at Waterville.   Now the head

master at New Coventry is a real good fellow, who
knows a Sanskrit root when he sees it, and often cracks
etymologies with me, — so that, in strictness, I ought to
go to their exhibitions. But think, reader, of sitting
through three long July days in that Academy chapel,
following the programme from

TUESDAY MORNING. *English Composition.* "SUNSHINE." Miss
Jones.

round to

Trio on Three Pianos. Duel from the Opera of "Midshipman
Easy." *Marryat.*

coming in at nine, Thursday evening! Think of this,
reader, for men who know the world is trying to go
backward, and who would give their lives if they could
help it on! Well! The double had succeeded so
well at the Board, that I sent him to the Academy.
(Shade of Plato, pardon!) He arrived early on
Tuesday, when, indeed, few but mothers and clergymen are generally expected, and returned in the evening to us, covered with honors. He had dined at the
right hand of the chairman, and he spoke in high
terms of the repast. The chairman had expressed his
interest in the French conversation. "I am very glad
you liked it," said Dennis; and the poor chairman,
abashed, supposed the accent had been wrong. At the
end of the day, the gentlemen present had been called
upon for speeches, — the Rev. Frederic Ingham first,
as it happened; upon which Dennis had risen, and

had said, "There has been so much said, and, on the whole, so well said, that I will not occupy the time." The girls were delighted, because Dr. Dabney, the year before, had given them at this occasion a scolding on impropriety of behavior at lyceum lectures. They all declared Mr. Ingham was a love, — and *so* handsome! (Dennis is good-looking.) Three of them, with arms behind the others' waists, followed him up to the wagon he rode home in; and a little girl with a blue sash had been sent to give him a rosebud. After this *début* in speaking, he went to the exhibition for two days more, to the mutual satisfaction of all concerned. Indeed, Polly reported that he had pronounced the trustees' dinners of a higher grade than those of the parsonage. When the next term began, I found six of the Academy girls had obtained permission to come across the river and attend our church. But this arrangement did not long continue.

After this he went to several Commencements for me, and ate the dinners provided; he sat through three of our Quarterly Conventions for me, — always voting judiciously, by the simple rule mentioned above, of siding with the minority. And I, meanwhile, who had before been losing caste among my friends, as holding myself aloof from the associations of the body, began to rise in everybody's favor. "Ingham's a good fellow, — always on hand"; "never talks much, but does the right thing at the right time"; "is not as unpunctual as he used to be, — he comes early, and sits through to the end." "He has got over his old talkative habit, too. I spoke to a friend of his about it once; and I think Ingham took it kindly," etc., etc.

This voting power of Dennis was particularly valuable at the quarterly meetings of the proprietors of the Naguadavick Ferry. My wife inherited from her father some shares in that enterprise, which is not yet fully developed, though it doubtless will become a very valuable property. The law of Maine then forbade stockholders to appear by proxy at such meetings. Polly disliked to go, not being, in fact, a "hens'-rights hen," transferred her stock to me. I, after going once, disliked it more than she. But Dennis went to the next meeting, and liked it very much. He said the arm-chairs were good, the collation good, and the free rides to stockholders pleasant. He was a little frightened when they first took him upon one of the ferry-boats, but after two or three quarterly meetings he became quite brave.

Thus far I never had any difficulty with him. Indeed, being, as I implied, of that type which is called shiftless, he was only too happy to be told daily what to do, and to be charged not to be forthputting or in any way original in his discharge of that duty. He learned, however, to discriminate between the lines of his life, and very much preferred these stockholders' meetings and trustees' dinners and Commencement collations to another set of occasions, from which he used to beg off most piteously. Our excellent brother, Dr. Fillmore, had taken a notion at this time that our Sandemanian churches needed more expression of mutual sympathy. He insisted upon it that we were remiss. He said, that, if the Bishop came to preach at Naguadavick, all the Episcopal clergy of the neighborhood were present; if Dr. Pond came, all the Congregational clergymen turned out to hear him; if Dr. Nichols, all the Unitarians; and he thought we owed it to each other, that, whenever there was an occasional service at a Sandemanian church, the other brethren should all, if possible, attend. "It looked well," if nothing more. Now this really meant that I had not been to hear one of Dr. Fillmore's lectures on the Ethnology of Religion. He forgot that he did not hear one of my course on the "Sandemanianism of Anselm." But I felt badly when he said it; and afterwards I always made Dennis go to hear all the brethren preach, when I was not preaching myself. This was what he took exceptions to, — the only thing, as I said, which he ever did except to. Now came the advantage of his long morning-nap, and of the green tea with which Polly supplied the kitchen. But he would plead, so humbly, to be let off, only from one or two! I never excepted him, however. I knew the lectures were of value, and I thought it best he should be able to keep the connection.

Polly is more rash than I am, as the reader has observed in the outset of this memoir. She risked Dennis one night under the eyes of her own sex. Governor Gorges had always been very kind to us, and, when he gave his great annual party to the town, asked us. I confess I hated to go. I was deep in the new volume of Pfeiffer's "Mystics," which Haliburton had just sent me from Boston. "But how rude," said Polly, "not to return the Governor's civility and Mrs. Gorges's, when they will be sure to ask why you are away!" Still I demurred, and at last she, with the wit of Eve and of Semiramis conjoined, let me off by saying that, if I would go in with her, and sustain the initial conversations with the Governor and the ladies staying there, she would risk Dennis for the rest of the evening. And that was just what we did. She took Dennis in training all that afternoon, instructed him in fashionable conversation, cautioned him against the temptations of the supper-table, — and at nine in the evening he drove us all down in the carryall. I made the grand star-*entrée* with Polly and the pretty Walton girls, who were staying with us. We had put Dennis into a great rough top-coat, without his glasses; and the girls never dreamed, in the darkness, of looking at him. He sat in the carriage, at the door, while we entered. I did the agreeable to Mrs. Gorges, was introduced to her niece, Miss Fernanda; I complimented Judge Jeffries on his decision in the great case of D'Aulnay *vs.* Laconia Mining Company; I stepped into the dressing-room for a moment, stepped out for another, walked home

after a nod with Dennis and tying the horse to a
pump; and while I walked home, Mr. Frederic Ingham, my double, stepped in through the library into the
Gorges's grand saloon.

Oh! Polly died of laughing as she told me of it at
midnight! And even here, where I have to teach my
hands to hew the beech for stakes to fence our cave,
she dies of laughing as she recalls it, — and says that
single occasion was worth all we have paid for it.
Gallant Eve that she is! She joined Dennis at the
library-door, and in an instant presented him to Dr.
Ochterlony, from Baltimore, who was on a visit in town,
and was talking with her as Dennis came in. "Mr.
Ingham would like to hear what you were telling us
about your success among the German population."
And Dennis bowed and said, in spite of a scowl from
Polly, "I'm very glad you liked it." But Dr. Ochterlony did not observe, and plunged into the tide of
explanation; Dennis listened like a prime-minister,
and bowing like a mandarin, which is, I suppose,
the same thing. Polly declared it was just like Haliburton's Latin conversation with the Hungarian minister, of which he is very fond of telling. " *Quæne
sit historia Reformationis in Ungariâ ?*" quoth Haliburton, after some thought. And his *confrère* replied
gallantly, " *In seculo decimo tertio,*" etc., etc., etc.;
and from *decimo tertio** to the nineteenth century and

---

* Which means, "In the thirteenth century," my dear little bell-
and-coral reader. You have rightly guessed that the question means,
" What is the history of the Reformation in Hungary ?"

a half lasted till the oysters came. So was it that before Dr. Ochterlony came to the " success," or near it, Governor Gorges came to Dennis, and asked him to hand Mrs. Jeffries down to supper, a request which he heard with great joy.

Polly was skipping round the room, I guess, gay as a lark. Auchmuty came to her " in pity for poor Ingham," who was so bored by the stupid pundit, — and Auchmuty could not understand why I stood it so long. But when Dennis took Mrs. Jeffries down, Polly could not resist standing near them. He was a little flustered, till the sight of the eatables and drinkables gave him the same Mercian courage which it gave Diggory. A little excited then, he attempted one or two of his speeches to the Judge's lady. But little he knew how hard it was to get in even a *promptu* there edgewise. " Very well, I thank you," said he, after the eating elements were adjusted ; " and you ? " And then did not he have to hear about the mumps, and the measles, and arnica, and belladonna, and chamomile-flower, and dodecatheon, till she changed oysters for salad ; and then about the old practice and the new, and what her sister said, and what her sister's friend said, and what the physician to her sister's friend said, and then what was said by the brother of the sister of the physician of the friend of her sister, exactly as if it had been in Ollendorff ? There was a moment's pause, as she declined Champagne. " I am very glad you liked it," said Dennis

again, which he never should have said but to one
who complimented a sermon. " Oh! you are so sharp,
Mr. Ingham! No! I never drink any wine at all,
— except sometimes in summer a little currant shrub,
— from our own currants, you know. My own mother, — that is, I call her my own mother, because, you
know, I do not remember," etc., etc., etc.; till they
came to the candid orange at the end of the feast,
when Dennis, rather confused, thought he must say
something, and tried No. 4, — " I agree, in general,
with my friend the other side of the room," — which
he never should have said but at a public meeting.
But Mrs. Jeffries, who never listens expecting to understand, caught him up instantly with " Well, I'm
sure my husband returns the compliment; he always
agrees with you, — though we do worship with the
Methodists; but you know, Mr. Ingham," etc., etc.,
etc., till the move up-stairs; and as Dennis led her
through the hall, he was scarcely understood by any
but Polly, as he said, " There has been so much said,
and, on the whole, so well said, that I will not occupy
the time."

His great resource the rest of the evening was
standing in the library, carrying on animated conversations with one and another in much the same way.
Polly had initiated him in the mysteries of a discovery of mine, that it is not necessary to finish your
sentences in a crowd, but by a sort of mumble,
omitting sibilants and dentals. This, indeed, if your

words fail you, answers even in public extempore speech, but better where other talking is going on. Thus: " We missed you at the Natural History Society, Ingham." Ingham replies, " I am very gligloglum, that is, that you were mmmmm." By gradually dropping the voice, the interlocutor is compelled to supply the answer. " Mrs. Ingham, I hope your friend Augusta is better." Augusta has not been ill. Polly cannot think of explaining, however, and answers, " Thank you, Ma'am ; she is very rearason wewahwewoh," in lower and lower tones. And Mrs. Throckmorton, who forgot the subject of which she spoke as soon as she asked the question, is quite satisfied. Dennis could see into the card-room, and came to Polly to ask if he might not go and play all-fours. But, of course, she sternly refused. At midnight they came home delighted, — Polly, as I said, wild to tell me the story of the victory ; only both the pretty Walton girls said, " Cousin Frederic, you did not come near me all the evening."

We always called him Dennis at home, for convenience, though his real name was Frederic Ingham, as I have explained. When the election-day came round, however, I found that by some accident there was only one Frederic Ingham's name on the voting-list ; and as I was quite busy that day in writing some foreign letters to Halle, I thought I would forego my privilege of suffrage, and stay quietly at home, telling Dennis that he might use the record on the voting-list, and vote. I gave him a ticket, which I told him he might use, if he liked to. That was that very sharp election in Maine which the readers of the Atlantic so well remember, and it had been intimated in public that the ministers would do well not to appear at the polls. Of course, after that, we had to appear by self or proxy. Still, Naguadavick was not then a city, and this standing in a double queue at town-meeting several hours to vote was a bore of the first water; and so when I found that there was but one Frederic Ingham on the list, and that one of us must give up, I stayed at home and finished the letters (which, indeed, procured for Fothergill his coveted appointment of Professor of Astronomy at Leavenworth), and I gave Dennis, as we called him, the chance. Something in the matter gave a good deal of popularity to the Frederic Ingham name; and at the adjourned election, next week, Frederic Ingham was chosen to the legislature. Whether this was I or Dennis I never really knew. My friends seemed to think it was I; but I felt that as Dennis had done the popular thing, he was entitled to the honor; so I sent him to Augusta when the time came, and he took the oaths. And a very valuable member he made. They appointed him on the Committee on Parishes; but I wrote a letter for him, resigning, on the ground that he took an interest in our claim to the stumpage in the minister's sixteenths of Gore A, next No. 7, in the 10th Range. He never made any speeches, and always voted with the minority, which was what he was sent to do. He made me and himself a great many good friends, some of whom I did not afterwards recognize as quickly as Dennis did my parishioners. On one or two occasions, when there was wood to saw at home, I kept him at home; but I took those occasions to go to Augusta myself. Finding myself often in his vacant seat at these times, I watched the proceedings with a good deal of care; and once was so much excited that I delivered my somewhat celebrated speech on the Central School-District question, a speech of which the " State of Maine" printed some extra copies. I believe there is no formal rule permitting strangers to speak; but no one objected.

Dennis himself, as I said, never spoke at all. But our experience this session led me to think that if, by some such "general understanding" as the reports speak of in legislation daily, every member of Congress might leave a double to sit through those deadly sessions and answer to roll-calls and do the legitimate party-voting, which appears stereotyped in the regular list of Ashe, Bocock, Black, etc., we should gain decidedly in working-power. As things stand, the saddest State prison I ever visit is that Representatives' Chamber in Washington. If a man leaves for an hour, twenty " correspondents" may be howling, " Where was Mr. Pendergrast when the Oregon bill passed?" And if poor Pendergrast stays there! Certainly the worst use you can make of a man is to put him in prison !

I know, indeed, that public men of the highest rank
have resorted to this expedient long ago. Dumas's
novel of the " Iron Mask " turns on the brutal imprisonment of Louis the Fourteenth's double. There
seems little doubt, in our own history, that it was the
real General Pierce who shed tears when the dele-
gate from Lawrence explained to him the sufferings of
the people there, and only General Pierce's double
who had given the orders for the assault on that town,
which was invaded the next day. My charming
friend, George Withers, has, I am almost sure, a
double, who preaches his afternoon sermons for him.
This is the reason that the theology often varies so
from that of the forenoon. But that double is almost
as charming as the original. Some of the most well-
defined men, who stand out most prominently on the
background of history, are in this way stereoscopic
men, who owe their distinct relief to the slight differ-
ences between the doubles. All this I know. My
present suggestion is simply the great extension of the
system, so that all public machine-work may be done
by it.

But I see I loiter on my story, which is rushing to
the plunge. Let me stop an instant more, however,
to recall, were it only to myself, that charming year
while all was yet well. After the double had become
a matter of course, for nearly twelve months before he
undid me, what a year it was! Full of active life, full
of happy love, of the hardest work, of the sweetest

sleep, and the fulfilment of so many of the fresh aspi-
rations and dreams of boyhood! Dennis went to
every school-committee meeting, and sat through all
those late wranglings which used to keep me up till
midnight and awake till morning. He attended all
the lectures to which foreign exiles sent me tickets
begging me to come for the love of Heaven and of
Bohemia. He accepted and used all the tickets for
charity concerts which were sent to me. He appeared
everywhere where it was specially desirable that " our
denomination," or " our party," or " our class," or
" our family," or " our street," or " our town," or
" our country," or " our State," should be fully represented. And I fell back to that charming life which
in boyhood one dreams of, when he supposes he shall
do his own duty and make his own sacrifices, without
being tied up with those of other people. My rusty
Sanskrit, Arabic, Hebrew, Greek, Latin, French,
Italian, Spanish, German, and English began to take
polish. Heavens! how little I had done with them
while I attended to my *public* duties ! My calls on my
parishioners became the friendly, frequent, homelike
sociabilities they were meant to be, instead of the hard
work of a man goaded to desperation by the sight of
his lists of arrears. And preaching! what a luxury
preaching was when I had on Sunday the whole result of an individual, personal week, from which to
speak to a people whom all that week I had been
meeting as hand-to-hand friend ; — I, never tired on

Sunday, and in condition to leave the sermon at home, if I chose, and preach it extempore, as all men should do always. Indeed, I wonder, when I think that a sensible people, like ours, — really more attached to their clergy than they were in the lost days, when the Mathers and Nortons were noblemen, — should choose to neutralize so much of their ministers' lives, and destroy so much of their early training, by this undefined passion for seeing them in public. It springs from our balancing of sects. If a spirited Episcopalian takes an interest in the almshouse, and is put on the Poor Board, every other denomination must have a minister there, lest the poorhouse be changed into St. Paul's Cathedral. If a Sandemanian is chosen president of the Young Men's Library, there must be a Methodist vice-president and a Baptist secretary. And if a Universalist Sunday-School Convention collects five hundred delegates, the next Congregationalist Sabbath-School Conference must be as large, " lest ' they ' — whoever *they* may be — should think ' we ' — whoever *we* may be — are going down."

Freed from these necessities, that happy year I began to know my wife by sight. We saw each other sometimes. In those long mornings, when Dennis was in the study explaining to map-peddlers that I had eleven maps of Jerusalem already, and to school-book agents that I would see them hanged before I would be bribed to introduce their text-books into the schools, — she and I were at work together, as in those old

dreamy days, — and in these of our log-cabin again.
But all this could not last, — and at length poor Dennis, my double, overtasked in turn, undid me.

It was thus it happened.   There is an excellent
fellow, once a minister, — I will call him Isaacs, —
who deserves well of the world till he dies, and after,
because he once, in a real exigency, did the right
thing, in the right way, at the right time, as no other
man could do it.   In the world's great football match,
the ball by chance found him loitering on the outside
of the field ; he closed with it, " camped " it, charged
it home, — yes, right through the other side, — not
disturbed, not frightened by his own success, — and
breathless found himself a great man, as the Great
Delta rang applause.   But he did not find himself
a rich man ; and the football has never come in his
way again.   From that moment to this moment he
has been of no use, that one can see at all.   Still, for
that great act we speak of Isaacs gratefully and remember him kindly ; and he forges on, hoping to
meet the football somewhere again.   In that vague
hope, he had arranged a " movement " for a general
organization of the human family into Debating-Clubs,
County Societies, State Unions, etc., etc., with a view
of inducing all children to take hold of the handles of
their knives and forks, instead of the metal.   Children
have bad habits in that way.   The movement, of
course, was absurd ; but we all did our best to forward,
not it, but him.   It came time for the annual county-

meeting on this subject to be held at Naguadavick.
Isaacs came round, good fellow! to arrange for it, —
got the town-hall, got the Governor to preside (the
saint! — he ought to have triplet doubles provided
him by law), and then came to get me to speak.
"No," I said, " I would not speak, if ten Governors
presided. I do not believe in the enterprise. If I
spoke, it should be to say children should take hold of
the prongs of the forks and the blades of the knives.
I would subscribe ten dollars, but I would not speak a
mill." So poor Isaacs went his way sadly, to coax
Auchmuty to speak, and Delafield. I went out.
Not long after he came back, and told Polly that they
had promised to speak, the Governor would speak,
and he himself would close with the quarterly report,
and some interesting anecdotes regarding Miss Bif-
fin's way of handling her knife and Mr. Nellis's way
of footing his fork. " Now if Mr. Ingham will only
come and sit on the platform, he need not say one
word ; but it will show well in the paper, — it will
show that the Sandemanians take as much interest in
the movement as the Armenians or the Mesopotamians,
and will be a great favor to me." Polly, good soul!
was tempted, and she promised. She knew Mrs. Isaacs
was starving, and the babies, — she knew Dennis
was at home, — and she promised ! Night came, and
I returned. I heard her story. I was sorry. I
doubted. But Polly had promised to beg me, and I
dared all ! I told Dennis to hold his peace, under all
circumstances, and sent him down.

It was not half an hour more before he returned, wild with excitement, — in a perfect Irish fury, — which it was long before I understood. But I knew at once that he had undone me!

What happened was this. The audience got together, attracted by Governor Gorges's name. There were a thousand people. Poor Gorges was late from Augusta. They became impatient. He came in direct from the train at last, really ignorant of the object of the meeting. He opened it in the fewest possible words, and said other gentlemen were present who would entertain them better than he. The audience were disappointed, but waited. The Governor, prompted by Isaacs, said, "The Honorable Mr. Delafield will address you." Delafield had forgotten the knives and forks, and was playing the Ruy Lopez opening at the chess-club. "The Rev. Mr. Auchmuty will address you." Auchmuty had promised to speak late, and was at the school-committee. "I see Dr. Stearns in the hall; perhaps he will say a word." Dr. Stearns said he had come to listen and not to speak The Governor and Isaacs whispered. The Governor looked at Dennis, who was resplendent on the platform; but Isaacs, to give him his due, shook his head. But the look was enough. A miserable lad, ill-bred, who had once been in Boston, thought it would sound well to call for me, and peeped out, "Ingham!" A few more wretches cried, "Ingham! Ingham!" Still Isaacs was firm; but the Governor, anxious, in-

deed, to prevent a row, knew I would say something, and said, " Our friend Mr. Ingham is always
prepared; and, though we had not relied upon him,
he will say a word perhaps." Applause followed,
which turned Dennis's head. He rose, fluttered, and
tried No. 3 : " There has been so much said, and, on
the whole, so well said, that I will not longer occupy
the time ! " and sat down, looking for his hat; for
things seemed squally. But the people cried, " Go
on ! go on ! " and some applauded. Dennis, still confused, but flattered by the applause, to which neither
he nor I are used, rose again, and this time tried No.
2 : " I am very glad you liked it ! " in a sonorous,
clear delivery. My best friends stared. All the people who did not know me personally yelled with delight at the aspect of the evening ; the Governor was
beside himself, and poor Isaacs thought he was undone !
Alas, it was I ! A boy in the gallery cried in a loud
tone, " It's all an infernal humbug," just as Dennis,
waving his hand, commanded silence, and tried No. 4 :
" I agree, in general, with my friend the other side of
the room." The poor Governor doubted his senses,
and crossed to stop him, — not in time, however.
The same gallery-boy shouted, " How's your mother ? " and Dennis, now completely lost, tried, as his
last shot, No. 1, vainly : " Very well, thank you ; and
you ? "

I think I must have been undone already. But
Dennis, like another Lockhard, chose " to make sicker."

The audience rose in a whirl of amazement, rage, and sorrow. Some other impertinence, aimed at Dennis, broke all restraint, and, in pure Irish, he delivered himself of an address to the gallery, inviting any person who wished to fight to come down and do so, — stating, that they were all dogs and cowards and the sons of dogs and cowards, — that he would take any five of them single-handed. " Shure, I have said all his Riverence and the Misthress bade me say," cried he, in defiance ; and, seizing the Governor's cane from his hand, brandished it, quarter-staff fashion, above his head. He was, indeed, got from the hall only with the greatest difficulty by the Governor, the City Marshal, who had been called in, and the Superintendent of my Sunday-School.

The universal impression, of course, was, that the Rev. Frederic Ingham had lost all command of himself in some of those haunts of intoxication which for fifteen years I have been laboring to destroy. Till this moment, indeed, that is the impression in Naguadavick. This number of the Atlantic will relieve from it a hundred friends of mine who have been sadly wounded by that notion now for years; but I shall not be likely ever to show my head there again.

No! My double has undone me.

We left town at seven the next morning. I came to No. 9, in the Third Range, and settled on the Minister's Lot. In the new towns in Maine, the first settled minister has a gift of a hundred acres of land.

I am the first settled minister in No. 9. My wife and little Paulina are my parish. We raise corn enough to live on in summer. We kill bear's meat enough to carbonize it in winter. I work on steadily on my "Traces of Sandemanianism in the Sixth and Seventh Centuries," which I hope to persuade Phillips, Sampson, & Co. to publish next year. We are very happy, but the world thinks we are undone.

THE MAN WITHOUT A COUNTRY.

FROM THE INGHAM PAPERS.

[THIS story was written in the summer of 1863, as a contribution, however humble, towards the formation of a just and true national sentiment, or sentiment of love to the nation. It was at the time when Mr. Vallandigham had been sent across the border. It was my wish, indeed, that the story might be printed before the autumn elections of that year, — as my "testimony" regarding the principles involved in them, — but circumstances delayed its publication till the December number of the Atlantic appeared.

It is wholly a fiction, "founded on fact." The facts on which it is founded are these, — that Aaron Burr sailed down the Mississippi River in 1805, again in 1806, and was tried for treason in 1807. The rest, with one exception to be noticed, is all fictitious.

It was my intention that the story should have been published with no author's name, other than that of Captain Frederic Ingham, U. S. N. Whether writing under his name or my own, I have taken no liberties with history other than such as every writer of fiction is privileged to take, — indeed, must take, if fiction is to be written at all.

The story having been once published, it passed out of my hands. From that moment it has gradually acquired different accessories, for which I am not responsible. Thus I have heard it said, that at one bureau of the Navy Department they say that

Nolan was pardoned, in fact, and returned home to die. At another bureau, I am told, the answer to questions is, that, though it is true that an officer was kept abroad all his life, his name was not Nolan. A venerable friend of mine in Boston, who discredits all tradition, still recollects this "Nolan court-martial." One of the most accurate of my younger friends had noticed Nolan's death in the newspaper, but recollected "that it was in September, and not in August." A lady in Baltimore writes me, I believe in good faith, that Nolan has two widowed sisters residing in that neighborhood. A correspondent of the Philadelphia Despatch believed "the article untrue, as the United States corvette 'Levant' was lost at sea nearly three years since, between San Francisco and San Juan." I may remark that this uncertainty as to the place of her loss rather adds to the probability of her turning up after three years in Lat. 2° 11' S., Long. 131° W. A writer in the New Orleans Picayune, in a careful historical paper, explained at length that I had been mistaken all through; that Philip Nolan never went to sea, but to Texas; that there he was shot in battle, March 21, 1801, and by orders from Spain every fifth man of his party was to be shot, had they not died in prison. Fortunately, however, he left his papers and maps, which fell into the hands of a friend of the Picayune's correspondent. This friend proposes to publish them, — and the public will then have, it is to be hoped, the true history of Philip Nolan, the man without a country.

With all these continuations, however, I have nothing to do. I can only repeat that my Philip Nolan is pure fiction. I cannot send his scrap-book to my friend who asks for it, because I have it not to send.

I remembered, when I was collecting material for my story, that in General Wilkinson's galimatias, which he calls his "Memoirs," is frequent reference to a Jorkins-like partner of his, of the name of Nolan, who, at some time near the beginning of this century, was killed in Texas. Whenever Wilkinson found himself in

rather a deeper bog than usual, he used to justify himself by saying that he could not explain such or such a charge because
"the papers referring to it were lost when *Mr. Nolan* was imprisoned in Texas." Finding this mythical character in the
mythical legends of a mythical time, I took the liberty to give
him a brother, rather more mythical, whose adventures should be
on the seas. I had the impression that Wilkinson's friend was
named Stephen, — and as such he is spoken of in this story at
page 232. But long after this was printed, I found that the New
Orleans paper was right in saying that the Texan hero was named
Philip. I am very sorry that I changed him inadvertently to
Stephen. It is too late for me to change him back again. I
remember to have heard a distinguished divine preach on St.
Philip's day, by accident, a discourse on the life of the Evange-
list Stephen. If such a mistake can happen in the best regulated
of pulpits, I must be pardoned for mistaking Philip for Stephen
Nolan. The reader must observe that he was dead some years
before the action of this story begins. In the same connection I
must add that Mr. P. Nolan, the teamster in Boston, whose horse
and cart I venture to recommend to an indulgent public, is no
relation of the hero of this tale.

If any reader considers the invention of a brother too great a
liberty to take in fiction, I venture to remind him that "'T is
sixty years since"; and that I should have the highest authority
in literature even for much greater liberties taken with annals so
far removed from our time.

A Boston paper, in noticing the story of "My Double," contained in another part of this collection, said it was highly *improbable*. I have always agreed with that critic. I confess I
have the same opinion of the story of Philip Nolan. It passes on
ships which had no existence, is vouched for by officers who never
lived. Its hero is in two or three places at the same time, under
a process wholly impossible under any conceivable administration of affairs. In reply, therefore, to a kind adviser in Con-

necticut, who told me that the story must be apologized for, because it was doing great injury to the national cause by asserting such continued cruelty of the Federal Government through a half-century, I must be permitted to say that the public, being the Supreme Court of the United States, "may be supposed to know something."]

I suppose that very few casual readers of the New York Herald of August 13th observed, in an obscure corner, among the "Deaths," the announcement, —

"Nolan. Died, on board U. S. Corvette Levant, Lat. 2° 11' S., Long. 131° W., on the 11th of May, Philip Nolan."

I happened to observe it, because I was stranded at the old Mission-House in Mackinaw, waiting for a Lake Superior steamer which did not choose to come, and I was devouring to the very stubble all the current literature I could get hold of, even down to the deaths and marriages in the Herald. My memory for names and people is good, and the reader will see, as he goes on, that I had reason enough to remember Philip Nolan. There are hundreds of readers who would have paused at that announcement, if the officer of the Levant who reported it had chosen to make it thus: — "Died, May 11th, THE MAN WITHOUT A COUNTRY." For it was as "The Man without a Country" that poor Philip Nolan had generally been known by the officers who had him in charge during some fifty years, as, indeed, by all the men who sailed under them. I dare say there is many a man who has taken wine with him once a fortnight, in a three years' cruise, who never knew that his name was "Nolan," or whether the poor wretch had any name at all.

There can now be no possible harm in telling this poor creature's story. Reason enough there has been till now, ever since Madison's administration went out in 1817, for very strict secrecy, the secrecy of honor itself, among the gentlemen of the navy who have had Nolan in successive charge. And certainly it speaks well for the *esprit de corps* of the profession, and the personal honor of its members, that to the press this man's story has been wholly unknown, — and, I think, to the country at large also. I have reason to think, from some investigations I made in the Naval Archives when I was attached to the Bureau of Construction, that every official report relating to him was burned when Ross burned the public buildings at Washington. One of the Tuckers, or possibly one of the Watsons, had Nolan in charge at the end of the war ; and when, on returning from his cruise, he reported at Washington to one of the Crowninshields, — who was in the Navy Department when he came home, — he found that the Department ignored the whole business. Whether they really knew nothing about it or whether it was a "*Non mi ricordo*," determined on as a piece of policy, I do not know. But this I do know, that since 1817, and possibly before, no naval officer has mentioned Nolan in his report of a cruise.

But, as I say, there is no need for secrecy any longer. And now the poor creature is dead, it seems to me worth while to tell a little of his story, by way of showing young Americans of to-day what it is to be A MAN WITHOUT A COUNTRY.

Philip Nolan was as fine a young officer as there was in the " Legion of the West," as the Western division of our army was then called. When Aaron Burr made his first dashing expedition down to New Orleans in 1805, at Fort Massac, or somewhere above on the river, he met, as the Devil would have it, this gay, dashing, bright young fellow, at some dinner-party, I think. Burr marked him, talked to him, walked with him, took him a day or two's voyage in his flat-boat, and, in short, fascinated him. For the next year, barrack-life was very tame to poor Nolan. He occasionally availed himself of the permission the great man had given him to write to him. Long, high-worded, stilted-letters the poor boy wrote and rewrote and copied. But never a line did he have in reply from the gay deceiver. The other boys in the garrison sneered at him, because he sacrificed in this unrequited affection for a politician the time which they devoted to Monongahela, hazard, and high-low-jack. Bourbon, euchre, and poker were still unknown. But one day Nolan had his revenge. This time Burr came down the river, not as an attorney seeking a place for his office, but as a disguised conqueror. He had defeated I know not how many district-attorneys; he had dined at I know not how many public dinners; he had been heralded in I know not how many Weekly Arguses, and it was rumored that he had an army behind him and an empire before him.   It was a great day — his arrival — to poor Nolan.   Burr had not been at the fort an hour before he sent for him.   That evening he asked Nolan to take him out in his skiff, to show him a canebrake or a cotton-wood tree, as he said, — really to seduce him; and by the time the sail was over, Nolan was enlisted body and soul. From that time, though he did not yet know it, he lived as A MAN WITHOUT A COUNTRY.

What Burr meant to do I know no more than you, dear reader.   It is none of our business just now.   Only, when the grand catastrophe came, and Jefferson and the House of Virginia of that day undertook to break on the wheel all the possible Clarences of the then House of York, by the great treason-trial at Richmond, some of the lesser fry in that distant Mississippi Valley, which was farther from us than Puget's Sound is to-day, introduced the like novelty on their provincial stage, and, to while away the monotony of the summer at Fort Adams, got up, for *spectacles*, a string of court-martials on the officers there.   One and another of the colonels and majors were tried, and, to fill out the list, little Nolan, against whom, Heaven knows, there was evidence enough, — that he was sick of the service, had been willing to be false to it, and would have obeyed any order to march any-whither with

any one who would follow him had the order been
signed, "By command of His Exc. A. Burr." The
courts dragged on. The big flies escaped, — rightly
for all I know. Nolan was proved guilty enough, as I
say; yet you and I would never have heard of him,
reader, but that, when the president of the court
asked him at the close, whether he wished to say anything to show that he had always been faithful to the
United States, he cried out, in a fit of frenzy, —

"D—n the United States! I wish I may never
hear of the United States again!"

I suppose he did not know how the words shocked
old Colonel Morgan, who was holding the court.
Half the officers who sat in it had served through the
Revolution, and their lives, not to say their necks, had
been risked for the very idea which he so cavalierly
cursed in his madness. He, on his part, had grown
up in the West of those days, in the midst of "Spanish
plot," "Orleans plot," and all the rest. He had been
educated on a plantation where the finest company
was a Spanish officer or a French merchant from Orleans. His education, such as it was, had been per-
fected in commercial expeditions to Vera Cruz, and I
think he told me his father once hired an Englishman
to be a private tutor for a winter on the plantation.
He had spent half his youth with an older brother,
hunting horses in Texas; and, in a word, to him
"United States" was scarcely a reality. Yet he had
been fed by "United States" for all the years since

he had been in the army. He had sworn on his faith as a Christian to be true to " United States." It was " United States " which gave him the uniform he wore, and the sword by his side. Nay, my poor Nolan, it was only because " United States " had picked you out first as one of her own confidential men of honor that " A. Burr " cared for you a straw more than for the flat-boat men who sailed his ark for him. I do not excuse Nolan ; I only explain to the reader why he damned his country, and wished he might never hear her name again.

He never did hear her name but once again. From that moment, September 23, 1807, till the day he died, May 11, 1863, he never heard her name again. For that half-century and more he was a man without a country.

Old Morgan, as I said, was terribly shocked. If Nolan had compared George Washington to Benedict Arnold, or had cried, " God save King George," Morgan would not have felt worse. He called the court into his private room, and returned in fifteen minutes, with a face like a sheet, to say, —

" Prisoner, hear the sentence of the Court! The Court decides, subject to the approval of the President, that you never hear the name of the United States again."

Nolan laughed. But nobody else laughed. Old Morgan was too solemn, and the whole room was hushed dead as night for a minute. Even Nolan lost his swagger in a moment. Then Morgan added, —

"Mr. Marshal, take the prisoner to Orleans in an armed boat, and deliver him to the naval commander there."

The Marshal gave his orders and the prisoner was taken out of court.

"Mr. Marshal," continued old Morgan, "see that no one mentions the United States to the prisoner. Mr. Marshal, make my respects to Lieutenant Mitchell at Orleans, and request him to order that no one shall mention the United States to the prisoner while he is on board ship. You will receive your written orders from the officer on duty here this evening. The court is adjourned without day."

I have always supposed that Colonel Morgan himself took the proceedings of the court to Washington City, and explained them to Mr. Jefferson. Certain it is that the President approved them, — certain, that is, if I may believe the men who say they have seen his signature. Before the Nautilus got round from New Orleans to the Northern Atlantic coast with the prisoner on board the sentence had been approved, and he was a man without a country.

The plan then adopted was substantially the same which was necessarily followed ever after. Perhaps it was suggested by the necessity of sending him by water from Fort Adams and Orleans. The Secretary of the Navy — it must have been the first Crowninshield, though he is a man I do not remember — was requested to put Nolan on board a government vessel

bound on a long cruise, and to direct that he should
be only so far confined there as to make it certain that
he never saw or heard of the country. We had few
long cruises then, and the navy was very much out
of favor; and as almost all of this story is traditional,
as I have explained, I do not know certainly what
his first cruise was. But the commander to whom he
was intrusted, — perhaps it was Tingey or Shaw, though
I think it was one of the younger men, — we are all
old enough now, — regulated the etiquette and the
precautions of the affair, and according to his scheme
they were carried out, I suppose, till Nolan died.

When I was second officer of the " Intrepid," some
thirty years after, I saw the original paper of instructions. I have been sorry ever since that I did not
copy the whole of it. It ran, however, much in this
way : —

> " WASHINGTON (with a date, which
> must have been late in 1807).

" SIR, — You will receive from Lieutenant Neale
the person of Philip Nolan, late a Lieutenant in the
United States Army.

" This person on his trial by court-martial expressed
with an oath the wish that he might ' never hear of
the United States again.'

" The Court sentenced him to have his wish fulfilled.

" For the present, the execution of the order is intrusted by the President to this Department.

N

" You will take the prisoner on board your ship, and keep him there with such precautions as shall prevent his escape.

" You will provide him with such quarters, rations, and clothing as would be proper for an officer of his late rank, if he were a passenger on your vessel on the business of his Government.

" The gentlemen on board will make any arrangements agreeable to themselves regarding his society. He is to be exposed to no indignity of any kind, nor is he ever unnecessarily to be reminded that he is a prisoner.

" But under no circumstances is he ever to hear of his country or to see any information regarding it; and you will specially caution all the officers under your command to take care, that, in the various indulgences which may be granted, this rule, in which his punishment is involved, shall not be broken.

" It is the intention of the Government that he shall never again see the country which he has disowned. Before the end of your cruise you will receive orders which will give effect to this intention.

" Respectfully yours,

" W. SOUTHARD, for the

Secretary of the Navy."

If I had only preserved the whole of this paper, there would be no break in the beginning of my sketch of this story. For Captain Shaw, if it were he, handed it to his successor in the charge, and he to his, and I suppose the commander of the Levant has it to-day as his authority for keeping this man in this mild custody.

The rule adopted on board the ships on which I have met "the man without a country" was, I think, transmitted from the beginning. No mess liked to have him permanently, because his presence cut off all talk of home or of the prospect of return, of politics or letters, of peace or of war, — cut off more than half the talk men liked to have at sea. But it was always thought too hard that he should never meet the rest of us, except to touch hats, and we finally sank into one system. He was not permitted to talk with the men, unless an officer was by. With officers he had unrestrained intercourse, as far as they and he chose. But he grew shy, though he had favorites: I was one. Then the captain always asked him to dinner on Monday. Every mess in succession took up the invitation in its turn. According to the size of the ship, you had him at your mess more or less often at dinner. His breakfast he ate in his own state-room, — he always had a state-room, — which was where a sentinel or somebody on the watch could see the door. And whatever else he ate or drank, he ate or drank alone. Sometimes, when the marines or sailors had any special jollification, they were permitted to invite "Plain-Buttons," as they called him. Then Nolan was sent with some officer, and the men were forbidden to speak of home while he was there. I believe the theory was that the sight of his punishment did them good. They called him " Plain-Buttons," because, while he always chose to wear a regulation army-uniform, he was not permitted to wear the army-button, for the reason that it bore either the initials or the insignia of the country he had disowned.

I remember, soon after I joined the navy, I was on shore with some of the older officers from our ship and from the Brandywine, which we had met at Alexandria. We had leave to make a party and go up to Cairo and the Pyramids. As we jogged along (you went on donkeys then), some of the gentlemen (we boys called them " Dons," but the phrase was long since changed) fell to talking about Nolan, and some one told the system which was adopted from the first about his books and other reading. As he was almost never permitted to go on shore, even though the vessel lay in port for months, his time at the best hung heavy; and everybody was permitted to lend him books, if they were not published in America and made no allusion to it. These were common enough in the old days, when people in the other hemisphere talked of the United States as little as we do of Paraguay. He had almost all the foreign papers that came into the ship, sooner or later; only somebody must go over them first, and cut out any advertisement or stray paragraph that alluded to America. This was a little cruel sometimes, when the back of what was cut out might be as innocent as Hesiod.   Right in the midst of one of Napoleon's battles, or one of Canning's speeches, poor Nolan would find a great hole, because on the back of the page of that paper there had been an advertisement of a packet for New York, or a scrap from the President's message.   I say this was the first time I ever heard of this plan, which afterwards I had enough and more than enough to do with.   I remember it, because poor Phillips, who was of the party, as soon as the allusion to reading was made, told a story of something which happened at the Cape of Good Hope on Nolan's first voyage; and it is the only thing I ever knew of that voyage.   They had touched at the Cape, and had done the civil thing with the English Admiral and the fleet, and then, leaving for a long cruise up the Indian Ocean, Phillips had borrowed a lot of English books from an officer, which, in those days, as indeed in these, was quite a windfall. Among them, as the Devil would order, was the " Lay of the Last Minstrel," which they had all of them heard of, but which most of them had never seen.   I think it could not have been published long.   Well, nobody thought there could be any risk of anything national in that, though Phillips swore old Shaw had cut out the " Tempest " from Shakespeare before he let Nolan have it, because he said " the Bermudas ought to be ours, and, by Jove, should be one day."   So Nolan was permitted to join the circle one afternoon when a lot of them sat on deck smoking and reading aloud.

People do not do such things so often now ; but when
I was young we got rid of a great deal of time so.
Well, so it happened that in his turn Nolan took the
book and read to the others; and he read very well,
as I know.   Nobody in the circle knew a line of the
poem, only it was all magic and Border chivalry, and
was ten thousand years ago.   Poor Nolan read steadily
through the fifth canto, stopped a minute and drank
something, and then began, without a thought of what
was coming, —

> "Breathes there the man, with soul so dead,
>   Who never to himself hath said," —

It seems impossible to us that anybody ever heard this
for the first time ; but all these fellows did then, and
poor Nolan himself went on, still unconsciously or
mechanically, —

> " This is my own, my native land ! "

Then they all saw something was to pay ; but he expected to get through, I suppose, turned a little pale,
but plunged on, —

> " Whose heart hath ne'er within him burned,
>   As home his footsteps he hath turned
>   From wandering on a foreign strand ? —
>   If such there breathe, go, mark him well," —

By this time the men were all beside themselves, wishing there was any way to make him turn over two
pages ; but he had not quite presence of mind for
that ; he gagged a little, colored crimson, and stag-
gered on, —

"For him no minstrel raptures swell;
High though his titles, proud his name,
Boundless his wealth as wish can claim,
Despite these titles, power, and pelf,
The wretch, concentred all in self," —

and here the poor fellow choked, could not go on, but
started up, swung the book into the sea, vanished into
his state-room, " And by Jove," said Phillips, " we did
not see him for two months again. And I had to
make up some beggarly story to that English surgeon
why I did not return his Walter Scott to him."

That story shows about the time when Nolan's
braggadocio must have broken down. At first, they
said, he took a very high tone, considered his imprisonment a mere farce, affected to enjoy the voyage, and
all that; but Phillips said that after he came out of
his state-room he never was the same man again. He
never read aloud again, unless it was the Bible or
Shakespeare, or something else he was sure of. But
it was not that merely. He never entered in with
the other young men exactly as a companion again.
He was always shy afterwards, when I knew him, —
very seldom spoke, unless he was spoken to, except to
a very few friends. He lighted up occasionally, — I
remember late in his life hearing him fairly eloquent
on something which had been suggested to him by
one of Fléchier's sermons, — but generally he had the
nervous, tired look of a heart-wounded man.

When Captain Shaw was coming home, — if, as I
say, it was Shaw, — rather to the surprise of every-

body they made one of the Windward Islands, and lay
off and on for nearly a week. The boys said the officers were sick of salt-junk, and meant to have turtle-
soup before they came home. But after several days
the Warren came to the same rendezvous ; they exchanged signals ; she sent to Phillips and these home-
ward-bound men letters and papers, and told them she
was outward-bound, perhaps to the Mediterranean,
and took poor Nolan and his traps on the boat back to
try his second cruise. He looked very blank when he
was told to get ready to join her. He had known
enough of the signs of the sky to know that till that
moment he was going " home." But this was a distinct evidence of something he had not thought of,
perhaps, — that there was no going home for him,
even to a prison. And this was the first of some
twenty such transfers, which brought him sooner or
later into half our best vessels, but which kept him
all his life at least some hundred miles from the country he had hoped he might never hear of again.

It may have been on that second cruise, — it was
once when he was up the Mediterranean, — that Mrs.
Graff, the celebrated Southern beauty of those days,
danced with him. They had been lying a long time
in the Bay of Naples, and the officers were very intimate in the English fleet, and there had been great
festivities, and our men thought they must give a great
ball on board the ship. How they ever did it on board
the " Warren " I am sure I do not know. Perhaps it

was not the " Warren," or perhaps ladies did not take up so much room as they do now. They wanted to use Nolan's state-room for something, and they hated to do it without asking him to the ball; so the captain said they might ask him, if they would be responsible that he did not talk with the wrong people, "who would give him intelligence." So the dance went on, the finest party that had ever been known, I dare say; for I never heard of a man-of-war ball that was not. For ladies they had the family of the American consul, one or two travellers who had adventured so far, and a nice bevy of English girls and matrons, perhaps Lady Hamilton herself.

Well, different officers relieved each other in standing and talking with Nolan in a friendly way, so as to be sure that nobody else spoke to him. The dancing went on with spirit, and after a while even the fellows who took this honorary guard of Nolan ceased to fear any *contretemps*. Only when some English lady — Lady Hamilton, as I said, perhaps — called for a set of "American dances," an odd thing happened. Everybody then danced contra-dances. The black band, nothing loath, conferred as to what " American dances " were, and started off with " Virginia Reel," which they followed with " Money-Musk," which, in its turn in those days, should have been followed by " The Old Thirteen." But just as Dick, the leader, tapped for his fiddles to begin, and bent forward, about to say, in true negro state, "'The Old Thirteen,' gentlemen and ladies!" as he had said "'Virginny Reel,' if you please!" and "'Money-Musk,' if you please!" the captain's boy tapped him on the shoulder, whispered to him, and he did not announce the name of the dance; he merely bowed, began on the air, and they all fell to, — the officers teaching the English girls the figure, but not telling them why it had no name.

But that is not the story I started to tell. — As the dancing went on, Nolan and our fellows all got at ease, as I said, — so much so, that it seemed quite natural for him to bow to that splendid Mrs. Graff, and say, —

"I hope you have not forgotten me, Miss Rutledge. Shall I have the honor of dancing?"

He did it so quickly, that Fellows, who was by him, could not hinder him. She laughed and said, —

"I am not Miss Rutledge any longer, Mr. Nolan; but I will dance all the same," just nodded to Fellows, as if to say he must leave Mr. Nolan to her, and led him off to the place where the dance was forming.

Nolan thought he had got his chance. He had known her at Philadelphia, and at other places had met her, and this was a Godsend. You could not talk in contra-dances, as you do in cotillons, or even in the pauses of waltzing; but there were chances for tongues and sounds, as well as for eyes and blushes. He began with her travels, and Europe, and Vesuvius, and the French; and then, when they had worked down, and had that long talking-time at the bottom

of the set, he said, boldly, — a little pale, she said, as
she told me the story, years after, —

"And what do you hear from home, Mrs. Graff?"

And that splendid creature looked through him.
Jove! how she must have looked through him!

"Home!! Mr. Nolan!!! I thought you were the
man who never wanted to hear of home again!" —
and she walked directly up the deck to her husband,
and left poor Nolan alone, as he always was. — He did
not dance again.

I cannot give any history of him in order; nobody
can now; and, indeed, I am not trying to. These
are the traditions, which I sort out, as I believe them,
from the myths which have been told about this man
for forty years. The lies that have been told about
him are legion. The fellows used to say he was the
"Iron Mask"; and poor George Pons went to his
grave in the belief that this was the author of "Junius,"
who was being punished for his celebrated libel on
Thomas Jefferson. Pons was not very strong in the
historical line. A happier story than either of these I
have told is of the War. That came along soon after.
I have heard this affair told in three or four ways, —
and, indeed, it may have happened more than once.
But which ship it was on I cannot tell. However,
in one, at least, of the great frigate-duels with the
English, in which the navy was really baptized, it
happened that a round-shot from the enemy entered
one of our ports square, and took right down the of-

fier of the gun himself, and almost every man of the gun's crew. Now you may say what you choose about courage, but that is not a nice thing to see. But, as the men who were not killed picked themselves up, and as they and the surgeon's people were carrying off the bodies, there appeared Nolan, in his shirt-sleeves, with the rammer in his hand, and, just as if he had been the officer, told them off with authority, — who should go to the cockpit with the wounded men, who should stay with him, — perfectly cheery, and with that way which makes men feel sure all is right and is going to be right. And he finished loading the gun with his own hands, aimed it, and bade the men fire. And there he stayed, captain of that gun, keeping those fellows in spirits, till the enemy struck, — sitting on the carriage while the gun was cooling, though he was exposed all the time, — showing them easier ways to handle heavy shot, — making the raw hands laugh at their own blunders, — and when the gun cooled again, getting it loaded and fired twice as often as any other gun on the ship. The captain walked forward by way of encouraging the men, and Nolan touched his hat and said, —

"I am showing them how we do this in the artillery, sir."

And this is the part of the story where all the legends agree; and the Commodore said, —

"I see you do, and I thank you, sir; and I shall never forget this day, sir, and you never shall, sir."

And after the whole thing was over, and he had the Englishman's sword, in the midst of the state and ceremony of the quarter-deck, he said, —

"Where is Mr. Nolan? Ask Mr. Nolan to come here."

And when Nolan came, the captain said, —

"Mr. Nolan, we are all very grateful to you to-day; you are one of us to-day; you will be named in the despatches."

And then the old man took off his own sword of ceremony, and gave it to Nolan, and made him put it on. The man told me this who saw it. Nolan cried like a baby, and well he might. He had not worn a sword since that infernal day at Fort Adams. But always afterwards on occasions of ceremony, he wore that quaint old French sword of the Commodore's.

The captain did mention him in the despatches. It was always said he asked that he might be pardoned. He wrote a special letter to the Secretary of War. But nothing ever came of it. As I said, that was about the time when they began to ignore the whole transaction at Washington, and when Nolan's imprisonment began to carry itself on because there was nobody to stop it without any new orders from home.

I have heard it said that he was with Porter when he took possession of the Nukahiwa Islands. Not this Porter, you know, but old Porter, his father, Essex Porter, — that is, the old Essex Porter, not this Essex. As an artillery officer, who had seen service in the West, Nolan knew more about fortifications, embrasures, ravelins, stockades, and all that, than any of them did; and he worked with a right good-will in fixing that battery all right. I have always thought it was a pity Porter did not leave him in command there with Gamble. That would have settled all the question about his punishment. We should have kept the islands, and at this moment we should have one station in the Pacific Ocean. Our French friends, too, when they wanted this little watering-place, would have found it was preoccupied. But Madison and the Virginians, of course, flung all that away.

All that was near fifty years ago. If Nolan was thirty then, he must have been near eighty when he died. He looked sixty when he was forty. But he never seemed to me to change a hair afterwards. As I imagine his life, from what I have seen and heard of it, he must have been in every sea, and yet almost never on land. He must have known, in a formal way, more officers in our service than any man living knows. He told me once, with a grave smile, that no man in the world lived so methodical a life as he. "You know the boys say I am the Iron Mask, and you know how busy he was." He said it did not do for any one to try to read all the time, more than to do anything else all the time; but that he read just five hours a day. "Then," he said, "I keep up my note-books, writing in them at such and such hours from what I have been reading; and I include in these my scrap-books."

These were very curious indeed. He had six or eight, of different subjects. There was one of History, one of Natural Science, one which he called "Odds and Ends." But they were not merely books of extracts from newspapers. They had bits of plants and ribbons, shells tied on, and carved scraps of bone and wood, which he had taught the men to cut for him, and they were beautifully illustrated. He drew admirably. He had some of the funniest drawings there, and some of the most pathetic, that I have ever seen in my life. I wonder who will have Nolan's scrap-books.

Well, he said his reading and his notes were his profession, and that they took five hours and two hours respectively of each day. "Then," said he, "every man should have a diversion as well as a profession. My Natural History is my diversion." That took two hours a day more. The men used to bring him birds and fish, but on a long cruise he had to satisfy himself with centipedes and cockroaches and such small game. He was the only naturalist I ever met who knew anything about the habits of the house-fly and the mosquito. All those people can tell you whether they are *Lepidoptera* or *Steptopotera ;* but as for telling how you can get rid of them, or how they get away from you when you strike them, — why Linnæus knew as little of that as John Foy the idiot did. These nine hours made Nolan's regular daily " occupation." The rest of the time he talked or walked. Till he grew very old, he went aloft a great deal. He always kept up his exercise; and I never heard that he was ill. If any other man was ill, he was the kindest nurse in the world; and he knew more than half the surgeons do. Then if anybody was sick or died, or if the captain wanted him to, on any other occasion, he was always ready to read prayers. I have said that he read beautifully.

My own acquaintance with Philip Nolan began six or eight years after the War, on my first voyage after I was appointed a midshipman. It was in the first days after our Slave-Trade treaty, while the Reigning House, which was still the House of Virginia, had still a sort of sentimentalism about the suppression of the horrors of the Middle Passage, and something was sometimes done that way. We were in the South Atlantic on that business. From the time I joined, I believe I thought Nolan was a sort of lay chaplain, — a chaplain with a blue coat. I never asked about him. Everything in the ship was strange to me. I knew it was green to ask questions, and I suppose I thought there was a " Plain-Buttons " on every ship. We had him to dine in our mess once a week, and the caution was given that on that day nothing was to be said about home. But if they had told us not to say anything about the planet Mars or the Book of Deuteronomy, I should not have asked why; there were a great many things which seemed to me to have as little reason. I first came to understand anything about " the man without a country " one day when we overhauled a dirty little schooner which had slaves on board. An officer was sent to take charge of her, and, after a few minutes, he sent back his boat to ask that some one might be sent him who could speak Portuguese. We were all looking over the rail when the message came, and we all wished we could interpret, when the captain asked Who spoke Portuguese. But none of the officers did; and just as the captain was sending forward to ask if any of the people could, Nolan stepped out and said he should be glad to interpret, if the captain wished, as he understood the language. The captain thanked him, fitted out another boat with him, and in this boat it was my luck to go.

When we got there, it was such a scene as you seldom see, and never want to. Nastiness beyond account, and chaos run loose in the midst of the nastiness. There were not a great many of the negroes; but by way of making what there were understand that they were free, Vaughan had had their hand-cuffs and ankle-cuffs knocked off, and, for convenience' sake, was putting them upon the rascals of the schooner's crew. The negroes were, most of them, out of the hold, and swarming all round the dirty deck, with a central throng surrounding Vaughan and addressing him in every dialect, and *patois* of a dialect, from the Zulu click up to the Parisian of Beledeljereed.

As we came on deck, Vaughan looked down from a hogshead, on which he had mounted in desperation, and said: —

" For God's love, is there anybody who can make these wretches understand something ?   The men gave them rum, and that did not quiet them.   I knocked that big fellow down twice, and that did not soothe him.   And then I talked Choctaw to all of them together ; and I 'll be hanged if they understood that as well as they understood the English."

Nolan said he could speak Portuguese, and one or two fine-looking Kroomen were dragged out, who, as it had been found already, had worked for the Portuguese on the coast at Fernando Po.

" Tell them they are free," said Vaughan ; " and tell them that these rascals are to be hanged as soon as we can get rope enough."

Nolan " put that into Spanish," — that is, he explained it in such Portuguese as the Kroomen could understand, and they in turn to such of the negroes as could understand them.   Then there was such a yell of delight, clinching of fists, leaping and dancing, kissing of Nolan's feet, and a general rush made to the hogshead by way of spontaneous worship of Vaughan, as the *deus ex machina* of the occasion.

" Tell them," said Vaughan, well pleased, " that I will take them all to Cape Palmas."

This did not answer so well.   Cape Palmas was practically as far from the homes of most of them as New Orleans or Rio Janeiro was ; that is, they would be eternally separated from home there.   And their interpreters, as we could understand, instantly

said, "*Ah, non Palmas*," and began to propose infinite
other expedients in most voluble language. Vaughan
was rather disappointed at this result of his liberality,
and asked Nolan eagerly what they said. The drops
stood on poor Nolan's white forehead, as he hushed
the men down, and said : —

"He says, 'Not Palmas.' He says, 'Take us
home, take us to our own country, take us to our own
house, take us to our own pickaninnies and our own
women.' He says he has an old father and mother
who will die if they do not see him. And this one
says he left his people all sick, and paddled down to
Fernando to beg the white doctor to come and help
them, and that these devils caught him in the bay just
in sight of home, and that he has never seen anybody
from home since then. And this one says," choked
out Nolan, " that he has not heard a word from his
home in six months, while he has been locked up in
an infernal barracoon."

Vaughan always said he grew gray himself while
Nolan struggled through this interpretation. I, who
did not understand anything of the passion involved in
it, saw that the very elements were melting with fer-
vent heat, and that something was to pay somewhere.
Even the negroes themselves stopped howling, as they
saw Nolan's agony, and Vaughan's almost equal agony
of sympathy. As quick as he could get words, he
said : —

" Tell them yes, yes, yes ; tell them they shall go

to the Mountains of the Moon, if they will.   If I sail
the schooner through the Great White Desert, they
shall go home!"

And after some fashion Nolan said so.   And then
they all fell to kissing him again, and wanted to rub
his nose with theirs.

But he could not stand it long; and getting Vaughan
to say he might go back, he beckoned me down into
our boat.   As we lay back in the stern-sheets and
the men gave way, he said to me: "Youngster, let
that show you what it is to be without a family,
without a home, and without a country.   And if you
are ever tempted to say a word or to do a thing that
shall put a bar between you and your family, your
home, and your country, pray God in his mercy to
take you that instant home to his own heaven.   Stick
by your family, boy; forget you have a self, while
you do everything for them.   Think of your home,
boy; write and send, and talk about it.   Let it be
nearer and nearer to your thought, the farther you
have to travel from it; and rush back to it, when you
are free, as that poor black slave is doing now.   And
for your country, boy," and the words rattled in his
throat, "and for that flag," and he pointed to the
ship, "never dream a dream but of serving her as she
bids you, though the service carry you through a
thousand hells.   No matter what happens to you, no
matter who flatters you or who abuses you, never
look at another flag, never let a night pass but you

pray God to bless that flag. Remember, boy, that behind all these men you have to do with, behind officers, and government, and people even, there is the Country Herself, your Country, and that you belong to Her as you belong to your own mother. Stand by Her, boy, as you would stand by your mother, if those devils there had got hold of her to-day!"

I was frightened to death by his calm, hard passion; but I blundered out, that I would, by all that was holy, and that I had never thought of doing anything else. He hardly seemed to hear me; but he did, almost in a whisper, say: "O, if anybody had said so to me when I was of your age!"

I think it was this half-confidence of his, which I never abused, for I never told this story till now, which afterward made us great friends. He was very kind to me. Often he sat up, or even got up, at night, to walk the deck with me, when it was my watch. He explained to me a great deal of my mathematics, and I owe to him my taste for mathematics. He lent me books, and helped me about my reading. He never alluded so directly to his story again; but from one and another officer I have learned, in thirty years, what I am telling. When we parted from him in St. Thomas harbor, at the end of our cruise, I was more sorry than I can tell. I was very glad to meet him again in 1830; and later in life, when I thought I had some influence in Washington, I moved heaven and earth to have him discharged.

But it was like getting a ghost out of prison. They pretended there was no such man, and never was such a man. They will say so at the Department now! Perhaps they do not know. It will not be the first thing in the service of which the Department appears to know nothing!

There is a story that Nolan met Burr once on one of our vessels, when a party of Americans came on board in the Mediterranean. But this I believe to be a lie ; or, rather, it is a myth, *ben trovato*, involving a tremendous blowing-up with which he sunk Burr, — asking him how he liked to be " without a country." But it is clear from Burr's life, that nothing of the sort could have happened ; and I mention this only as an illustration of the stories which get a-going where there is the least mystery at bottom.

So poor Philip Nolan had his wish fulfilled. I know but one fate more dreadful; it is the fate reserved for those men who shall have one day to exile themselves from their country because they have attempted her ruin, and shall have at the same time to see the prosperity and honor to which she rises when she has rid herself of them and their iniquities. The wish of poor Nolan, as we all learned to call him, not because his punishment was too great, but because his repentance was so clear, was precisely the wish of every Bragg and Beauregard who broke a soldier's oath two years ago, and of every Maury and Barron who broke a sailor's. I do not know how often they have repented. I do know that they have done all that in them lay that they might have no country, — that all the honors, associations, memories, and hopes which belong to "country" might be broken up into little shreds and distributed to the winds. I know, too, that their punishment, as they vegetate through what is left of life to them in wretched Boulognes and Leicester Squares, where they are destined to upbraid each other till they die, will have all the agony of Nolan's, with the added pang that every one who sees them will see them to despise and to execrate them. They will have their wish, like him.

For him, poor fellow, he repented of his folly, and then, like a man, submitted to the fate he had asked for. He never intentionally added to the difficulty or delicacy of the charge of those who had him in hold. Accidents would happen; but they never happened from his fault. Lieutenant Truxton told me, that, when Texas was annexed, there was a careful discussion among the officers, whether they should get hold of Nolan's handsome set of maps, and cut Texas out of it, — from the map of the world and the map of Mexico. The United States had been cut out when the atlas was bought for him. But it was voted, rightly enough, that to do this would be virtually to reveal to him what had happened, or, as Harry Cole said, to make him think Old Burr had succeeded. So it was from no fault of Nolan's that a great botch happened at my own table, when, for a short time, I was in command of the George Washington corvette, on the South American station. We were lying in the La Plata, and some of the officers, who had been on shore, and had just joined again, were entertaining us with accounts of their misadventures in riding the half-wild horses of Buenos Ayres. Nolan was at table, and was in an unusually bright and talkative mood. Some story of a tumble reminded him of an adventure of his own, when he was catching wild horses in Texas with his brother Stephen, at a time when he must have been quite a boy. He told the story with a good deal of spirit, — so much so, that the silence which often follows a good story hung over the table for an instant, to be broken by Nolan himself. For he asked perfectly unconsciously: —

"Pray, what has become of Texas? After the Mexicans got their independence, I thought that province of Texas would come forward very fast. It is really one of the finest regions on earth; it is the Italy of this continent. But I have not seen or heard a word of Texas for near twenty years."

There were two Texan officers at the table. The reason he had never heard of Texas was that Texas and her affairs had been painfully cut out of his newspapers since Austin began his settlements; so that, while he read of Honduras and Tamaulipas, and, till quite lately, of California, — this virgin province, in which his brother had travelled so far, and, I believe, had died, had ceased to be to him. Waters and

Williams, the two Texas men, looked grimly at each other, and tried not to laugh. Edward Morris had his attention attracted by the third link in the chain of the captain's chandelier. Watrous was seized with a convulsion of sneezing. Nolan himself saw that something was to pay, he did not know what. And I, as master of the feast, had to say, —

" Texas is out of the map, Mr. Nolan. Have you seen Captain Back's curious account of Sir Thomas Roe's Welcome ? "

After that cruise I never saw Nolan again. I wrote to him at least twice a year, for in that voyage we became even confidentially intimate ; but he never wrote to me. The other men tell me that in those fifteen years he *aged* very fast, as well he might indeed, but that he was still the same gentle, uncomplaining, silent sufferer that he ever was, bearing as best he could his self-appointed punishment, — rather less social, perhaps, with new men whom he did not know, but more anxious, apparently, than ever to serve and befriend and teach the boys, some of whom fairly seemed to worship him. And now it seems the dear old fellow is dead. He has found a home at last, and a country.

Since writing this, and while considering whether or no I would print it, as a warning to the young Nolans and Vallandighams and Tatnalls of to-day of what it is to throw away a country, I have received from Danforth, who is on board the Levant, a letter which

gives an account of Nolan's last hours. It removes
all my doubts about telling this story.

To understand the first words of the letter, the non-
professional reader should remember that after 1817,
the position of every officer who had Nolan in charge
was one of the greatest delicacy. The government
had failed to renew the order of 1807 regarding him.
What was a man to do? Should he let him go?
What, then, if he were called to account by the Department for violating the order of 1807? Should he
keep him? What, then, if Nolan should be liberated
some day, and should bring an action for false imprisonment or kidnapping against every man who had had
him in charge? I urged and pressed this upon Southard,
and I have reason to think that other officers did the
same thing. But the Secretary always said, as they so
often do at Washington, that there were no special orders to give, and that we must act on our own judgment.
That means, " If you succeed, you will be sustained ;
if you fail, you will be disavowed." Well, as Danforth
says, all that is over now, though I do not know but I
expose myself to a criminal prosecution on the evidence
of the very revelation I am making.

Here is the letter : —

"LEVANT, 2° 2' S. @ 131° W.

" DEAR FRED : — I try to find heart and life to tell
you that it is all over with dear old Nolan. I have
been with him on this voyage more than I ever was,

and I can understand wholly now the way in which you used to speak of the dear old fellow. I could see that he was not strong, but I had no idea the end was so near. The doctor has been watching him very carefully, and yesterday morning came to me and told me that Nolan was not so well, and had not left his state-room, — a thing I never remember before. He had let the doctor come and see him as he lay there, — the first time the doctor had been in the state-room, — and he said he should like to see me. O dear! do you remember the mysteries we boys used to invent about his room, in the old Intrepid days? Well, I went in, and there, to be sure, the poor fellow lay in his berth, smiling pleasantly as he gave me his hand, but looking very frail. I could not help a glance round, which showed me what a little shrine he had made of the box he was lying in. The stars and stripes were triced up above and around a picture of Washington, and he had painted a majestic eagle, with lightnings blazing from his beak and his foot just clasping the whole globe, which his wings overshadowed. The dear old boy saw my glance, and said, with a sad smile, 'Here, you see, I have a country!' And then he pointed to the foot of his bed, where I had not seen before a great map of the United States, as he had drawn it from memory, and which he had there to look upon as he lay. Quaint, queer old names were on it, in large letters: 'Indiana Territory,' 'Mississippi Territory,' and 'Louisiana Territory,' as I suppose our fa-

thers learned such things: but the old fellow had
patched in Texas, too; he had carried his western
boundary all the way to the Pacific, but on that shore
he had defined nothing.

"'O Danforth,' he said, 'I know I am dying. I
cannot get home. Surely you will tell me something
now? — Stop! stop! Do not speak till I say what I
am sure you know, that there is not in this ship, that
there is not in America, — God bless her! — a more
loyal man than I. There cannot be a man who loves
the old flag as I do, or prays for it as I do, or hopes
for it as I do. There are thirty-four stars in it now,
Danforth. I thank God for that, though I do not
know what their names are. There has never been
one taken away: I thank God for that. I know by
that that there has never been any successful Burr.
O Danforth, Danforth,' he sighed out, 'how like a
wretched night's dream a boy's idea of personal fame
or of separate sovereignty seems, when one looks
back on it after such a life as mine! But tell me, —
tell me something, — tell me everything, Danforth,
before I die!'

"Ingham, I swear to you that I felt like a monster
that I had not told him everything before. Danger
or no danger, delicacy or no delicacy, who was I, that
I should have been acting the tyrant all this time over
this dear, sainted old man, who had years ago expiated,
in his whole manhood's life, the madness of a boy's
treason? 'Mr. Nolan,' said I, 'I will tell you everything you ask about. Only, where shall I begin?'

" O the blessed smile that crept over his white face!
and he pressed my hand and said, ' God bless you!'
' Tell me their names,' he said, and he pointed to the
stars on the flag. ' The last I know is Ohio. My
father lived in Kentucky. But I have guessed Michi-
gan and Indiana and Mississippi, — that was where
Fort Adams is, — they make twenty. But where
are your other fourteen ? You have not cut up any
of the old ones, I hope ? '

" Well, that was not a bad text, and I told him the
names in as good order as I could, and he bade me
take down his beautiful map and draw them in as I
best could with my pencil. He was wild with delight
about Texas, told me how his brother died there ; he
had marked a gold cross where he supposed his brother's grave was ; and he had guessed at Texas. Then
he was delighted as he saw California and Oregon ; —
that, he said, he had suspected partly, because he had
never been permitted to land on that shore, though
the ships were there so much. ' And the men,' said
he, laughing, ' brought off a good deal besides furs.'
Then he went back — heavens, how far ! — to ask
about the Chesapeake, and what was done to Barron
for surrendering her to the Leopard, and whether
Burr ever tried again, — and he ground his teeth with
the only passion he showed. But in a moment that
was over, and he said, ' God forgive me, for I am sure
I forgive him.' Then he asked about the old war, —
told me the true story of his serving the gun the day

we took the Java, — asked about dear old David Porter, as he called him. Then he settled down more quietly, and very happily, to hear me tell in an hour the history of fifty years.

"How I wished it had been somebody who knew something! But I did as well as I could. I told him of the English war. I told him about Fulton and the steamboat beginning. I told him about old Scott, and Jackson; told him all I could think of about the Mississippi, and New Orleans, and Texas, and his own old Kentucky. And do you think, he asked who was in command of the 'Legion of the West.' I told him it was a very gallant officer named Grant, and that, by our last news, he was about to establish his head-quarters at Vicksburg. Then, ' Where was Vicksburg?.' I worked that out on the map; it was about a hundred miles, more or less, above his old Fort Adams; and I thought Fort Adams must be a ruin now. ' It must be at old Vick's plantation,' said he: ' well, that is a change!'

"I tell you, Ingham, it was a hard thing to condense the history of half a century into that talk with a sick man. And I do not now know what I told him, — of emigration, and the means of it, — of steamboats, and railroads, and telegraphs, — of inventions, and books, and literature, — of the colleges, and West Point, and the Naval School, — but with the queerest interruptions that ever you heard. You see it was Robinson Crusoe asking all the accumulated questions of fifty-six years!

" I remember he asked, all of a sudden, who was President now ; and when I told him, he asked if Old Abe was General Benjamin Lincoln's son. He said he met old General Lincoln, when he was quite a boy himself, at some Indian treaty. I said no, that Old Abe was a Kentuckian like himself, but I could not tell him of what family ; he had worked up from the ranks. ' Good for him ! ' cried Nolan ; ' I am glad of that. As I have brooded and wondered, I have thought our danger was in keeping up those regular successions in the first families.' Then I got talking about my visit to Washington. I told him of meeting the Oregon Congressman, Harding ; I told him about the Smithsonian, and the Exploring Expedition ; I told him about the Capitol, and the statues for the pediment, and Crawford's Liberty, and Greenough's Washington : Ingham, I told him everything I could think of that would show the grandeur of his country and its prosperity ; but I could not make up my mouth to tell him a word about this infernal Rebellion !

" And he drank it in, and enjoyed it as I cannot tell you. He grew more and more silent, yet I never thought he was tired or faint. I gave him a glass of water, but he just wet his lips, and told me not to go away. Then he asked me to bring the Presbyterian ' Book of Public Prayer,' which lay there, and said, with a smile, that it would open at the right place, — and so it did. There was his double red mark down the page ; and I knelt down and read, and he repeated with me, 'For ourselves and our country, O gracious God, we thank Thee, that, notwithstanding our manifold transgressions of Thy holy laws, Thou hast continued to us Thy marvellous kindness,' — and so to the end of that thanksgiving. Then he turned to the end of the same book, and I read the words more familiar to me : 'Most heartily we beseech Thee with Thy favor to behold and bless Thy servant, the President of the United States, and all others in authority,' — and the rest of the Episcopal collect. 'Danforth,' said he, 'I have repeated those prayers night and morning, it is now fifty-five years.' And then he said he would go to sleep. He bent me down over him and kissed me ; and he said, 'Look in my Bible, Danforth, when I am gone.' And I went away.

" But I had no thought it was the end. I thought he was tired and would sleep. I knew he was happy and I wanted him to be alone.

" But in an hour, when the doctor went in gently, he found Nolan had breathed his life away with a smile. He had something pressed close to his lips. It was his father's badge of the Order of the Cincinnati.

" We looked in his Bible, and there was a slip of paper at the place where he had marked the text : —

" ' They desire a country, even a heavenly : wherefore God is not ashamed to be called their God : for he hath prepared for them a city.'

" On this slip of paper he had written : —

" ' Bury me in the sea ; it has been my home, and

I love it.   But will not some one set up a stone for my memory at Fort Adams or at Orleans, that my disgrace may not be more than I ought to bear ?   Say on it : —

"'*In Memory of*

"'PHILIP NOLAN,

"'*Lieutenant in the Army of the United States.*

"'He loved his country as no other man has loved her ; but no man deserved less at her hands.'"

THE LAST OF THE FLORIDA.

FROM THE INGHAM PAPERS.

[THE Florida, Anglo-Rebel pirate, after inflicting horrible injuries on the commerce of America and the good name of England, was cut out by Captain Collins, from the bay of Bahia, by one of those fortunate mistakes in international law which endear brave men to the nations in whose interest they are committed. When she arrived here the government was obliged to disavow the act. The question then was, as we had her by mistake, what we should do with her. At that moment the National Sailors' Fair was in full blast at Boston, and I offered my suggestion in answer in the following article, which was published November 19, 1864, in the "Boatswain's Whistle," a little paper issued at the fair.

The government did not take the suggestion. Very unfortunately, before the Florida was got ready for sea, she was accidentally sunk in a collision with a tug off Fort Monroe, and the heirs of the Confederate government or the English bond-holders must look there for her, if the Brazilian government will give them permission.

For the benefit of the New York Observer I will state that a despatch sent round the world in a spiral direction westward 1,200 times, would not really arrive at its destination four years before it started. It is only a joke which suggests it.]

SPECIAL DESPATCH.

LETTER FROM CAPTAIN INGHAM, IN COMMAND OF THE FLORIDA.

[Received four years in advance of the mail by a lightning express, which has gained that time by running round the world 1,200 times

in a spiral direction westward on its way from Brazil to our publica-
tion-office. Mrs. Ingham's address not being known, the letter is
printed for her information.]

No. 29.

BAHIA, BRAZIL, April 1, 1868.

MY DEAR WIFE: — We are here at last, thank fortune; and I shall surrender the old pirate to-day to
the officers of government. We have been saluted,
are to be fêted, and perhaps I shall be made a Knight
Commander of the Golden Goose. I never was so
glad as when I saw the lights on the San Esperitu
head-land, which makes the south point of this Bahia
or bay.

You will not have received my No. 28 from Loando,
and may have missed 26 and 24, which I gave to *outward* bound whalemen. I always doubted whether
you got 1, 7, 9, and 11. And for me I have no word
of you since you waved your handkerchief from the
window in Springfield Street on the morning of the
1st of June, 1865, nearly four years. My dear child,
you will not know me.

Let me then repeat, very briefly, the outline of this
strange cruise; and when the letters come, you can
fill in the blanks.

The government had determined that the Florida
must be returned to the neutral harbor whence she
came. They had put her in complete repair, and six
months of diplomacy had made the proper apologies
to the Brazilian government. Meanwhile Collins,
who had captured her by mistake, had, by another

mistake, been made an admiral, and was commanding a squadron; and to insure her safe and respectful delivery, I, who had been waiting service, was unshelved, and, as you know, bidden to take command.

She was in apple-pie order. The engines had been cleaned up; and I thought we could make a quick thing of it. I was a little dashed when I found the crew was small; but I have been glad enough since that we had no more mouths. No one but myself knew our destination. The men thought we were to take despatches to the Gulf squadron.

You remember I had had only verbal orders to take command, and after we got outside the bay I opened my sealed despatches. The gist of them was in these words: —

"You will understand that the honor of this government is pledged for the *safe* delivery of the Florida to the government of Brazil. You will therefore hazard nothing to gain speed. The quantity of your coal has been adjusted with the view to give your vessel her best trim, and the supply is not large. You will husband it with care, — taking every precaution to arrive in Bahia *safely* with your charge, in such time as *your best discretion* may suggest to you."

" *Your best discretion* " was underscored.

I called Prendergast, and showed him the letter. Then we called the engineer and asked about the coal. He had not been into the bunkers, but went and returned with his face white, through the black grime, to report "not four days' consumption." By some cursed accident, he said, the bunkers had been filled with barrels of salt-pork and flour!

On this, I ordered a light and went below. There had been some fatal misunderstanding somewhere. The vessel was fitted out as for an arctic voyage. Everywhere hard-bread, flour, pork, beef, vinegar, sour-krout; but, clearly enough, not, at the very best, five days of coal!

And I was to get to Brazil with this old pirate transformed into a provision ship, "at my best discretion."

"Prendergast," said I, "we will take it easy. Were you ever in Bahia?"

"Took flour there in '55, and lay waiting for India-rubber from July to October. Lost six men by yellow-jack."

Prendergast was from the merchant marine. I had known him since we were children. "Ethan," said I, "in my best discretion it would be bad to arrive there before the end of October. Where would you go?"

I cannot say he took the responsibility. He would not take it. You know, my dear, of course, that it was I who suggested Upernavik. From the days of the old marbled paper Northern Regions, — through the quarto Ross and Parry and Back and the nephew Ross and Kane and McClure and McClintock, you know, my dear, what my one passion has been, — to

see those floes and icebergs for myself. Surely you
forgive me, or at least excuse me. Do not you?
Here was this fast steamer under me. I ought not to
be in Bahia before October 25. It was June 1. Of
course we went to Upernavik.

I will not say I regret it now. Yet I will say that
on that decision, cautiously made, though it was " on
my discretion," all our subsequent misfortunes hang.
The Danes were kind to us, — the Governor especially, though I had to carry the poor fellow bad news
about the Duchies and the Danish war, which was all
fresh then. He got up a dance for us, I remember,
and there I wrote No. 1 to you. I could not of course
help — when we left him — running her up a few de-
grees to the north, just to see whether there is or is
not that passage between Igloolik and Prince Rupert's
Headland (and by the way there *is*). After we
passed Igloolik, there was such splendid weather, that
I just used up a little coal to drive her along the coast
of King William's Land; and there, as we waited for
little duck-shooting on the edge of a floe one day, as
our luck ordered, a party of natives came on board,
and we treated them with hard-tack crumbs and whale-
oil. They fell to dancing, and we to laughing, —
they danced more and we laughed more, till the oldest
woman tumbled in her bear-skin bloomers, and came
with a smash right on the little cast-iron frame by the
wheel, which screened binnacle and compass. My
dear child, there was such a hullalu and such a mess

together as I remember now. We had to apologize ; the doctor set her head as well as he could. We gave them gingerbread from the cabin, to console them, and got them off without a fight. But the next morning when I cast off from the floe, it proved the beggars had stolen the compass card, needle and all.

My dear Mary, there was not another bit of magnetized iron in the ship. The government had been very shy of providing instruments of any kind for Confederate cruisers. Poor Ethan had traded off two compasses only the day before for whalebone spears and skin breeches, neither of which knew the north star from the ace of spades. And this thing proved of more importance than you will think ; it really made me feel that the stuff in the books and the sermons about the mariners' needle was not quite poetry.

As you shall see, if I ever get through. (Since I began, I have seen the Consul, — and heard the glorious news from home, — and am to be presented to the port authorities to-morrow.) It was the most open summer, Mary, ever known there. If I had not had to be here in October, I would have driven right through Lancaster Sound, by Baring's Island, and come out into the Pacific. But here was the honor of the country, and we merely stole back through the Straits. It was well enough there, — all daylight, you know. But after we passed Cape Farewell, we worked her into such fogs, child, as you never saw out of Hyde Park. Did not I long for that compass-card !

We sailed, and we sailed, and we sailed. For thirty-
seven days I did not get an observation, nor speak a
ship! October! It was October before we were
warm. At noon we used to sail where we thought it
was lightest. At night I used to keep two men up
for a lookout, lash the wheel, and let her drift like a
Dutchman. One way as good as another. Mary,
when I saw the sun at last, enough to get any kind of
observation, we were wellnigh three hundred miles
northeast of Iceland! Talk of fogs to me!

Well, I set her south again, but how long can you
know if you are sailing south, in those places where
the northeast winds and Scotch mists come from!
Thank Heaven, we got south, or we should have frozen
to death. We got into November, and we got into
December. We were as far south as 37° 29'; and
were in 31° 17' west on New Year's Day, 1866, when
the second officer wished me a happy new year, con-
gratulated me on the fine weather, said we should get
a good observation, and asked me for the new nautical
almanac! You know they are only calculated for five
years. We had two Greenwich ones on board, and
they ran out December 31, 1865. But the government had been as stingy in almanacs as in coal and
compasses. They did not mean to keep the Confederacy in almanacs.

That was the beginning of our troubles. I had to
take the old almanac, with Prendergast, and we fig-
ured like Cocker, and always kept ahead with a

month's tables. But somehow, — I feel sure we were right, — but something was wrong; and after a few weeks the lunars used to come out in the most beastly way, and we always proved to be on the top of the Andes or in the Marquesas Islands, or anywhere but in the Atlantic Ocean. Well then, by good luck, we spoke the Winged Batavian; could not speak a word of Dutch, nor he a word of English; but he let Ethan copy his tables, and so we ran for St. Sacrament. I posted 8, 9, and 10 there; I gave the Dutchman 7, which I hope you got, but fear.

Well, this story is running long; but at St. Sacrament we started again, but, as ill-luck would have it, without a clean bill of health. At that time I could have run into Bahia with coal — of which I had bought some — in a week. But there was fever on shore, — and bad, — and I knew we must make pratique when we came into the outer harbor here; so, rather than do that, we stretched down the coast, and met that cyclone I wrote you about, and had to put into Loando. Understand, this was the first time we went into Loando. I have learned that wretched hole well enough since. And it was as we were running out of Loando, that, in reversing the engine too suddenly, lest we should smash up an old Portuguese woman's bum-boat, that the slides or supports of the piston-rod just shot out of the grooves they run in on the top, came cleverly down on the outside of the carriage, gave that odious *g-r-r-r*, which I can hear

now, and then, *dump*, — down came the whole weight
of the walking-beam, bent rod and carriages all into
three figure 8's, and there we were! I had as lief
run the boat with a clothes-wringer as with that engine, any day, from then to now.

Well, we tinkered, and the Portuguese dock-yard
people tinkered. We took out this, and they took out
that. It was growing sickly, and I got frightened,
and finally I shipped the propeller and took it on board,
and started under such canvas as we had left, — not
much after the cyclone, — for the North and the
South together had rather rotted the original duck.

Then, — as I wrote you in No. 11, — it was too late
to get to Bahia before that summer's sickly season,
and I stretched off to cooler regions again, " in my
best discretion." That was the time when we had the
fever so horribly on board; and but for Wilder the
surgeon, and the Falkland Islands, we should be dead,
every man of us, now. But we touched in Queen's
Bay just in time. The Governor (who is his own
only subject) was very cordial and jolly and kind.
We all went ashore, and pitched tents, and ate ducks
and penguins till the men grew strong. I scraped
her, nearly down to the bends, for the grass floated
by our side like a mermaid's hair as we sailed, and
the once swift Florida would not make four knots an
hour on the wind; — and this was the ship I was to
get into Bahia in good order, at my best discretion!

Meanwhile none of these people had any news from

America. The last paper at the Falkland Islands was a London Times of 1864, abusing the Yankees. As for the Portuguese, they were like the people Logan saw at Vicksburg. "They don't know anything good!" said he; "they don't know anything at all!" It was really more for news than for water I put into Sta. Lucia, — and a pretty mess I made of it there. We looked so like pirates (as at bottom the old tub is), that they took all of us who landed to the guard-house. None of us could speak Sta. Lucia, whatever that tongue may be, nor understand it. And it was not till Ethan fired a shell from the 100-pound Parrott over the town that they let us go. I hope the dogs sent you my letters. I suppose there was another infringement of neutrality. But if the Brazilian government sends this ship to Sta. Lucia, I shall not command her, that's all!

Well! what happened at Loando the second time, Valencia, and Puntos Pimos, and Nueva Salamanca, and Loando this last time, you know and will know, and why we loitered so. At last, thank fortune, here we are. Actually, Mary, this ship logged on the average only thirty-two knots a day for the last week before we got her into port.

Now think of the ingratitude of men! I have brought her in here, "according to my best discretion," and do you believe, these hidalgos, or dons, or señores, or whatever they are, had forgotten she existed. And when I showed them to her, they said in good Portugal that I was a liar.   Fortunately the Consul is our old friend Kingsley.   He was delighted to see me; thought I was at the bottom of the sea. From him we learned that the Confederacy was blown sky-high long ago.   And from all I can learn, I may have the Florida back again for my own private yacht or peculium, unless she goes to Sta. Lucia.

Not I, my friends!   Scrape her, and mend her, and give her to the marines, — and tell them her story; but do not intrust her again to my own Polly's own

FREDERIC INGHAM.

THE SKELETON IN THE CLOSET.

By J. THOMAS DARRAGH (late C. C. S.).

[This paper was first published in the " Galaxy," in 1866.]

I SEE that an old chum of mine is publishing bits of
confidential Confederate History in Harper's Magazine. It would seem to be time, then, for the pivots
to be disclosed on which some of the wheelwork of
the last six years has been moving. The science of
history, as I understand it, depends on the timely dis-
closure of such pivots, which are apt to be kept out
of view while things are moving.

I was in the Civil Service at Richmond. Why I
was there, or what I did, is nobody's affair. And I
do not in this paper propose to tell how it happened
that I was in New York in October, 1864, on confidential business. Enough that I was there, and that
it was honest business. That business done, as far as
it could be with the resources intrusted to me, I prepared to return home. And thereby hangs this tale,
and, as it proved, the fate of the Confederacy.

For, of course, I wanted to take presents home to
my family. Very little question was there what these
presents should be, — for I had no boys nor brothers.

The women of the Confederacy had one want, which overtopped all others. They could make coffee out of beans; pins they had from Columbus; straw hats they braided quite well with their own fair hands; snuff we could get better than you could in "the old concern." But we had no hoop-skirts, — skeletons, we used to call them. No ingenuity had made them. No bounties had forced them. The Bat, the Greyhound, the Deer, the Flora, the J. C. Cobb, the Varuna, and the Fore-and-Aft all took in cargoes of them for us in England. But the Bat and the Deer and the Flora were seized by the blockaders, the J. C. Cobb sunk at sea, the Fore-and-Aft and the Greyhound were set fire to by their own crews, and the Varuna (our Varuna) was never heard of. Then the State of Arkansas offered sixteen townships of swamp land to the first manufacturer who would exhibit five gross of a home-manufactured article. But no one ever competed. The first attempts, indeed, were put to an end, when Schofield crossed the Blue Lick, and destroyed the dams on Yellow Branch. The consequence was, that people's crinoline collapsed faster than the Confederacy did, of which that brute of a Grierson said there was never anything of it but the outside.

Of course, then, I put in the bottom of my new large trunk in New York, not a "duplex elliptic," for none were then made, but a "Belmonte," of thirty springs, for my wife. I bought, for her more common wear, a good "Belle-Fontaine." For Sarah and Susy each, I got two "Dumb-Belles." For Aunt Eunice and Aunt Clara, maiden sisters of my wife, who lived with us after Winchester fell the fourth time, I got the "Scotch Harebell," two of each. For my own mother I got one "Belle of the Prairies" and one "Invisible Combination Gossamer." I did not forget good old Mamma Chloe and Mamma Jane. For them I got substantial cages, without names. With these, tied in the shapes of figure eights in the bottom of my trunk, as I said, I put in an assorted cargo of dry-goods above, and, favored by a pass, and Major Mulford's courtesy on the flag-of-truce boat, I arrived safely at Richmond before the autumn closed.

I was received at home with rapture. But when, the next morning, I opened my stores, this became rapture doubly enraptured. Words cannot tell the silent delight with which old and young, black and white, surveyed these fairy-like structures, yet unbroken and unmended.

Perennial summer reigned that autumn day in that reunited family. It reigned the next day, and the next. It would have reigned till now if the Belmontes and the other things would last as long as the advertisements declare; and, what is more, the Confederacy would have reigned till now, President Davis and General Lee! but for that great misery, which all families understand, which culminated in our great misfortune.

I was up in the cedar closet one day, looking for an
old parade cap of mine, which I thought, though it
was my third best, might look better than my second
best, which I had worn ever since my best was lost at
the Seven Pines.   I say I was standing on the lower
shelf of the cedar closet, when, as I stepped along in
the darkness, my right foot caught in a bit of wire,
my left did not give way in time, and I fell, with a
small wooden hat-box in my hand, full on the floor.
The corner of the hat-box struck me just below the
second frontal sinus, and I fainted away.

When I came to myself I was in the blue chamber;
I had vinegar on a brown paper on my forehead; the
room was dark, and I found mother sitting by me,
glad enough indeed to hear my voice, and to know
that I knew her.   It was some time before I fully understood what had happened.   Then she brought me
a cup of tea, and I, quite refreshed, said I must go to
the office.

"Office, my child!" said she.   "Your leg is broken above the ankle; you will not move these six
weeks.   Where do you suppose you are?"

Till then I had no notion that it was five minutes
since I went into the closet.   When she told me the
time, five in the afternoon, I groaned in the lowest
depths.   For, in my breast pocket in that innocent
coat, which I could now see lying on the window-seat,
were the duplicate despatches to Mr. Mason, for which,
late the night before, I had got the Secretary's signa-

ture. They were to go at ten that morning to Wilmington, by the Navy Department's special messenger.
I had taken them to insure care and certainty. I had
worked on them till midnight, and they had not been
signed till near one o'clock. Heavens and earth, and
here it was five o'clock! The man must be half-way
to Wilmington by this time. I sent the doctor for
Lafarge, my clerk. Lafarge did his prettiest in rushing to the telegraph. But no! A freshet on the
Chowan River, or a raid by Foster, or something, or
nothing, had smashed the telegraph wire for that night.
And before that despatch ever reached Wilmington the
navy agent was in the offing in the Sea Maid.

"But perhaps the duplicate got through?" No,
breathless reader, the duplicate did not get through.
The duplicate was taken by Faucon, in the Ino. I
saw it last week in Dr. Lieber's hands, in Washington.
Well, all I know is, that if the duplicate had got
through, the Confederate government would have
had in March a chance at eighty-three thousand two
hundred and eleven muskets, which, as it was, never left
Belgium. So much for my treading into that blessed
piece of wire on the shelf of the cedar closet, up stairs.

"What was the bit of wire?"

Well, it was not telegraph wire. If it had been, it
would have broken when it was not wanted to.
Don't you know what it was? Go up in your own
cedar closet, and step about in the dark, and see what
brings up round your ankles. Julia, poor child, cried

Q

her eyes out about it. When I got well enough to sit up, and as soon as I could talk and plan with her, she brought down seven of these old things, antiquated Belmontes and Simplex Elliptics, and horrors without a name, and she made a pile of them in the bedroom, and asked me in the most penitent way what she should do with them.

"You can't burn them," said she; "fire won't touch them. If you bury them in the garden, they come up at the second raking. If you give them to the servants, they say, 'Thank-e, missus,' and throw them in the back passage. If you give them to the poor, they throw them into the street in front, and do not say, 'Thank-e.' Sarah sent seventeen over to the sword factory, and the foreman swore at the boy, and told him he would flog him within an inch of his life if he brought any more of his sauce there; and so — and so," sobbed the poor child, "I just rolled up these wretched things, and laid them in the cedar closet, hoping, you know, that some day the government would want something, and would advertise for them. You know what a good thing I made out of the bottle corks."

In fact, she had sold our bottle corks for four thousand two hundred and sixteen dollars of the first issue. We afterward bought two umbrellas and a corkscrew with the money.

Well, I did not scold Julia. It was certainly no fault of hers that I was walking on the lower shelf of her cedar closet. I told her to make a parcel of the things, and the first time we went to drive I hove the whole shapeless heap into the river, without saying mass for them.

But let no man think, or no woman, that this was the end of troubles. As I look back on that winter, and on the spring of 1865 (I do not mean the steel spring), it seems to me only the beginning. I got out on crutches at last; I had the office transferred to my house, so that Lafarge and Hepburn could work there nights, and communicate with me when I could not go out; but mornings I hobbled up to the Department, and sat with the Chief, and took his orders. Ah me! shall I soon forget that damp winter morning, when we all had such hope at the office. One or two of the army fellows looked in at the window as they ran by, and we knew that they felt well; and though I would not ask Old Wick, as we had nick-named the Chief, what was in the wind, I knew the time had come, and that the lion meant to break the net this time. I made an excuse to go home earlier than usual; rode down to the house in the Major's ambulance, I remember; and hopped in, to surprise Julia with the good news, only to find that the whole house was in that quiet uproar which shows that some-thing bad has happened of a sudden.

"What is it, Chloe?" said I, as the old wench rushed by me with a bucket of water.

"Poor Mr. George, I 'fraid he 's dead, sah!"

And there he really was, — dear handsome, bright George Schaff, — the delight of all the nicest girls of Richmond ; he lay there on Aunt Eunice's bed on the ground floor, where they had brought him in. He was not dead, — and he did not die. He is making cotton in Texas now. But he looked mighty near it then. "The deep cut in his head" was the worst I then had ever seen, and the blow confused everything. When McGregor got round, he said it was not hopeless ; but we were all turned out of the room, and with one thing and another he got the boy out of the swoon, and somehow it proved his head was not broken.

No, but poor George swears to this day it were better it had been, if it could only have been broken the right way and on the right field. For that evening we heard that everything had gone wrong in the surprise. There we had been waiting for one of those early fogs, and at last the fog had come. And Jubal Early had, that morning, pushed out every man he had, that could stand ; and they lay hid for three mortal hours, within I don't know how near the picket line at Fort Powhatan, only waiting for the shot which John Streight's party were to fire at Wilson's Wharf, as soon as somebody on our left centre advanced in force on the enemy's line above Turkey Island stretching across to Nansemond. I am not in the War Department, and I forget whether he was to advance *en barbette* or by *échelon* of infantry. But he was to advance somehow, and he knew how ; and when he advanced, you see, that other man lower down was to rush in, and as soon as Early heard him he was to surprise Powhatan, you see ; and then, if you have understood me, Grant and Butler and the whole rig of them would have been cut off from their supplies, would have had to fight a battle for which they were not prepared, with their right made into a new left, and their old left unexpectedly advanced at an oblique angle from their centre, and would not that have been the end of them ?

Well, that never happened. And the reason it never happened was, that poor George Schaff, with the last fatal order for this man whose name I forget (the same who was afterward killed the day before High Bridge), undertook to save time by cutting across behind my house, from Franklin to Green Streets. You know how much time he saved, — they waited all day for that order. George told me afterwards that the last thing he remembered was kissing his hand to Julia, who sat at her bedroom window. He said he thought she might be the last woman he ever saw this side of heaven. Just after that, it must have been, — his horse — that white Messenger colt old Williams bred — went over like a log, and poor George was pitched fifteen feet head-foremost against a stake there was in that lot. Julia saw the whole. She rushed out with all the women, and had just brought him in when I got home. And that was the reason that the great promised combination of December, 1864, never came off at all.

I walked out in the lot, after McGregor turned me
out of the chamber, to see what they had done with
the horse. There he lay, as dead as old Messenger
himself. His neck was broken. And do you think, I
looked to see what had tripped him. I supposed it
was one of the boys' bandy holes. It was no such
thing. The poor wretch had tangled his hind legs in
one of those infernal hoop-wires that Chloe had thrown
out in the piece when I gave her her new ones.
Though I did not know it then, those fatal scraps of
rusty steel had broken the neck that day of Robert
Lee's army.

That time I made a row about it. I felt too badly
to go into a passion. But before the women went to
bed, — they were all in the sitting-room together, — I
talked to them like a father. I did not swear. I had
got over that for a while, in that six weeks on my back.
But I did say the old wires were infernal things, and
that the house and premises must be made rid of them.
The aunts laughed, — though I was so serious, — and
tipped a wink to the girls. The girls wanted to laugh,
but were afraid to. And then it came out that the
aunts had sold their old hoops, tied as tight as they
could tie them, in a great mass of rags. They had
made a fortune by the sale, — I am sorry to say it
was in other rags, but the rags they got were new instead of old, — it was a real Aladdin bargain. The
new rags had blue backs, and were numbered, some
as high as fifty dollars. The rag-man had been in a

hurry, and had not known what made the things so
heavy. I frowned at the swindle, but they said all
was fair with a pedler, — and I own I was glad the
things were well out of Richmond. But when I
said I thought it was a mean trick, Lizzie and Sarah
looked demure, and asked what in the world I would
have them do with the old things. Did I expect them
to walk down to the bridge themselves with great parcels to throw into the river, as I had done by Julia's ?
Of course it ended, as such things always do, by my
taking the work on my own shoulders. I told them
to tie up all they had in as small a parcel as they could,
and bring them to me.

Accordingly, the next day, I found a handsome
brown paper parcel, not so very large, considering,
and strangely square, considering, which the minxes
had put together and left on my office table. They
had a great frolic over it. They had not spared red
tape nor red wax. Very official it looked, indeed,
and on the left-hand corner, in Sarah's boldest and
most contorted hand, was written, " Secret service."
We had a great laugh over their success. And, indeed, I should have taken it with me the next time I
went down to the Tredegar, but that I happened to
dine one evening with young Norton of our gallant
little navy, and a very curious thing he told us.

We were talking about the disappointment of the
combined land attack. I did not tell what upset poor
Schaff's horse ; indeed, I do not think those navy men

knew the details of the disappointment. O'Brien had told me, in confidence, what I have written down probably for the first time now. But we were speaking, in a general way, of the disappointment. Norton finished his cigar rather thoughtfully, and then said: " Well, fellows, it is not worth while to put in the newspapers, but what do you suppose upset our grand naval attack, the day the Yankee gunboats skittled down the river so handsomely ? "

" Why," said Allen, who is Norton's best-beloved friend, " they say that you ran away from them as fast as they did from you."

" Do they ? " said Norton, grimly. " If you say that, I 'll break your head for you. Seriously, men," continued he, " that was a most extraordinary thing. You know I was on the ram. But why she stopped when she stopped I knew as little as this wineglass does; and Callender himself knew no more than I. We had not been hit. We were all right as a trivet for all we knew, when, skree ! she began blowing off steam, and we stopped dead, and began to drift down under those batteries. Callender had to telegraph to the little Mosquito, or whatever Walter called his boat, and the spunky little thing ran down and got us out of the scrape. Walter did it right well ; if he had had a monitor under him he could not have done better. Of course we all rushed to the engine-room. What in thunder were they at there ? All they knew was they could get no water into her boiler.

"Now, fellows, this is the end of the story. As soon as the boilers cooled off they worked all right on those supply pumps. May I be hanged if they had not sucked in, somehow, a long string of yarn, and cloth, and, if you will believe me, a wire of some woman's crinoline. And that French folly of a sham Empress cut short that day the victory of the Confederate navy, and old Davis himself can't tell when we shall have such a chance again!"

Some of the men thought Norton lied. But I never was with him when he did not tell the truth. I did not mention, however, what I had thrown into the water the last time I had gone over to Manchester. And I changed my mind about Sarah's "secret-service" parcel. It remained on my table.

That was the last dinner our old club had at the Spotswood, I believe. The spring came on, and the plot thickened. We did our work in the office as well as we could; I can speak for mine, and if other people — but no matter for that! The 3d of April came, and the fire, and the right wing of Grant's army. I remember I was glad then that I had moved the office down to the house, for we were out of the way there. Everybody had run away from the Department; and so, when the powers that be took possession, my little sub-bureau was unmolested for some days. I improved those days as well as I could, — burning carefully what was to be burned, and hiding carefully what was to be hidden. One thing that happened then belongs to this story. As I was at work on the private bureau, — it was really a bureau, as it happened, one I had made Aunt Eunice give up when I broke my leg, — I came, to my horror, on a neat parcel of coast-survey maps of Georgia, Alabama, and Florida. They were not the same Maury stole when he left the National Observatory, but they were like them. Now I was perfectly sure that on that fatal Sunday of the flight I had sent Lafarge for these, that the President might use them, if necessary, in his escape. When I found them, I hopped out and called for Julia, and asked her if she did not remember his coming for them. "Certainly," she said, "it was the first I knew of the danger. Lafarge came, asked for the key of the office, told me all was up, walked in, and in a moment was gone."

And here, on the file of April 3d, was Lafarge's line to me : —

"I got the secret-service parcel myself, and have put it in the President's own hands. I marked it, 'Gulf coast,' as you bade me."

What could Lafarge have given to the President? Not the soundings of Hatteras Bar. Not the working-drawings of the first monitor. I had all these under my hand. Could it be, — "Julia, what did we do with that stuff of Sarah's that she marked *secret service?*"

As I live, we had sent the girls' old hoops to the President in his flight.

And when the next day we read how he used them,

and how Pritchard arrested him, we thought if he had only had the right parcel he would have found the way to Florida.

That is really the end of this memoir. But I should not have written it, but for something that happened just now on the piazza. You must know, some of us wrecks are up here at the Berkeley baths. My uncle has a place near here. Here came to-day John Sisson, whom I have not seen since Memminger ran and took the clerks with him. Here we had before, both the Richards brothers, the great paper men, you know, who started the Edgerly Works in Prince George's County, just after the war began. After dinner, Sisson and they met on the piazza. Queerly enough, they had never seen each other before, though they had used reams of Richards's paper in correspondence with each other, and the treasury had used tons of it in the printing of bonds and bank-bills. Of course we all fell to talking of old times, — old they seem now, though it is not a year ago. " Richards," said Sisson at last, " what became of that last order of ours for water-lined, pure linen government-callendered paper of *sureté ?* We never got it, and I never knew why."

" Did you think Kilpatrick got it ? " said Richards, rather gruffly.

" None of your chaff, Richards. Just tell where the paper went, for in the loss of that lot of paper, as it proved, the bottom dropped out of the Treasury tub. On that paper was to have been printed our new issue of ten per cent, convertible, you know, and secured on that up-country cotton, which Kirby Smith had above the Big Raft. I had the printers ready for near a month waiting for that paper. The plates were really very handsome. I 'll show you a proof when we go up stairs. Wholly new they were, made by some Frenchmen we got, who had worked for the Bank of France. I was so anxious to have the thing well done, that I waited three weeks for that paper, and, by Jove, I waited just too long. We never got one of the bonds off, and that was why we had no money in March."

Richards threw his cigar away. I will not say he swore between his teeth, but he twirled his chair round, brought it down on all fours, both his elbows on his knees and his chin in both hands.

"Mr. Sisson," said he, "if the Confederacy had lived, I would have died before I ever told what became of that order of yours. But now I have no secrets, I believe, and I care for nothing. I do not know now how it happened. We knew it was an extra nice job. And we had it on an elegant little new French Fourdrinier, which cost us more than we shall ever pay. The pretty thing ran like oil the day before. That day, I thought all the devils were in it. The more power we put on the more the rollers screamed; and the less we put on, the more sulkily the jade stopped. I tried it myself every way; back current, I tried; forward current; high feed; low freed , I tried it on old stock, I tried it on new ; and, Mr. Sisson, I would have made better paper in a coffee-mill ! We drained off every drop of water. We washed the tubs free from size. Then my brother, there, worked all night with the machinists, taking down the frame and the rollers. You would not believe it, sir, but that little bit of wire," — and he took out of his pocket a piece of this hateful steel, which poor I knew so well by this time, — " that little bit of wire had passed in from some hoop-skirt, passed the pickers, passed the screens, through all the troughs, up and down through what we call the lacerators, and had got itself wrought in, where, if you know a Fourdrinier machine, you may have noticed a brass ring riveted to the cross-bar, and there this cursed little knife — for you see it was a knife, by that time — had been cutting to pieces the endless wire web every time the machine was started. You lost your bonds, Mr. Sisson, because some Yankee woman cheated one of my rag-men."

On that story I came up stairs. Poor Aunt Eunice! She was the reason I got no salary on the 1st of April. I thought I would warn other women by writing down the story.

That fatal present of mine, in those harmless hourglass parcels, was the ruin of the Confederate navy, army, ordnance, and treasury ; and it led to the capture of the poor President too.

But, Heaven be praised, no one shall say that my office did not do its duty !

CHRISTMAS WAITS IN BOSTON.

FROM THE INGHAM PAPERS.

[WHEN my friends of the Boston Daily Advertiser asked me last year to contribute to their Christmas number, I was very glad to recall this scrap of Mr. Ingham's memoirs.

For in most modern Christmas stories I have observed that the rich wake up of a sudden to befriend the poor, and that the moral is educed from such compassion. The incidents in this story show, what all life shows, that the poor befriend the rich as truly as the rich the poor: that, in the Christian life, each needs all.

I have been asked a dozen times how far the story is true. Of course no such series of incidents has ever taken place in this order in four or five hours. But there is nothing told here which has not parallels perfectly fair in my experience or in that of any working minister.]

I ALWAYS give myself a Christmas present.

And on this particular year the present was a carol party, which is about as good fun, all things consenting kindly, as a man can have.

Many things must consent, as will appear. First of all, there must be good sleighing; and second, a fine night for Christmas eve. Ours are not the carollings of your poor shivering little East Angles or South Mercians, where they have to plod round afoot in countries which do not know what a sleigh-ride is.

I had asked Harry to have sixteen of the best voices in the chapel school to be trained to five or six good carols, without knowing why. We did not care to disappoint them if a February thaw setting in on the 24th of December should break up the spree before it began. Then I had told Howland that he must reserve for me a span of good horses, and a sleigh that I could pack sixteen small children into, tight-stowed. Howland is always good about such things, knew what the sleigh was for, having done the same in other years, and made the span four horses of his own accord, because the children would like it better, and "it would be no difference to him." Sunday night, as the weather nymphs ordered, the wind hauled round to the northwest and everything froze hard. Monday night, things moderated and the snow began to fall steadily, — so steadily ; and so Tuesday night the Metropolitan people gave up their unequal contest, all good men and angels rejoicing at their discomfiture, and only a few of the people in the very lowest *Bolgie* being ill-natured enough to grieve. And thus it was, that by Thursday evening was one hard compact roadway from Copp's Hill to the Bone-burner's Gehenna, fit for good men and angels to ride over, without jar, without noise, and without fatigue to horse or man. So it was that when I came down with Ly-

cidas to the chapel at seven o'clock, I found Harry
had gathered there his eight pretty girls and his eight
jolly boys, and had them practising for the last time,

> " Carol, carol, Christians,
> Carol joyfully ;
> Carol for the coming
> Of Christ's nativity."

I think the children had got inkling of what was
coming, or perhaps Harry had hinted it to their mothers. Certainly they were warmly dressed, and when,
fifteen minutes afterwards, Howland came round himself with the sleigh, he had put in as many rugs and
bear-skins as if he thought the children were to be
taken new-born from their respective cradles. Great
was the rejoicing as the bells of the horses rang beneath the chapel windows, and Harry did not get his
last *da capo* for his last carol. Not much matter indeed, for they were perfect enough in it before midnight.

Lycidas and I tumbled in on the back seat, each
with a child in his lap to keep us warm ; I flanked
by Sam Perry, and he by John Rich, both of the
mercurial age, and therefore good to do errands.
Harry was in front somewhere flanked in like wise,
and the other children lay in miscellaneously between,
like sardines when you have first opened the box.
I had invited Lycidas, because, besides being my best
friend, he is the best fellow in the world, and so deserves the best Christmas eve can give him. Under

the full moon, on the still white snow, with sixteen children at the happiest, and with the blessed memories of the best the world has ever had, there can be nothing better than two or three such hours.

"First, driver, out on Commonwealth Avenue. That will tone down the horses. Stop on the left after you have passed Fairfield Street." So we dashed up to the front of Haliburton's palace, where he was keeping his first Christmas tide. And the children, whom Harry had hushed down for a square or two, broke forth with good full voice under his strong lead in

"Shepherd of tender sheep,"

singing with all that unconscious pathos with which children do sing, and starting the tears in your eyes in the midst of your gladness. The instant the horses' bells stopped their voices began. In an instant more we saw Haliburton and Anna run to the window and pull up the shades, and in a minute more faces at all the windows. And so the children sung through Clement's old hymn. Little did Clement think of bells and snow, as he taught it in his Sunday school there in Alexandria. But perhaps to-day, as they pin up the laurels and the palm in the chapel at Alexandria, they are humming the words, not thinking of Clement more than he thought of us. As the children closed with

"Swell the triumphant song
To Christ, our King,"

Haliburton came running out, and begged me to bring them in. But I told him, "No," as soon as I could hush their shouts of "Merry Christmas"; that we had a long journey before us, and must not alight by the way. And the children broke out with

> " Hail to the night,
> Hail to the day,"

rather a favorite, — quicker and more to the childish taste perhaps than the other, — and with another " Merry Christmas" we were off again.

Off, the length of Commonwealth Avenue, to where it crosses the Brookline branch of the Mill-Dam, dashing along with the gayest of the sleighing-parties as we came back into town, up Chestnut Street, through Louisburg Square; ran the sleigh into a bank on the slope of Pinckney Street in front of Walter's house; and, before they suspected there that any one had come, the children were singing

> " Carol, carol, Christians,
> Carol joyfully."

Kisses flung from the window; kisses flung back from the street. " Merry Christmas" again with a good-will, and then one of the girls began,

> " When Anna took the baby,
> And pressed his lips to hers,"

and all of them fell in so cheerily. O dear me! it is a scrap of old Ephrem the Syrian, if they did but know it! And when, after this, Harry would fain have driven

on, because two carols at one house was the rule, how
the little witches begged that they might sing just one
song more there, because Mrs. Alexander had been so
kind to them, when she showed them about the German stitches. And then up the hill and over to the
North End, and as far as we could get the horses up
into Moon Court, that they might sing to the Italian
image-man who gave Lucy the boy and dog in plaster,
when she was sick in the spring. For the children
had, you know, the choice of where they would go, and
they select their best friends, and will be more apt to
remember the Italian image-man than Chrysostom
himself, though Chrysostom should have " made a few
remarks " to them seventeen times in the chapel.
Then the Italian image-man heard for the first time in
his life

" Now is the time of Christmas come,"

and

" Jesus in his babes abiding."

And then we came up Hanover Street and stopped
under Mr. Gerry's chapel, where they were dressing
the walls with their evergreens, and gave them

" Hail to the night,
Hail to the day " ;

and so down State Street and stopped at the Advertiser office, because, when the boys gave their " Literary Entertainment," Mr. Hale put in their advertisement for nothing, and up in the old attic there the
compositors were relieved to hear

and
> "Nor war nor battle sound,"
>
> "The waiting world was still";

so that even the leading editor relaxed from his gravity, and the "In-General" man from his more serious views, and the Daily the next morning wished everybody a merry Christmas with even more unction, and resolved that in coming years it would have a supplement, large enough to contain all the good wishes. So away again to the houses of confectioners who had given the children candy, — to Miss Simonds's house, because she had been so good to them in school, — to the palaces of millionnaires who had prayed for these children with tears if the children only knew it, — to Dr. Frothingham's in Summer Street, I remember, where we stopped because the Boston Association of Ministers met here, — and out on Dover Street Bridge, that the poor chair-mender might hear our carols sung once more before he heard them better sung in another world where nothing needs mending.

> "King of glory, king of peace!"
>
> "Hear the song, and see the Star!"
>
> "Welcome be thou, heavenly King!"
>
> "Was not Christ our Saviour?"

and all the others, rung out with order or without order, breaking the hush directly as the horses' bells were stilled, thrown into the air with all the gladness of childhood, selected sometimes as Harry happened to think best for the hearers, but more often as the jubilant and uncontrolled enthusiasm of the children bade them break out in the most joyous, least studied, and purely lyrical of all. O, we went to twenty places that night, I suppose! We went to the grandest places in Boston, and we went to the meanest. Everywhere they wished us a merry Christmas, and we them. Everywhere a little crowd gathered round us, and then we dashed away far enough to gather quite another crowd; and then back, perhaps, not sorry to double on our steps if need were, and leaving every crowd with a happy thought of

"The star, the manger, and the Child!"

At nine we brought up at my house, D Street, three doors from the corner, and the children picked their very best for Polly and my six little girls to hear, and then for the first time we let them jump out and run in. Polly had some hot oysters for them, so that the frolic was crowned with a treat. There was a Christmas cake cut into sixteen pieces, which they took home to dream upon; and then hoods and muffs on again, and by ten o'clock, or a little after, we had all the girls and all the little ones at their homes. Four of the big boys, our two flankers and Harry's right and left hand men, begged that they might stay till the last moment. They could walk back from the stable, and "rather walk than not, indeed." To which we assented, having gained parental permission, as we left younger sisters in their respective homes.

II.

Lycidas and I both thought, as we went into these modest houses, to leave the children, to say they had been good and to wish a "Merry Christmas" ourselves to fathers, mothers, and to guardian aunts, that the welcome of those homes was perhaps the best part of it all. Here was the great stout sailor-boy whom we had not seen since he came back from sea. He was a mere child when he left our school years on years ago, for the East, on board Perry's vessel, and had been round the world. Here was brave Mrs. Masury. I had not seen her since her mother died. " Indeed, Mr. Ingham, I got so used to watching then, that I cannot sleep well yet o' nights ; I wish you knew some poor creature that wanted me to-night, if it were only in memory of Bethlehem." " You take a deal of trouble for the children," said Campbell, as he crushed my hand in his ; "but you know they love you, and you know I would do as much for you and yours," — which I knew was true. " What can I send to your children ? " said Dalton, who was finishing sword-blades. (Ill wind was Fort Sumter, but it blew good to poor Dalton, whom it set up in the world with his sword-factory.) " Here 's an old-fashioned tape-measure for the girl, and a Sheffield wimble for the boy. What, there is no boy? Let one of the girls have it then ; it will count one more present for her." And so he pressed his brown-paper parcel into my hand. From every house, though it were the humblest, a word of love, as sweet, in truth, as if we could have heard the voice of angels singing in the sky.

I bade Harry good night; took Lycidas to his lodgings, and gave his wife my Christmas wishes and good night; and, coming down to the sleigh again, gave way to the feeling which I think you will all understand, that this was not the time to stop, but just the time to begin. For the streets were stiller now, and the moon brighter than ever, if possible, and the blessings of these simple people and of the grand people, and of the very angels in heaven, who are not bound to the misery of using words when they have anything worth saying, — all these wishes and blessings were round me, all the purity of the still winter night, and I did n't want to lose it all by going to bed to sleep. So I put the boys all together, where they could chatter, took one more brisk turn on the two avenues, and then, passing through Charles Street, I believe I was even thinking of Cambridge, I noticed the lights in Woodhull's house, and, seeing they were up, thought I would make Fanny a midnight call. She came to the door herself. I asked if she were waiting for Santa Claus, but saw in a moment that I must not joke with her. She said she had hoped I was her husband. In a minute was one of those contrasts which make life, life. God puts us into the world that we may try them and be tried by them.

Poor Fanny's mother had been blocked up on the Springfield train as she was coming on to Christmas. The old lady had been chilled through, and was here in bed now with pneumonia. Both Fanny's children had been ailing when she came, and this morning the doctor had pronounced it scarlet fever. Fanny had not undressed herself since Monday, nor slept, I thought, in the same time. So while we had been singing carols and wishing merry Christmas, the poor child had been waiting, and hoping that her husband or Edward, both of whom were on the tramp, would find for her and bring to her the model nurse, who had not yet appeared. But at midnight this unknown sister had not arrived, nor had either of the men returned. When I rang, Fanny had hoped I was one of them. Professional paragons, dear reader, are shy of scarlet fever. I told the poor child that it was better as it was. I wrote a line for Sam Perry to take to his aunt, Mrs. Masury, in which I simply said: "Dear mamma, I have found the poor creature who wants you to-night. Come back in this carriage." I bade him take a hack at Gates's, where they were all up waiting for the assembly to be done at Papanti's. I sent him over to Albany Street; and really as I sat there trying to soothe Fanny, it seemed to me less time than it has taken to dictate this little story about her, before Mrs. Masury rang gently, and I left them, having made Fanny promise that she would consecrate the day, which at that moment was born, by trusting

God, by going to bed and going to sleep, knowing
that her children were in much better hands than
hers. As I passed out of the hall, the gas-light fell
on a print of Correggio's Adoration, where Woodhull
had himself written years before,

" Ut appareat iis qui in tenebris et umbra mortis positi sunt."

" Darkness and the shadow of death " indeed, and
what light like the light and comfort such a woman as
my Mary Masury brings!

And so, but for one of the accidents, as we call
them, I should have dropped the boys at the corner
of Dover Street, and gone home with my Christmas
lesson.

But it happened, as we irreverently say, — it happened as we crossed Park Square, so called from
its being an irregular pentagon of which one of the
sides has been taken away, that I recognized a tall
man, plodding across in the snow, head down, round-
shouldered, stooping forward in walking, with his
right shoulder higher than his left; and by these tokens
I knew Tom Coram, prince among Boston princes.
Not Thomas Coram that built the Foundling Hospital,
though he was of Boston too; but he was longer
ago. You must look for him in Addison's contribution to a supplement to the Spectator, — the old Spectator, I mean, not the Thursday Spectator, which is
more recent. Not Thomas Coram, I say, but Tom
Coram, who would build a hospital to-morrow, if you

showed him the need, without waiting to die first, and
always helps forward, as a prince should, whatever is
princely, be it a statue at home, a school in Richmond, a newspaper in Florida, a church in Exeter, a
steam-line to Liverpool, or a widow who wants a hundred dollars. I wished him a merry Christmas, and
Mr. Howland, by a fine instinct, drew up the horses
as I spoke. Coram shook hands; and, as it seldom
happens that I have an empty carriage while he is on
foot, I asked him if I might not see him home. He
was glad to get in. We wrapped him up with spoils
of the bear, the fox, and the bison, turned the horses'
heads again, — five hours now since they started on
this entangled errand of theirs, — and gave him his
ride. "I was thinking of you at the moment," said
Coram, — "thinking of old college times, of the mystery of language as unfolded by the Abbé Faria to
Edmond Dantes in the depths of the Chateau d'If.
I was wondering if you could teach me Japanese, if I
asked you to a Christmas dinner." I laughed. Japan
was really a novelty then, and I asked him since when
he had been in correspondence with the sealed country.
It seemed that their house at Shanghae had just sent
across there their agents for establishing the first house
in Edomo, in Japan, under the new treaty. Everything
looked promising, and the beginnings were made for
the branch which has since become Dot and Trevilyan
there. Of this he had the first tidings in his letters
by the mail of that afternoon. John Coram, his

brother, had written to him, and had said that he
enclosed for his amusement the Japanese bill of particulars, as it had been drawn out, on which they had
founded their orders for the first assorted cargo ever
to be sent from America to Edomo.   Bill of particulars
there was, stretching down the long tissue-paper in
exquisite chirography.   But by some freak of the "total
depravity of things," the translated order for the assorted cargo was not there.   John Coram, in his care
to fold up the Japanese writing nicely, had left on his
own desk at Shanghae the more intelligible English.
"And so I must wait," said Tom philosophically, "till
the next East India mail for my orders, certain that
seven English houses have had less enthusiastic and
philological correspondents than my brother."

I said I did not see that.   That I could not teach
him to speak the Taghalian dialects so well, that he
could read them with facility before Saturday.   But I
could do a good deal better.   Did he remember writing a note to old Jack Percival for me five years ago?
No, he remembered no such thing; he knew Jack
Percival, but never wrote a note to him in his life.
Did he remember giving me fifty dollars, because I
had taken a delicate boy, whom I was going to send
to sea, and I was not quite satisfied with the government outfit?   No, he did not remember that, which
was not strange, for that was a thing he was doing
every day.   "Well, I don't care how much you remember, but the boy about whom you wrote to Jack

Percival, for whose mother's ease of mind you provided the half-hundred, is back again, — strong, straight, and well; what is more to the point, he had the whole charge of Perry's commissariat on shore at Yokohama, was honorably discharged out there, reads Japanese better than you read English; and if it will help you at all, he shall be here at your house at breakfast." For as I spoke we stopped at Coram's door. " Ingham," said Coram, " if you were not a parson, I should say you were romancing." " My child," said I, " I sometimes write a parable for the Atlantic; but the words of my lips are verity, as all those of the Sandemanians. Go to bed; do not even dream of the Taghalian dialects; be sure that the Japanese interpreter will breakfast with you, and the next time you are in a scrape send for the nearest minister. George, tell your brother Ezra that Mr. Coram wishes him to breakfast here to-morrow morning at eight o'clock; don't forget the number, Pemberton Square, you know." " Yes, sir," said George; and Thomas Coram laughed, said " Merry Christmas," and we parted.

It was time we were all in bed, especially these boys. But glad enough am I as I write these words that the meeting of Coram set us back that dropped-stitch in our night's journey. There was one more delay. We were sweeping by the Old State House, the boys singing again, " Carol, carol, Christians," as we dashed along the still streets, when I caught sight of Adams

Todd, and he recognized me. He had heard us singing when we were at the Advertiser office. Todd is an old fellow-apprentice of mine, — and he is now, or rather was that night, chief pressman in the Argus office. I like the Argus people, — it was there that I was South American Editor, now many years ago, — and they befriend me to this hour. Todd hailed me, and once more I stopped. "What sent you out from your warm steam-boiler?" "Steam-boiler, indeed," said Todd. "Two rivets loose, — steam-room full of steam, — police frightened, — neighborhood in a row, — and we had to put out the fire. She would have run a week without hurting a fly, — only a little puff in the street sometimes. But there we are, Ingham. We shall lose the early mail as it stands. Seventy-eight tokens to be worked now." They always talked largely of their edition at the Argus. Saw it with many eyes, perhaps; but this time, I am sure, Todd spoke true. I caught his idea at once. In younger and more muscular times, Todd and I had worked the Adams press by that fly-wheel for full five minutes at a time, as a test of strength; and in my mind's eye, I saw that he was printing his paper at this moment with relays of grinding stevedores. He said it was so. "But think of it to-night," said he. "It is Christmas eve, and not an Irishman to be hired, though one paid him ingots. Not a man can stand the grind ten minutes." I knew that very well from old experience, and I thanked him inwardly

for not saying " the demnition grind," with Mantilini.
" We cannot run the press half the time," said he ;
" and the men we have are giving out now. We
shall lose all our carrier delivery." " Todd," said I,
" is this a night to be talking of ingots, or hiring, or
losing, or gaining? When will you learn that Love
rules the court, the camp, and the Argus office. And
I wrote on the back of a letter to Campbell: " Come
to the Argus office, No. 2 Dassett's Alley, with seven
men not afraid to work " ; and I gave it to John and
Sam, bade Howland take the boys to Campbell's
house, — walked down with Todd to his office, — chal-
lenged him to take five minutes at the wheel, in memory of old times, — made the tired relays laugh as
they saw us take hold ; and then, — when I had cooled
off, and put on my Cardigan, — met Campbell, with
his seven sons of Anak, tumbling down the stairs,
wondering what round of mercy the parson had found
for them this time. I started home, knowing I should
now have my Argus with my coffee.

III.

And so I walked home. Better so, perhaps, after
all, than in the lively sleigh, with the tinkling bells.

> " It was a calm and silent night ! —
> Seven hundred years and fifty-three
> Had Rome been growing up to might,
> And now was queen of land and sea !

No sound was heard of clashing wars, —
  Peace brooded o'er the hushed domain ;
Apollo, Pallas, Jove, and Mars
  Held undisturbed their ancient reign
    In the solemn midnight,
        Centuries ago ! "

What an eternity it seemed since I started with those children singing carols. Bethlehem, Nazareth, Calvary, Rome, Roman senators, Tiberius, Paul, Nero, Clement, Ephrem, Ambrose, and all the singers, — Vincent de Paul, and all the loving wonder-workers, Milton and Herbert and all the carol-writers, Luther and Knox and all the prophets, — what a world of people had been keeping Christmas with Sam Perry and Lycidas and Harry and me ; and here were Yokohama and the Japanese, the Daily Argus and its ten million tokens and their readers, — poor Fanny Woodhull and her sick mother there, keeping Christmas too ! For a finite world, these are a good many " waits " to be singing in one poor fellow's ears on one Christmas-tide.

" 'T was in the calm and silent night ! —
  The senator of haughty Rome,
Impatient urged his chariot's flight,
  From lordly revel, rolling home.
Triumphal arches gleaming swell
  His breast, with thoughts of boundless **sway.**
What recked the *Roman* what befell
  A paltry province far away,
    In the solemn midnight,
        Centuries ago !

" Within that province far away
   Went plodding home a weary boor ;
A streak of light before him lay,
   Fallen through a half-shut stable door
Across his path. He passed, — for naught
   Told *what was going on within ;*
How keen the stars, his only thought,
   The air how calm and cold and thin,
     In the solemn midnight,
        Centuries ago ! "

"Streak of light " — Is there a light in Lycidas's
room ? They not in bed ! That is making a night of
it ! Well, there are few hours of the day or night
when I have not been in Lycidas's room, so I let myself in by the night-key he gave me, ran up the stairs,
— it is a horrid seven-storied, first-class lodging-house.
For my part, I had as lief live in a steeple. Two
flights I ran up, two steps at a time, — I was younger
then than I am now, — pushed open the door which
was ajar, and saw such a scene of confusion as I never
saw in Mary's over-nice parlor before. Queer ! I
remember the first thing that I saw was wrong was
a great ball of white German worsted on the floor.
Her basket was upset. A great Christmas-tree lay
across the rug, quite too high for the room ; a large
sharp-pointed Spanish clasp-knife was by it, with
which they had been lopping it ; there were two
immense baskets of white papered presents, both upset ; but what frightened me most was the centre-
table. Three or four handkerchiefs on it, — towels,
napkins, I know not what, — all brown and red and

almost black with blood! I turned, heart-sick, to look into the bedroom, — and I really had a sense of relief when I saw somebody. Bad enough it was, however. Lycidas, but just now so strong and well, lay pale and exhausted on the bloody bed, with the clothing removed from his right thigh and leg, while over him bent Mary and Morton. I learned afterwards that poor Lycidas, while trimming the Christmas-tree, and talking merrily with Mary and Morton, — who, by good luck, had brought round his presents late, and was staying to tie on glass balls and apples, — had given himself a deep and dangerous wound with the point of the unlucky knife, and had lost a great deal of blood before the hemorrhage could be controlled. Just before I entered, the stick tourniquet which Morton had improvised had slipped in poor Mary's unpractised hand, at the moment he was about to secure the bleeding artery, and the blood followed in such a gush as compelled him to give his whole attention to stopping its flow. He only knew my entrance by the "Ah, Mr. Ingham," of the frightened Irish girl, who stood useless behind the head of the bed.

"O Fred," said Morton, without looking up, "I am glad you are here."

"And what can I do for you?"

"Some whiskey, — first of all."

"There are two bottles," said Mary, who was holding the candle, — "in the cupboard behind his dressing-glass."

I took Bridget with me, struck a light in the dressing-room (how she blundered about the match), and found the cupboard door locked! Key doubtless in Mary's pocket, — probably in pocket of "another dress." I did not ask. Took my own bunch, willed tremendously that my account-book drawer key should govern the lock, and it did. If it had not, I should have put my fist through the panels. Bottle of bed-bug poison; bottle marked "bay rum"; another bottle with no mark; two bottles of Saratoga water. "Set them all on the floor, Bridget." A tall bottle of Cologne. Bottle marked in MS. What in the world is it? "Bring that candle, Bridget." "Eau destillée. Marron, Montreal." What in the world did Lycidas bring distilled water from Montreal for? And then Morton's clear voice in the other room, "As quick as you can, Fred." "Yes! in one moment. Put all these on the floor, Bridget." Here they are at last. "Bourbon whiskey." "Corkscrew, Bridget."

"Indade, sir, and where is it?" "Where? I don't know. Run down as quick as you can, and bring it. His wife cannot leave him." So Bridget ran, and the first I heard was the rattle as she pitched down the last six stairs of the first flight headlong. Let us hope she has not broken her leg. I meanwhile am driving a silver pronged fork into the Bourbon corks, and the blade of my own penknife on the other side.

"Now, Fred," from George within. (We all call

Morton "George.") "Yes, in one moment," I replied. Penknife blade breaks off, fork pulls right out, two crumbs of cork come with it. Will that girl never come?

I turned round; I found a goblet on the washstand; I took Lycidas's heavy clothes-brush, and knocked off the neck of the bottle. Did you ever do it, reader, with one of those pressed glass bottles they make now? It smashed like a Prince Rupert's drop in my hand, crumbled into seventy pieces, — a nasty smell of whiskey on the floor, — and I, holding just the hard bottom of the thing with two large spikes running worthless up into the air. But I seized the goblet, poured into it what was left in the bottom, and carried it in to Morton as quietly as I could. He bade me give Lycidas as much as he could swallow; then showed me how to substitute my thumb for his, and compress the great artery. When he was satisfied that he could trust me, he began his work again, silently; just speaking what must be said to that brave Mary, who seemed to have three hands because he needed them. When all was secure, he glanced at the ghastly white face, with beads of perspiration on the forehead and upper lip, laid his finger on the pulse, and said: "We will have a little more whiskey. No, Mary, you are overdone already; let Fred bring it." The truth was that poor Mary was almost as white as Lycidas. She would not faint, — that was the only reason she did not, — and at the moment I wondered that she did not fall. I believe George and I were both expecting it, now the excitement was over. He called her Mary and me Fred, because we were all together every day of our lives. Bridget, you see, was still nowhere.

So I retired for my whiskey again, — to attack that other bottle. George whispered quickly as I went, "Bring enough, — bring the bottle." Did he want the bottle corked? Would that Kelt ever come up stairs? I passed the bell-rope as I went into the dressing-room, and rang as hard as I could ring. I took the other bottle, and bit steadily with my teeth at the cork, only, of course, to wrench the end of it off. George called me, and I stepped back. "No," said he, " bring your whiskey."

Mary had just rolled gently back on the floor. I went again in despair. But I heard Bridget's step this time. First flight, first passage ; second flight, second passage. She ran in in triumph at length, with a *screw-driver !*

"No!" I whispered, — "no. The crooked thing you draw corks with," and I showed her the bottle again. "Find one somewhere and don't come back without it." So she vanished for the second time.

"Frederic!" said Morton. I think he never called me so before. Should I risk the clothes-brush again? I opened Lycidas's own drawers, — papers, boxes, everything in order, — not a sign of a tool.

"Frederic !" "Yes," I said. But why did I

say "Yes"? "Father of Mercy, tell me what to do."

And my mazed eyes, dim with tears,—did you ever shed tears from excitement?—fell on an old razor-strop of those days of shaving, made by C. WHITTAKER, SHEFFIELD. The "Sheffield" stood in black letters out from the rest like a vision. They make corkscrews in Sheffield too. If this Whittaker had only made a corkscrew! And what is a "Sheffield wimble?"

Hand in my pocket,—brown paper parcel.

"Where are you, Frederic?" "Yes," said I, for the last time. Twine off! brown paper off. And I learned that the "Sheffield wimble" was one of those things whose name you never heard before, which people sell you in Thames Tunnel, where a hoof-cleaner, a gimlet, a screw-driver, and a *corkscrew* fold into one handle.

"Yes," said I, again. "Pop," said the cork. "Bubble, bubble, bubble," said the whiskey. Bottle in one hand, full tumbler in the other, I walked in. George poured half a tumblerful down Lycidas's throat that time. Nor do I dare say how much he poured down afterwards. I found that there was need of it, from what he said of the pulse, when it was all over. I guess Mary had some, too.

This was the turning-point. He was exceedingly weak, and we sat by him in turn through the night, giving, at short intervals, stimulants and such food as he could swallow easily ; for I remember Morton was very particular not to raise his head more than we could help.   But there was no real danger after this.

As we turned away from the house on Christmas morning, — I to preach and he to visit his patients, — he said to me, " Did you make that whiskey ? "

" No," said I, " but poor Dod Dalton had to furnish the corkscrew."

And I went down to the chapel to preach.   The sermon had been lying ready at home on my desk, — and Polly had brought it round to me, — for there had been no time for me to go from Lycidas's home to D Street and to return.   There was the text, all as it was the day before : —

" They helped every one his neighbor, and every one said to his brother, Be of good courage. So the carpenter encouraged the gold-smith, and he that smootheth with the hammer him that smote the anvil."

And there were the pat illustrations, as I had finished them yesterday; of the comfort Mary Magdalen gave Joanna, the court lady; and the comfort the court lady gave Mary Magdalen, after the mediator of a new covenant had mediated between them; how Simon the Cyrenian, and Joseph of Arimathea, and the beggar Bartimeus comforted each other, gave each other strength, common force, *com-fort*, when the One Life flowed in all their veins; how on board the ship the Tent-Maker proved to be Captain, and the Centurion learned his duty from his

Prisoner, and how they " *All* came safe to shore," because the New Life was there. But as I preached, I caught Frye's eye. Frye is always critical; and I said to myself, " Frye would not take his illustrations from eighteen hundred years ago." And I saw dear old Dod Dalton trying to keep awake, and Campbell hard asleep after trying, and Jane Masury looking round to see if her mother did not come in ; and Ezra Sheppard, looking, not so much at me, as at the window beside me, as if his thoughts were the other side of the world. And I said to them all, " O, if I could tell you, my friends, what every twelve hours of my life tells me, — of the way in which woman helps woman, and man helps man, when only the ice is broken, — how we are all rich so soon as we find out that we are all brothers, and how we are all in want, unless we can call at any moment for a brother's hand, — then I could make you understand something, in the lives you lead every day, of what the New Covenant, the New Commonwealth, the New Kingdom is to be."

But I did not dare tell Dod Dalton what Campbell had been doing for Todd, nor did I dare tell Campbell by what unconscious arts old Dod had been helping Lycidas. Perhaps the sermon would have been better had I done so.

But, when we had our tree in the evening at home, I did tell all this story to Polly and the bairns, and I gave Alice her measuring-tape, — precious with a spot of Lycidas's blood, — and Bertha her Sheffield wimble.

"Papa," said old Clara, who is the next child, "all the people gave presents, did not they, as they did in the picture in your study?"

"Yes," said I, "though they did not all know they were giving them."

"Why do they not give such presents every day?" said Clara.

"O child," I said, "it is only for thirty-six hours of the three hundred and sixty-five days, that all people remember that they are all brothers and sisters, and those are the hours that we call, therefore, Christmas eve and Christmas day."

"And when they always remember it," said Bertha, "it will be Christmas all the time! What fun!"

"What fun, to be sure; but Clara, what is in the picture?"

"Why, an old woman has brought eggs to the baby in the manger, and an old man has brought a sheep. I suppose they all brought what they had."

"I suppose those who came from Sharon brought roses," said Bertha. And Alice, who is eleven, and goes to the Lincoln School, and therefore knows everything, said, "Yes, and the Damascus people brought Damascus wimbles."

"This is certain," said Polly, "that nobody tried to give a straw, but the straw, if he really gave it, carried a blessing."